THE
BUSINESS
OF BLOOD

A FIONA MAHONEY MYSTERY

· USA Today Bestselling Author ·

KERRIGAN
BYRNE

OLIVER HEBER BOOKS

GNARLY WOOL PUBLISHING
EST. 2015

To you, who thrived in a world that was not considered yours.
Who proved them wrong and demanded respect.
Who lost everything, and found a reason to keep going.
Who were told to believe, but still searched for the truth.
To you, the ones who forged the path so others could follow.
Who would not be silent. Would not be silenced.
To you.
The ones who were first to do what they said couldn't be done
by someone like you.

CHAPTER 1

LONDON, 1890

The arrangement of Frank Sawyer's corpse was queer enough to lend me pause. He hung upside down in the common room, suspended from the rafter by one foot, the other bent behind him, his spindly legs forming a strange triangle.

I'd seen too many bodies to recall the exact number but, in my experience, those hanging from a rope most often did so by their throats. In this case, there didn't seem to be enough left of a throat to manage a proper hanging.

"You should know better than to linger at a threshold, Fiona, lest a demon take you."

I whirled to face the voice behind me with my hand over my startled heart, thanking all the saints I could conjure that it was *not* Inspector Croft who'd caught me snooping at a murder scene before a body had been removed.

Especially after he'd told me some time ago, in no uncertain terms, to *not* enter a structure until the evidence of a crime had been conducted forth. And I hadn't. *Technically,* the threshold was still out on the street.

"Aidan, you startled me," I reproached. "What are you doing here?"

Whitechapel was a long way from Limerick, Ireland, where Aidan Fitzpatrick and I had been whelped and raised. It'd been an eternity since my elder brothers, Flynn and Finnegan, followed Aidan around like two identical twin shadows.

And not because they'd fallen out with each other, but because neither Aidan nor I believed in ghosts. And chances were good that Finn and Flynn had conned St. Peter into letting them be angels, though they scarcely did anything in their tragically short lifetimes to deserve the designation.

"I'm here for the same reason as you, I suspect. To clean up after death." He looked past me into the common house, and his winsome smile died a slow death, taking with it the rogue I'd known before he donned the cassock. "I have to keep telling you, Fiona. Call me Father Fitzpatrick," he reminded me with idle distraction.

"Just so, *Father Fitzpatrick*." I cringed at the taste the title left on my tongue—like bitter herbs and disappointed expectations. "And you can call me Miss Mahoney if we're being proper folk."

One shouldn't look at a priest the way I looked at Aidan. But surely God forgave me, because every other lady in his congregation did the same. He had the countenance and figure of a fallen angel, not to mention the voice of a seraph.

I knew that he'd pledged his life—his heart—to God. But he'd promised it to me first upon a day and, saints preserve me, I felt downright proprietary about it sometimes. I supposed a vow of fidelity was easier to break to your best mate's freckled and bespectacled little sister than to the Almighty.

"I thought a man of the cloth wasn't supposed to pay mind to superstitious pagan beliefs like thresholds and the in-between," I chided.

"Perhaps not, but we do believe in demons, and

there are plenty to be found hereabouts." All traces of good humor vanished, and we locked eyes for a solemn moment before his big, tentative hand settled on my shoulder.

He knew what this place did to me. He understood the demons that awaited me here.

I hated that he could identify my weakness. That he knew what it looked like because he'd seen it before. He'd witnessed me at my worst.

I was no stranger to Father Aidan Fitzpatrick's touch. There was a time that his hands thrilled me with carnal delight. They sent me to my own priest to confess when they'd found their illicit way beneath my bodice when we were young and, I'd thought, in love.

Now, his touch was simply offered as a balm. A comfort. The only familiar warmth to be found in a cold, pitiless world.

He scrutinized the gruesome corpse with dark eyes that had always seemed incongruous with the gold in his hair. Aidan didn't cringe at the inky sight of Mr. Sawyer's blood, all drained from his open throat onto the floorboards. I would give him that much. I imagined him being a soldier contributed to his stoic mien. He'd witnessed countless wounds and plenty of blood. Perhaps even sinew and bone, like that of Mr. Sawyer's spine, visible through his open throat.

I winced at the sight, more because I felt I ought to, rather than out of sympathy.

I wouldn't identify my feelings about this murder until much, much later. Not because I didn't possess them, mind, but because something inside of me long ago decided I didn't get to have emotions in the presence of death.

They came for me later, when I least expected them.

"They told me Frank Sawyer died when they summoned me here, not that he'd been murdered," Aidan said with grave solemnity. "Where's Agnes?"

"Agnes, who?"

"Agnes Sawyer." He glanced at me as though I were daft. "Frank Sawyer's wife."

"I imagine she's being guarded by Constable Fanshaw over there." I pointed in the direction of a dozen doorways, indicating one boasting a sentinel from the London Metropolitan Police.

Aidan took a step toward it, instantly alert. "Is she alone?"

I blinked. Weren't we all alone at a time like this?

"Jesus, Mary, and Joseph, Fiona, how could you leave her at such a time?"

"I only just arrived." I scowled up at him, not appreciating the censure in his voice one bit. I didn't know Agnes Sawyer, and she wasn't acquainted with me. What possible comfort could I offer to her now? "She has her husband's blood on her clothes and shoes. That's evidence, isn't it?"

"You could be all sorts of comfort to her, Fiona." He leveled me with his most priestly look. "You understand exactly what she's going through at this moment."

"I didn't know she was part of your congregation." I crossed defensive arms over my chest, unwilling to open that door right now. "Or I'd have sent for you myself."

"You would have known if you ever came to church. Sometimes, Fiona, I worry for your soul." He cast me a damning look before he hurried toward the next door.

Aye, well. Sometimes, I worried for my soul, too. God knew I'd committed enough sins to procure my place in Hell.

Aidan went to the door next to the one in which I stood and held an urgent, *sotto voce* conversation with Constable Fanshaw. The lawman nodded, shook Aidan's hand, and led the priest inside.

I watched Aidan's features transform just before he

disappeared into the gloom, sharp angles arranging from exasperation to compassion with practiced ease.

I drifted toward the threshold and eavesdropped, as I had naught to do until the body was conveyed to the coroner.

Agnes Sawyer hadn't made so much as a peep until she saw Aidan.

After, her sobs could have roused the dead.

They say we Irish are cannier than most, that we are born with senses others don't possess. Maybe that's why I couldn't bring myself to budge once Agnes Sawyer began to cry because I heard the melody of horror in her weeping. I felt the shock and terror, the grief and pain of stumbling upon a slaughtered loved one as though it were my own.

And it had been. More than once.

I pictured what must have occurred as Agnes Sawyer came home to find her husband displayed in such a ghastly way, his blood slowed to a mere trickle from what little remained of his neck.

When they say that blood is thicker than water, it's valid in the most literal sense.

It's more slippery, as well.

That's likely why I noted the edge of the congealing puddle had been interrupted by the skid of a boot heel. Why Mr. Sawyer's open collar and vest bore the crimson smears and stains of dainty fingers.

Because his wife had held desperate hands to his neck. She'd clutched at her dead husband, kneeling in his gore. Anyone with the slightest powers of observation would have taken one glance at the scene and known that Mr. Sawyer was beyond hope.

Shock and grief made loonies of us all.

Mrs. Sawyer made my job harder by doing what she did. She spread the blood about, painting a macabre portrait of motion with the bottom of her skirts. But I didn't blame her a bit. I never did. During such a terrible mess, no one thought about who would have to clean it up later.

And why should they?

It had been my experience that most people couldn't bring themselves to bear witness to what I do. Often, if they tried, they ended up hating through their gratitude. No one else wanted to be on their knees scouring up parts of their loved ones.

I attempted to remember sometimes, as I scrubbed the blood and offal from my hands, the exact, lamentable instant that the horrific became commonplace. Try as I might to pin the moment in effigy, like a lepidopterist would a butterfly to his board, I found it quite impossible.

Countless corpses rolled through my recollection with photographic detail. Except, unlike a photograph, these images contained the startling third dimension, as one would see through the scopes of a stereograph.

To say nothing of the other sensory reminiscences. The odors. The...tactile.

I asked myself: why bother with the gruesome carcasses of the past when there is a right grisly one just in front of me? And there would be others. Death's business was a messy one.

And I made my living cleaning up after him. At least, here in London.

Aidan's tall shadow knelt behind a flimsy partition separating one side of the tiny, pathetic room from the other. A lone lamp cast his shadow against it, along with the hunched form of poor Mrs. Sawyer, perched on the edge of a sparse bed. A cold cookstove hunkered in the corner, and I could barely make out a well-worn table protecting four mismatched dining chairs. Despite my unkind estimation of the place, it was one of the more comfortable lodging houses in this particular part of Whitechapel, in that it was a dwelling for a single family rather than a cupboard for countless thieves, immigrants, workmen, and prostitutes who would pay four pence for a vermin-ridden bed.

I listened to the hypnotic sympathy in Aidan's voice. It seemed to calm the distraught woman. "Do you believe that your husband will meet God?" he asked gently. "That he'll receive his just reward?"

"I do, Father."

"As do I, Agnes. I believe it with all my heart and soul. Your husband's suffering in this life has ended, and that can be its own blessing."

I didn't have to be on their side of the partition to see his gentle, encouraging smile. I could hear it. I'd been the recipient of it more times than I deserved.

"Take comfort," he soothed. "Death is only anguish for those who believe it is truly the end." Aidan handed her a bottle of something I suspected to be a spirit of the unholy kind.

"You Irish are full of blarney." Inspector Croft's shadow slid over me like the cold specter of winter, and I had to suppress a shudder. "That man suffered plenty of anguish before he gave up the ghost."

If Aidan's presence was a balm to me, then Inspector Grayson Croft was the rash. My entire being prickled with defensive awareness. I mustered the most vitriolic glare I was capable of and retreated outside to where Hao Long, my assistant, patiently stood by the cart with our supplies.

Croft ambled after me, all loose limbs and hulking shoulders. He seemed uncomfortable in his gray suit. In any suit, really. With his slick, dark hair, and undignified jaw that always wanted shaving, he would fit in with the bruisers at the ironworker's union meetings rather than the upright fellows at Scotland Yard.

Perhaps that was more of a help than a hindrance to him here in Whitechapel.

"Shame on you, for saying such things within earshot of a grieving widow," I admonished him, plucking a scraper and pail from my cart with curt, angry movements.

"Shame on your priest for lying to her," Croft rumbled. "He didn't know Mr. Sawyer's secret sins. The ones he never dared to confess."

"Do you?"

"Nay, but a murder like this has a way of revealing them." He glanced to the door beyond which Frank Sawyer's corpse still swung in the darkness. "My point is, your priest can't promise the widow that her husband's gone to Heaven."

"He's not *my* priest," I snapped.

Listening to him was like traversing the gravel pits with only moonlight to guide me. Inspector Croft wasn't from London. Anyone could tell by the lilt of his accent that he had been born somewhere south of Scotland but north of Hadrian's Wall.

Armed with my scraper and pail, I stepped eye to eye with him. Which was to say, I stepped eye to throat, as he was somewhat tall, and I was on the short side of average. "Furthermore, you're supposed to give condolences and the like to grieving people, it's just what's done."

"*You* don't."

"Not generally," I admitted. "But that's not my job, is it?"

"Nor is it mine." Our glares clashed and held with mutual repugnance, and he lit a fragrant cigarette, which drove me to step around him. "My job is to collect evidence and apprehend murderers."

"Well then, Inspector Croft, why haven't you finished your job so I can do mine?" I asked. "If you've summoned me here, you're no doubt aware that I'm unable to clean up after the cadaver until it's gone, and I'd rather be away from Whitechapel sooner than later, all told."

His gaze flicked down the lane toward an address

we'd both like to forget. When eyes the color of the moss clinging to the cliffs of Moher met mine, an uncharacteristic humanity lurked in the verdant depths.

I'd come to be intrinsically wary of Inspector Croft as he gave the impression of a man with violent secrets buried beneath a rough but respectable façade. "Miss Mahoney, you must know that neither Aberline nor I would call you back to Dorset Street."

"Why not?" I challenged. "I answered the call, didn't I? Same as you." I'd returned to Dorset Street despite the fingers of ice gripping my spine.

Beneath their chill, a whisper of providence drew me toward the past.

I only dreamt in nightmares because of Dorset Street. If I were honest, I'd come because I wanted to prove that I was as stout-hearted and stalwart as the others who bore witness to the most infamous butchery in Whitechapel. Those few men who'd gained their life's notoriety from the death of my dearest childhood friend, Mary Kelly.

Without even solving her murder.

Some could argue—would argue—that I'd purchased my life from her death, as well...

Which is why I still searched for her murderer after everyone had given up.

My two-year quest for justice was not what had summoned me to the scene of my nightmares on that night. Indeed, it had been one of the bone-thin errand boys who flitted through the streets of London, delivering beatings, packages, threats, or summons in a network far wider and more economical than the newly implemented telephone lines. He'd eyes as hard as marble beneath his grimy cap as he relayed his midnight message. A death on Dorset Street needed seeing to immediately.

My presence had been requested.

He disappeared into the vapor of the Thames before I'd a chance to inquire as to who'd sent him to my door.

I figured I'd witnessed enough death and blood to inoculate myself against the malevolent memory of Mary Kelly's corpse.

Once I'd arrived, something about the way the night shifted, the darkness claiming the many nooks and alleys of Whitechapel, the most wretched borough of London, sent a thousand insects skittering across my skin.

Beleaguered gas lamps were few and far between, allowing the darkness to drift between their pallid spheres. A presence more insidious than the ghosts of the past regarded me from the shadows of the archway leading to the room that painted my nightmares with blood.

The fine hairs on my body vibrated. Lifted and crackled with the shocking energy that arced between two bodies in a painful zap. I felt as though, at any moment, someone would snatch me from my feet and pull me into the blood-soaked past.

Two years is a respectable distance where death is concerned, but an evil so potent leaves a trace behind. Echoes rippling through time like an iridescent overlay or carbonless copy paper. I tried to convince myself that it was the hour, the circumstances, or the gruesome murder in front of me that summoned the shifting specter of a killer in my periphery.

But I knew it was the place.

13 Miller's Court.

The archway beneath which I, Fiona Mahoney, had been well and truly broken.

I couldn't accurately claim that I'd been repaired after all this time, but let us say I'd salvaged myself. Repurposed, even.

I stared down to the dark horizon along the row of common houses, distinct in their tight quarters and shoddy craftsmanship. In these dwellings barely fit for pigs, several impoverished families would often huddle together for warmth, or drunkards, whores, and thieves would pay a ha'penny for a dingy, flea-ridden bed, anemic tea, and a crust of bread.

They'd cram inside smelling of sweat and sex and liquor in an untenable mélange of vice and villainy.

Lifting my chin, I refused to look toward that arch. I did my utmost to maintain my decisive focus on the murder in front of me, not the one in my history. I toed up to the threshold, tucking escaped wisps of my dark, sleep-tangled knot behind my ears as I surveyed the gruesome scene.

"Who do you think sent for me?" I asked after clearing a gather of nerves from my throat.

His exhale, thick with smoke, reminded me that autumn would soon give way to winter, and my business always thrived in that season.

"Someone who didn't know better." He gave the shadows another dark glance.

Most of the men who worked at Scotland Yard knew of the painful, sanguinary past I shared with Whitechapel. You see, it was there that I began my profession as a Post-Mortem Sanitation Specialist.

I couldn't shake the sense that I'd pleased the devil just by being here. That he observed me from his lair and smiled. A cold feeling, that. The coldest. It had me squinting over my shoulder into the night, searching for shades. For the demon I'd claimed as my own.

Because Dorset Street belonged to Jack the Ripper. Ask anyone.

I suspected it always would.

CHAPTER 2

Constable Hurst leaned on my cart and lifted the
burlap cover with his nightstick. He inspected
the contents with all the disgusted curiosity an
inquisitor owed a witch's lair. To be fair, it contained a
few less than potable concoctions.

And some less than legal, to boot.

He wrinkled his nose as he unstopped a vial and
sniffed. If you wanted my opinion, I'd say he had the olfactory abilities of a bloodhound with a nose as beakish
as his. He could simply sniff his way to a murderer. That
he remained a mere constable at forty years of age or
so, spoke volumes regarding his ineptitude. Men his age
were usually promoted.

"Hao Long is a Chinaman's name, Fanshaw?"

I tried not to shudder at how many of Hurst's chins
wobbled as he laughed.

"I dunno, Bob, 'ow long is it?" Constable Fanshaw
resembled a bundle of kindling leaned against the
chipped brick of the common house. All long, spindly
limbs and bristled whiskers.

"I'm telling you, Fanshaw, Hao Long is a Chinaman's
name."

"Sounds like you're asking me, Bob, and all I can
say's I don't rightly know."

"All's I know is their names are about half as long as their—"

"That's quite enough," Croft intoned from the doorway. He used his sinewy frame as a sort of bulwark, letting nothing in nor out, while still giving Mrs. Sawyer and Aidan some privacy.

I appreciated his terse brand of chivalry, though I didn't want to rely on it. So, I said, "I imagine you two lackwits think you're as clever as the last dozen people I've heard have this exact conversation." Tying my white apron around my trim waist kept me from gesturing at them, though I had a few particular gestures in mind. "I assure you both, it's as tedious now as it was the first time."

"Aw, we don't mean no'fing by it, Miss Mahoney." Fanshaw's whiskers lifted in an attempt at a conciliatory smile. "Besides, 'e don't understand us, do 'e?"

"My employee's origins do not give you leave to be so inconsiderate," I admonished. "If you use the pejorative again in his presence, I'll be taking it up with your superior."

Hurst muttered beneath his breath, "I'm not like to be in trouble over a bloody immigrant."

"*I am* a bloody immigrant," I reminded them, glancing at Hao Long, who stood patiently behind the cart in his silk vest and apron, hands clasped behind him.

The truth of it was, I didn't have any idea how much English he understood. In the several months he'd worked for me, we'd miraculously communicated in gestures and looks. The only time we had trouble understanding each other was when we attempted to use language. So, we avoided it whenever possible.

He didn't seem to be paying the uncouth constables any mind. Turned out, Hao Long watched Inspector Croft, who glared at *me* from beneath his felt hat as though the entire conversation were my fault.

I fought the urge to fix my untidy mahogany hair by rummaging in my things for the sleeve covers I used to protect my dress during such messy jobs. I tried to keep my movements unhurried as I pulled them on over my black frock.

"I'll thank you to keep your paws off my things," I snapped, grabbing for the bottle Fanshaw had extracted from its case.

He swung it high and out of my reach.

Even the taciturn Hao Long cringed perceptibly.

I planted both my hands on my hips, wishing my spectacles didn't hinder my withering glare. "Have it your way, but that's my concentrated hypochlorite powder. If any of that so much as touches the ammonia Hurst is currently mishandling, the fumes will melt the lungs right out of your chest, and you'll drown in your own blood whilst struggling to cough it onto the stones."

"We're doing no'fing but inspecting it," Fanshaw dismissed me. "Shew us the smelling salts in case you give over to hysterics?"

I did my best to ignore his jibe at my sex. "That vial is more likely to explode than I am. But if you break it, it'll take a month's wages to replace."

"Look at her," Hurst pointed. "Ears are the color of pickled beets."

"Calm down," Fanshaw put up a hand in an exaggerated gesture. "No need for a bird to get 'er feathers in a ruffle."

If there was anything more infuriating than a condescending male instructing me to remain calm when I am, indeed, already calm, I hadn't found it yet.

It'd taken me twenty years and six brothers to learn, but I'd discovered how to school most of the emotions a man could use against me out of my countenance. What I didn't have control of, however, was my skin. I blushed and flushed with alarming frequency. When emotions were high, my ears and my chest turned red as Robert Burns' rose, and the crimson melted up my throat and down my cheeks in a splash of damning color.

"Put. Them. Back." Croft's command was immediately obeyed by both abashed constables. I couldn't tell if I was more relieved that they'd minded him, or irritated that they'd heeded him over me.

Either way, I decided to mark this night as a ready example for the next time someone asked me why I wasn't married at nine and twenty.

Marching up to Inspector Croft, I noted in my periphery that Hao Long had gathered the things we'd need to lift the bloodstains from the aged wooden floor. I tried not to smile when he snatched the hypochlorite powder from Constable Fanshaw's hand as he trundled past.

"Has the photograph of the corpse been taken?" I asked Croft.

"It has." From this vantage point beneath the dim light of the gas lamp, his felt hat shadowed his eyes. That didn't stop me from sensing the darkness in his gaze.

"And the doctor's made the post-mortem report?" I made a show of searching our vicinity. "I don't see him about."

"He has." A cloud of smoke erupted from his mouth at the curt words, and I waved it away, pretending that the smell of cloves and chicory offended me.

"And you've conducted your murder scene investigation, then?" I pressed impatiently.

"I have." The nettle in his voice grated at nerves already raw.

I picked up the scraper and pail I'd leaned against the stoop and stood against him as he blocked my way into the house. "I'm trying to figure out why you haven't cut the body down yet to send to the mortuary."

He lifted his head to pierce me with a level stare. "I'm waiting on Aberline."

I must have looked like a right idiot blinking at him for as long as I did. "Aberline?" I echoed like a daft parrot. "Inspector Fredrick Aberline? He's coming *here*? To Whitechapel?"

"He is."

If you were anything like me, you'd likely spend most of your time wanting to slap a proper response out of Inspector Croft, and I'd not blame you for it. I'd worked around him enough to know that if the preponderance of his answers contained two syllables instead of one, it meant he was feeling downright chatty.

"But why?" I wondered aloud. "Aberline is assigned to the borough of London, he's not much been in Whitechapel since..." I paused, keenly aware of the dark arch to 13 Miller's Court behind me. It loomed like a cold gate to Hell, not a hundred paces away.

Or, more appropriately, *from Hell*, to steal the closing salutation from the Ripper's infamous letter.

Aberline hadn't much been to Whitechapel since he'd conducted the murder inquiry and investigation of Jack the Ripper during the Autumn of Terror in 1888.

It seemed like an eternity, or maybe yesterday.

"I don't often see you in these parts, either," Croft said, and I detected a note in his voice that a more fanciful girl might have called grim, and a cynical woman might label suspicious. "Not that I blame you, mind. Business must be good if you can afford a row house in Chelsea all on your own."

My business was none of his concern. Especially since some of my business could see me arrested.

Or hanged.

I tried to shoulder past him, using the handle of my scraper to avoid as much contact with his unyielding body as I could. "Do you know how much longer he'll be? I'd really like to get on with it. It's late enough to be early, and I'd like to be done before a crowd starts to gather at dawn, and an enterprising landlord starts charging admission for a view of the corpse—"

Croft's hand winching around my arm was enough to startle me into silence, and I gaped at him in shock and alarm. "Go *home*, Fiona." His low voice was astonishingly gentle, where his words were not. "You want no part of this."

I stared up into his serious expression, trying to discern his intention. If the law hadn't summoned me here. Then who?

A dark notion stabbed me in the gut, followed by a darker anticipation. What was Croft hiding from me? I understood that he disagreed with my choice of profession, but it was better than the alternative, and we both knew it.

Besides, I made more money than a prostitute.

Inspector Croft had never been friendly with me, never employed me, and had never called me Fiona. To him, I was Miss Mahoney. And only then if he acknowledged my presence at all.

It occurred to me in that moment, that the last time he'd physically held me back from a crime scene had, indeed, been almost two years ago in the doorway of 13 Miller's Court.

He'd been a newly promoted inspector then, before the tiny shards of silver ever threaded themselves through the perpetually dark stubble on his jaw. I remembered how strong he was, how inflexible. Like a mountain in a morning suit.

"Why don't you want me here, Inspector Croft?" I demanded, thoroughly studying the rough planes of his face, searching for a lie. "What aren't you telling me? What are you trying to protect me from?"

"Yourself." His grip tightened to painful on my arm.

"Why call Aberline to Whitechapel? Unless..."

My gaze swung back to the body of poor Mr. Sawyer. To the pool of blood beneath him. Blood that had long since ceased to disgust me. I devoured every visible detail the wan light allowed. The filthy tin basin of dark wash water perched on a rickety table. A few days' worth of dirty dishes stacked in a bin. An upturned chair next to a scratched, unused writing desk. And an open, dingy window—

"Wait!" I surged against Inspector Croft's hold, but it remained as secure as an iron shackle. "Let me go."

"No," he ground out. "There's nothing here for you. No one to pay your bill. Just. *Go*. Home."

But we both knew I'd seen what he hoped I wouldn't. Water in a washbasin shouldn't be so inky and dark when the dishes hadn't been cleaned.

The water wasn't water at all.

And it wasn't blood, either.

"Was Mr. Sawyer disemboweled?" I demanded loudly, itching to get my hands on his buttoned shirt, vest, and jacket in order to rip them open. Knowing that desire made me a monster. "Are those his innards in that pail?"

Frank Sawyer's throat had been cut in two neat motions, all the way to the bone. *Exactly* like the throats of more than six prostitutes during the Autumn of Terror. If I guessed right, he'd been sliced from pelvis to sternum, his organs removed. Organs that I was certain were piled neatly in the basin. Something I would confirm once I could see in better light.

Croft had called Aberline to Dorset Street because, even though the victim was a man, the wounds were too similar to the Ripper murders to ignore. Croft didn't want me here because he knew of my obsession. Of the way I spent my sleepless nights, attempting to solve the very murder that'd thwarted the brightest investigative minds of our modern age.

And also his.

Croft had listened to the vow I'd made to my dear friend, Mary Kelly, as I'd scooped ruined bits of her into the very pail I now gripped in my hand. I'd promised that I would avenge her death. That I wouldn't rest until I uncovered the identity of Jack the Ripper and saw to it that justice was done.

CHAPTER 3

I wasn't ashamed to say that I squirmed out of Croft's ham-fisted grip in a rather undignified manner.

I'd heard Inspector Grayson Croft's hands compared to iron hammers, and my smarting upper arm lent validation to the claim. I couldn't say I'd studied them before, but I certainly did now.

My father used to say that you could tell a lot about a person by looking at their hands. And not in the way my Aunt Nola did, reading palms and the like, but by studying the details.

Inspector Croft's hands matched the rest of him. Big, square, and rough, with old calluses, scars of dubious origin, and blunt fingers. Though his hands were clean, and his nails curiously well-kept, the skin of his knuckles bore the craggy confessions of recent violence. As I stared, I idly wondered what my father would have said about Croft after taking a look at his hands.

I even allowed myself to wonder what Aunt Nola would read in them, though I would bet a month's pay he'd never let her near them. The consummate skeptic was Croft.

"Why do you suppose it doesn't smell?" I wondered

aloud, hoping to buy myself the time it took for Aberline to arrive.

He glowered down at me, scrubbing the palm he'd maltreated me with on his suit coat before burrowing his fists into his pockets away from inspection. "It *does* smell. It smells like a ripe corpse and a lake of blood."

"Well, that's a given, isn't it?" I glowered right back, furrowing my brow to do him one better in the foul expression department. "But you know as well as I that the stench of a disemboweled body is a great deal worse than your average corpse. We'd not like to be standing in such poorly ventilated rooms without our suppers making a violent reappearance. What did the coroner have to say about that in the post-mortem report?"

His lips compressed into a white hyphen.

I marched over to the tin basin full of poor Mr. Sawyer's innards. If Croft sanctimoniously refused me answers, I'd find them myself. I was no medical expert by any means, but neither was I a fool. Building a business such as mine, I'd learned a few things the past couple of years.

Hao Long followed me like a shadow, and I handed him my pail before I snatched the lantern from the table.

Careful to keep my skirts out of the pool of blood, I peered down into the macabre stew, holding the lantern aloft. "Which surgeon conducted the post-mortem examination?" I queried. "Dr. Brown or Dr. Phillips?"

If I were lucky, it would be Dr. Phillips. He was more likely to let me take a peek at the post-mortem report. I'd met him right here on Dorset Street when he reported the findings on poor Mary. He'd explained to me that *post-mortem* is Latin for *after death*. I liked the sound of it so much, I decided to purloin it for my own professional title.

"Most women would faint at the very thought of

what is in this room," Croft muttered, more to himself than to me.

"As I am not a matron, factory girl, nor a prostitute, it's safe to assume I'm not like most women of your acquaintance, Inspector."

"You are unlike anyone I know," he confirmed.

I didn't glance back to gauge Croft's expression, mostly because I didn't have to. I knew what he thought of me. To say I confounded him was putting it too mildly, and to say I disgusted him was too harsh. But I was certain the dark, bemused tone of his voice accompanied an expression I'd seen on too many faces. A horrified rejection at the sight of a well-kempt woman scrubbing blood from the wallpaper, carrying a mattress soaked through with the leavings of death...

Or using the wrong end of a soiled fork to slide organs around in a basin to inventory them—as was my current occupation.

The inspector wasn't wrong when he said that ladies might be seized with the vapors at the sights and scents of death, but he wasn't altogether accurate, either. In the two years I'd been a Post-Mortem Sanitation Specialist, I'd calculated that about one in four men collapsed in a faint that would do a debutante proud—and all at the sight of a little blood. Never mind a ghastly scene such as this one. And let me tell you, it was the bigger and more braggadocious ones that were the most often afflicted by a loss of consciousness. Of course, they didn't call what a man did *fainting*. But it was the same bloomin' thing, if you asked me.

I turned to Hao Long and gestured at the next room, where Aidan sat with Mrs. Sawyer, then I pointed back at the basin. He nodded and set down the pail and the tray of supplies he'd brought in with him. He eyed Croft as he passed the inspector in a rustle of dark silks.

Whilst waiting for Mr. Long to carry out his task, I

refocused on the basin, doing my best to keep my heartbeat from galloping after my unruly thoughts.

It was all here as far as I could tell. Two kidneys with adrenal glands attached, two lungs, a heart, a liver, a spleen, a gallbladder with the bile duct still intact. I was extremely careful with the intestines as I nudged them aside with the handle of the fork. It wouldn't do to acquaint myself with the contents therein.

Sweet Christ and all the saints, was that a...? Was that his *shillelagh*? I cast a horrified glance back at the corpse and noted that the blue fabric of his trousers had darkened between his legs.

Dear Jesus, I wondered if he'd still been alive when his sex was cut from his body.

"You can't come in here, Father, this is a murder scene." I turned to find Croft's shoulders blocking Aidan from entering the room.

"I understand, Inspector, but the Chinaman fetched me," Aidan said congenially, nodding his head to where Hao Long lingered beside him.

Though he was the taller of the two, Aidan emitted a great deal less menace than Croft. He looked past the inspector to find me, an action I assumed Croft did not appreciate if his stance was ought to go by.

"Do you need something?" he asked.

"Your opinion." I pointed to the basin.

"Absolutely not." Croft remained where he was, as insurmountable as a Spartan shield wall. And just as prickly.

"Sorry, Fi." Aidan shrugged in that disarming way of his. "Besides,"—he wrinkled his nose at the scent of death— "I'd just as soon not join you in there."

Croft grunted his approval and whirled on me, thunder gathering above the Irish moss in his eyes. "Now, are *you* leaving, or do I have to physically escort you out?"

Throw me out, he meant.

Aidan's voice remained agreeable as he asked, "Are your hands clean, Fiona?"

I didn't miss the tic in Croft's temple every time Aidan said my Christian name.

The question surprised me so much, I studied my hands for an instant too long, wondering if he'd meant the query about blood in the existential sense, or the literal.

Some of the blood from the fork had made it onto my fingers, so I looked back up at him and shook my head in the negative.

My hands were unclean. I was glad he didn't know just how soiled they were in the eyes of his Lord.

"Mrs. Sawyer is requesting her shawl, a frock, and a few...delicates, as she's surrendering her garments for evidence," Aidan said. "Do you mind very much if I fetch them for her, Inspector Croft? Or would you rather do it?"

Croft set his jaw and looked at the ceiling. I imagined him silently asking the Almighty why he'd been cursed with the two most aggravating Catholics in London on top of such a nightmarish murder scene. I also imagined that he'd rather do anything but paw through a woman's unmentionables with her murdered husband still hanging from the rafters, and their priest looking on, besides.

"Be quick about it," Croft ordered gruffly, moving to the side just enough to allow Aidan room to shoulder through.

Once he'd gained access to the scene, Aidan gave me a victorious smile and a cheeky wink, reminding me of the days when we'd been each other's closest confidants and conspirators.

I turned away so Croft couldn't see my secret smile.

So Aidan couldn't see my secret pain.

"Fiona, would you show me what a crinoline is?" Aidan requested. "Mrs. Sawyer is very adamant that she cannot be considered modestly dressed without it."

"Certainly," I agreed, ignoring the irate sound Croft made as I drifted over to where Aidan stood in front of the wretched wardrobe.

He swung it open, supporting the door once it became readily apparent that only one of the hinges was capable of carrying out its vocation.

"What was your question?" Aidan grabbed the crinoline without instruction, sliding me an expectant glance.

This is why I love—*loved* him. Past tense. He would still bend the rules for me.

"Mr. Sawyer was disemboweled," I whispered. "All of his organs are in that basin over there."

He cast the basin a dismayed look. "It doesn't smell like it."

"Exactly," I said, fighting to keep the enthusiasm out of my voice. "The intestines weren't perforated one little bit. If they were, it'd smell like a shithouse in here."

"Language, Fiona," Aidan scowled.

I ignored him. "What do you make of that?"

It was common knowledge in Whitechapel that before Aidan had become a priest, he'd been the top medical student at Trinity College, only months away from becoming a doctor. He often nursed the sick as he ministered to them.

They didn't know he'd been months away from becoming my husband.

"Cutting a man's organs out so neatly is no easy feat," he said, interrupting the dangerous direction of my thoughts. "You'd need knowledge of just where and how to dissect the dermis to avoid organ damage and remove everything."

We looked at the body, the dark suit covering an empty cavity, and then back at each other. Our eyes widened in tandem as Aidan confirmed that he shared my suspicions. "You don't think this was done by..."

"This man is *not* a victim of Jack the Ripper," Croft snarled from behind us. "Now, get what you need and get *out*."

I faced him, shoulders squared, and guilt concealed firmly behind bravado. "Then why send for Aberline?" I challenged.

"Yes, Inspector Croft. Why summon me to this cursed street at this ungodly hour?"

Chief Inspector Frederick George Aberline appeared in the doorway, a weary crusader in a checkered suit and a billycock hat. Gleaming from his vest dangled a watch chain the Prince of Wales would lust after. It wasn't that the inspector was a particularly fashionable fellow, just an abidingly punctual one.

Whitechapel used to be his kingdom, as he'd been the local inspector in charge of H Division's Criminal Investigations Division.

Blunt features adorned with silver muttonchops and kind eyes provided a façade for a mind as precise and ruthless as the spinning cogs of Big Ben. Which explained why, two years ago, Aberline had been drafted to lead the inquest into the Ripper murders.

I always assumed that his acquaintance with the peculiar singularities of the Whitechapel district had something to do with his enlistment to the case.

Inspector Croft opened his mouth to debrief Aberline, but the chief inspector interrupted him.

"Why, Miss Mahoney. It's been too long since I've clapped these old eyes on such a beauty that in'nt my Emma."

He was being kind, of course, but I blushed anyway. Frederick Aberline loved his wife to distraction, but it didn't stop him from being a harmless flirt once in a while.

We spinsters lived upon the praise of harmless flirts.

He ducked past Croft with a friendly chuck on the arm and surveyed the scene with his characteristic shrewdness.

"It's a pleasure to see you again, Inspector," I said, though I didn't extend my hand to his on account of the utensil I still gripped, and the blood and whatnot on my fingers.

"I wish it was somewhere but Dorset Street." He echoed the sentiment heartily shared by everyone in the room.

"May I introduce an...old friend?" I hurried to keep the conversation from following the dark path to Miller's Court. "Chief Inspector Frederick Aberline, this is Father Aidan Fitzpatrick of St. Michael's off Leman Street. The victim and his wife are part of his congregation."

"St. Michael, the patron saint of soldiers," Aberline recalled aloud as the two shared a congenial handshake.

"Indeed, Inspector," Aidan said with a solemn nod.

"You've the look of a soldier, lad. Where'd you serve? South Africa? The Boer War?"

If his deduction surprised Aidan, he didn't show it. "Different army, I'm afraid," he admitted a little sheepishly. "I spent most of my youth as part of the *Sinn Fein*, fighting for an independent Ireland."

Aberline made an uncomfortable noise. "Terrible business, that."

I chanced a peek at Aidan's carefully impassive features, noting his pallor and the gathering of mist on his upper lip. Not for the first time, I *burned* to know what had happened to him during his short stint in the Irish Republican Army.

I was sure it was the reason he hadn't married me, though he'd never said as much.

"And a dreadful business, this." Aberline gestured to Mr. Sawyer, correctly deducing that he'd found Aidan at the shores of a mire he had no great need to forge. Instead, he toed to the edge of the spreading pool of blood that coagulation had begun to contain.

I sent Hao Long a morose look, and he nodded conspiratorially. Time was, indeed, of the essence, as the floor planks were old, porous, and feebly kept. Which meant, the longer the blood had to cling to the wood, the worse it would stain.

"I see now why I was summoned," Aberline muttered, a remembered darkness feathering across the lines of his face before it disappeared beneath a mask of nonchalance every inspector must practice at length. He crouched down on his haunches to get a better look, rather too certain of his balance if you asked me, as an upset in stability would plunk him right into the gruesome lake. "I've not seen a throat done like this since our old nemesis, eh, Croft? And am I to assume that's not laundry in that basin over there?"

Croft removed his hat, though I was sure it was only done to lend weight to the dark glare he directed at me rather than in any deference to decorum. "I'll clear the room and brief you on the particulars. Then I'd like to request that you accompany me to the morgue."

"I'll stay, if it's all the same to you." I quickly directed this to Aberline as he'd proven himself my ally more than once.

The regret in his eyes sent my hopes plummeting before he delivered his gentle rejection. "I'm sorry, Miss Mahoney, but it's against procedure, and this scene is already muddled enough. Once the body is cleared away, we'll invite you back to work your magic on the place. It's a good thing you do for these families visited by such horrors. I'm sure Mrs. Sawyer is grateful to employ you."

At this, confusion drew my brows together. "I was hoping you'd sent for me, Inspector."

"To Dorset Street?" He gasped as though I'd done him a personal affront. "I'd never! Not to within a stone's throw of where poor Miss Kelly—" He broke off, perceptibly reddening. "And to a scene like this? What must you think of me?"

"It's become a bit of a mystery just *who* sent for Miss Mahoney." Croft stood over Aberline, crossing his arms over his chest in a sardonic gesture. "The affair of the unpaid invoice."

I balled my fists and pursed my lips, fighting the spurt of Irish temper heating my blood.

"The church will cover it, of course, on behalf of poor Mrs. Sawyer." Aidan was at my side at once, his hand reclaiming its perch on my shoulder. "Come, Fiona. Let us leave the inspectors to their work." He clutched Agnes Sawyer's garments in his other hand as he attempted to steer me in the direction of the door.

Aberline sent him a grateful smile as Croft's hard mouth inverted the gesture.

"At least let me take the basin to the coroner's cart for you," I suggested, doing my best to hide precisely how keen I was to do so. If I could get that bit outside, perhaps Aidan could help me examine it for any pertinent clues. "It'll improve the smell."

"Not a chance—" Croft began.

"I'd be obliged," Aberline said simultaneously.

"But won't you need to inspect—?"

"I'm feeling a might peaky, Croft." Aberline patted his belly. "Anything you want to show me in that basin, you can report with the Queen's own English."

I did my best not to look smug as I motioned for Hao Long to help me heft the tub. Perhaps I didn't exactly smother *all* triumph from sparkling in my eyes, but let's call it a decent effort and move right along.

The coroner's cart was teamed by horses a bit too fresh for ghastly cargo with a propensity to slosh, but it wasn't my business to notice. They kept the antsy animals in line with a rough hand, too distracted by their task to pay us much mind as we perched the basin on the backboard.

"Aidan," I said excitedly, shooing Hao Long away to make room at my side. "Hurry and help me look through this. You can tell me if anything is missing."

"Dear God, why would you want to do that?" he asked, horrified.

"Because." My whisper escaped as a hiss. "The Ripper usually *took* something, didn't he? An ear, a womb, a bladder, a kidney, or what have you. If I'm not to hear what the detectives have to say, then maybe I can find something helpful in the evidence left behind." I poked my pilfered fork toward the contents of the basin, then gave the street a furtive glance, ensuring our privacy.

It was just before two in the morning, a time when the denizens of the night who plied their various seedy trades in the district began to seek refuge from the misery of the *matins*. To them, the insufficient gas lamps of Whitechapel only created more opportune shadows. But once dawn licked the stones with grey, the respectable and industrious citizens would emerge, and they didn't take kindly to seeing the illicit revenants of the dark. Most factory workers wouldn't rouse until five, so now was the time when the streets were nigh empty, and the shadows were full and long.

In fact, one shifted with a serpentine grace over by the Miller's Court arch, and I thought I got an impression of a top hat and a dark overcoat.

Stunned, I dropped the fork.

I grimaced with distaste as I retrieved it from where it slid between a kidney and the wall of the basin.

When I looked up again, the shadow had disappeared.

If it had ever been there to begin with.

So what if there had been a man in a top hat? I admonished myself. Such a sighting wasn't exactly a rarity, and the depictions in the papers of the gentleman Ripper with his top hat and smart mustache had no basis in reality or even hearsay. They were just the speculations of rabid journalists.

Still, I couldn't shake the sense that a killer stood nearby. That he watched me conduct my gruesome investigation. That he appreciated the sight of blood on my hands.

This place was driving me looney.

"I don't like this," Aidan lamented.

"Oh, come now," I goaded. "You don't expect me to believe that you've gone all squeamish, do you?"

"Of course, not. But, Jesus, Mary, and Joseph, Fiona, that's all that's left of a parishioner of mine in there. A man brutally murdered, possibly tortured, and his poor wife—widow— may be within earshot."

I used to like to watch emotion turn his dark eyes grey. But couldn't bring myself to look at them now.

"What if those were *my* bits in that basin?" he asked. "Would you just poke about at them with a dirty fork and get on with it?"

"No." My voice sounded churlish and ashamed all at once, and only served to fuel my ire. Had this been Aidan, I'd be nothing but a puddle on the ground. His death didn't bear consideration. Not even in the hypothetical.

Even though he wasn't *mine*...he was all I had left.

"What if we could help find the killer?" I challenged. "You know the Sawyers better than anyone in there, and Whitechapel is your home, isn't it? What if *he's* back, Aidan? What if this killing is the first of many?"

"I want justice done, same as you, for the Sawyers and for Mary." The genuine tenderness in his voice strung my nerves tight as a piano wire, and I hunched against it lest it breach my composure. "Two of Scotland Yard's finest inspectors are on the case. If Jack the

Ripper has returned, then Whitechapel isn't safe. And if he hasn't, then this is some...perverse imitation of what he's done. One that's not likely to be an isolated event."

I started when he touched my cheek, as I'd been too busy inspecting the darkness to notice his hand move. "Either way, it isn't a place for you. I don't want you involved in all of this—"

I slapped his hand away and jabbed the fork into the air between us. "You don't get to tell me my place, Aidan Fitzpatrick." There was no Irish fire in my tone this time, only ice. "I believe Mrs. Sawyer is waiting for her things." I adjusted my spectacles with my clean hand and turned back to the basin, summarily dismissing him.

He stood behind me for a moment, motionless and silent. I could hear every word ever spoken and unspoken between us spilling onto the ground at my back.

"I understand what the years have done to you, Fiona. I know all the reasons you do what you do." The pity in his voice summoned a scream from deep, deep in my soul, and I swallowed three times to keep it from escaping. "I appreciate that you have to be cold sometimes. But have a care this profession of yours doesn't make you heartless."

Heartless.

Struck by an idea, I frantically searched until I found Frank Sawyer's heart in the center of the basin. An unceasingly strong muscle upon which one's entire existence depended. I counted four chambers. Four valves. I stared hard, unblinking in the wan light until Aidan's retreating footsteps plodded away.

I'd never found Mary Kelly's heart.

Every single part of her had been catalogued in all its exposed and grotesque exactitude. But not her heart. Jack had taken that, along with her life.

I searched for the palpitations to prove Aidan

wrong and found them, faint and fluttering, against my ribcage. *I* still had a heart, even though he owned pieces of it. And yet, I'd stood over too many corpses of those I loved, each time expecting my bleeding heart to just...stop. It should, I think. When a heart was broken as many times as mine, it shouldn't work anymore. But somehow, it still did. It kept going.

And so long as it beat in its chamber, I'd search for the Ripper.

CHAPTER 4

As it turned out, I identified all of Frank Sawyer's organs without enlisting aid, and in short order. I tossed a canvas over the basin of innards and managed to look busy as Constable Hurst and Aidan ushered the frail Mrs. Sawyer toward Baker Street.

The yearning to seize upon Mrs. Sawyer and interrogate her about her husband caused my fingers to curl and bite into the meat of my palms. Where had he been during the Autumn of Terror? Who did he know? What were his sins, his proclivities, his nocturnal desires?

Did he do anything that might have angered the Ripper?

If anyone would know of or suspect a connection of any kind, it would be the woman who shared his life. His bed.

I asked Mrs. Sawyer nothing.

The poor widow's capabilities seemed stretched to their limits by the task of placing one foot in front of the other.

She'd be useless to me now. To anyone.

I should know. I was intimately acquainted with the weight of the loss curling her shoulders forward. I understood the defeat echoed in every trudge of her work-worn boots. I sincerely hoped she had kind relatives with a warm hearth and a place where she could fall apart for a time. It would be difficult for her to return and face the home where she'd lost her family.

I'd never been able to. I'd left my entire island behind, and doubted I'd ever return.

Aidan paused as he passed me, his doe-brown eyes full of grace and sorrow. "I'm going to accompany Agnes to her sister's in Lambeth. If you hear anything, Fiona..."

I nodded a silent promise to keep him informed, even as I searched for something else to gaze upon. Anything but his perfection.

Hao Long stood at the cart, mixing a solution of sodium bicarbonate to battle the deep stains in the porous wood.

Constable Fanshaw seemed chummy with the coroner's carriage drivers if his level of absorption with their conversation were any judge.

I glanced over to the door of the common house and found it momentarily free of a guard.

As stout as the men were, no one dared shut a door through which the stench of death escaped on a crosswind.

I drifted away from Aidan and his sad charge and moved toward said cross breeze, which carried the solemn tones of Inspectors Croft and Aberline. I leaned against the brick under the guise of patiently awaiting permission to conduct my business.

As the fifth of seven children, and the only girl, I'd perfected the dubious art of eavesdropping at an early age. I posted myself against the wall adjacent to the door, taking care not to cast my shadow upon the scene.

"...position of the corpse that confounds me." I identified Aberline by his East End accent filtered through his impressive mustache. "The grisly way he was done does mirror a Ripper murder. His throat slashed twice by a thin knife, sharp as you please. But that's not what killed him, was it? There's no arterial spray in the room."

"Think you he was strangled first?" Croft speculated.

"That I do," Aberline said. "I agree with Dr. Phillips' post-mortem assessment. In'nt enough tissue left on the neck to assess ligature marks, but it remains the only way to explain the cause of death. The blood was drained, the torso most precisely vivisected, organs extracted. After which, the more...sadistic sexual wounds were inflicted."

The room fell silent for a moment, and I imagined a cold shiver of male sympathy shared amongst the inspectors at the thought of poor Mr. Sawyer's intimate dismemberment.

"But that he's hanging inverted by only one ankle stymies me quite." I pictured the circumspect Aberline, his hands clasped behind him, a ponderous posture he was often wont to assume. "Posing the victims thus was something the Ripper never did, and I don't at all know what to make of it."

I identified a dark, speculative sound as that of Inspector Croft. He was more often than not the last to speak. "The particulars of the Ripper murders were much detailed by the press and easy to replicate," Croft stated. "I'm not at all convinced this is his work."

"Though neither can we rule it out, can we?" said Aberline. "However, the question remains, be the killer the Ripper or an imposter, why hang *this* blighter upside down?"

"Dr. Phillips noted that hardly enough blood remained in the corpse to constitute a drip once the killer opened the body cavity to extract the organs," Croft said. "It all drained from the neck first."

"Do you suppose exsanguination was the murderer's only intent?" Aberline sounded skeptical as his boots seemed to find every uneven floorboard as he paced around the circle of blood. "Perhaps someone with a penchant for Penny Dreadfuls and an inability to separate reality from evil and horror."

"Reality is enough of a horror," Croft muttered, and I felt the verity of his statement to the marrow of my very bones.

"How are there no footprints, other than the wife's, leading from this mess?" Aberline redirected.

"The course of my next conjecture," Croft said. "Have we completely cleared the wife of suspicion?"

Aberline tsked loudly. "It would be difficult for a woman of such small stature to string up a man of this size, but she could have had an accomplice."

"She has an alibi," Croft said. "But if she had an accomplice, it doesn't matter where she was physically."

"What do we know about her?"

"She works in a factory and took an extra night shift. Apparently, the couple recently found out Agnes Sawyer had conceived, and they were saving for a holiday to visit her parents in Bournemouth."

A blade of distress slid between my ribs and hit its mark. The joy of a new child smothered by a tragedy such as this.

Poor Agnes Sawyer.

"I see." Disappointment colored Aberline's voice, but he didn't dwell. "So, why dress him back up after the grisly work is done? And how did the killer manage to get the guts in the basin without making a bloody mess?"

They were quiet a moment, presumably examining the scene for any clues as to how the killer had done his deeds, and in what order.

Their silence gave me a chance to digest the information pertinent to my own motivations. Dr. Phillips, a local coroner, had done the post-mortem examination, which was excellent news for me. Since there was no sign of him about, I imagined he'd gone home. Proper autopsies were done during business hours, and one rarely found a coroner before eight o'clock.

What the good inspectors didn't know was that the doctor and I had an understanding of a financial nature. A respectable man of *almost* unimpeachable morals, Dr. Phillips was also a scientist and tended to be swayed by logic above ethics.

I'd certainly be attending the autopsy, and because he was just as clever and cunning as he was principled, Dr. Phillips would be expecting me.

I shared the inspectors' confusion over the obviously significant placement of Mr. Sawyer's body.

In all the murders attributed to Jack the Ripper, the violence had a very precise chronological order. First, he strangled the victims to unconsciousness if not death, after which he slashed their throats in two clean slices almost to the point of decapitation. That done, he'd commence with the mutilations. They began with thirty-nine stab wounds to the torso and genitals of Martha Tabrum and intensified in their unspeakable gruesomeness with each murder until Mary Kelly.

There was little you could do to a body that he *hadn't* done to Mary's.

Even Mr. Sawyer's murder was only half as gruesome as most of what the Ripper had done. And, as Scotland Yard's finest pointed out, Jack the Ripper's victims were women.

All prostitutes.

He'd posed them on their backs, skirts flung above their waists, and their knees drawn up and parted as though to accept a lover.

Or a customer, as was most often the case.

In my darkest moments, I fervently hoped the knife was the only thing he'd penetrated their bodies with. When stuck in those moments, I was grateful that there was no way to assess if he'd defiled their corpses with his own body... I didn't know what I might have done with that knowledge.

"Poor blighter's lucky he's so lean." Aberline's voice broke my dark reverie. "Can't figure why he's strung up by only one ankle, and the bent knee of the other leg behind the body, makes for a strange triangle, don't it?"

"Indeed."

I froze like a bunny in a hedge as Inspector Croft's heavy footfalls told me he'd approached the threshold.

I held my breath and pressed my body against the outer wall as he leaned his shoulder on the doorjamb.

"I've more than a passing suspicion that the place-ment of the body is invariably more consequential than just the drainage of blood," Croft surmised.

"Yes," Aberline agreed. "But what the message could be, I can hardly make out. Do you have any ideas, Croft?"

The young inspector was close enough for me to hear the sandpaper rasp of his rough hand running over his evening beard. In the slant of light on the ground cast by the lantern within, I watched his shadow rum-mage about in his pocket and put something in his mouth. I flinched at the loud scrape and flare of a match.

He really did smoke too much.

Inhaling alongside him, I did my best not to wince when the match hit my boot. It blessedly went out in-stead of catching the wool of my skirts aflame.

"*Pittura infamante.*" In a voice as cavernous as Croft's, the words invoked a Gregorian chant echoing in the halls of an old cathedral. The sacrosanct language spoken in a voice crafted for profanity lifted the fine hairs on my body.

"What's that you say?"

"*Pittura infamante,*" Croft repeated louder on an ex-hale of smoke that disseminated into the pall of coal, steam, and mist of the London night with no more consequence than a tear would into the ocean. "It's Latin for *defaming portrait*. A common enough practice in Italy from Ancient Rome all the way through the Renaissance, especially in the wealthy states of Florence and Milan."

Aberline snorted. "I've heard of the Romans doing some rather dodgy, brutal things, but never this."

"Well, the practice wasn't known to be deadly. It was used as a form of public humiliation for crimes in which there was no true legal recourse. Things like bad debts, forgeries, libel, the defamation of an innocent woman, that sort of thing. The perpetrator would hang upside down from one foot until he could be sketched. Then, that sketch would be painted on a fresco in the square or disseminated somehow with the name of the subject and his offense."

"Remarkable." Aberline harrumphed, and I could hear the tiny clicks of his watch as he checked it. "How on earth do you know this?"

I wondered, as well. Croft had never struck me as a history enthusiast, but then I didn't know what he did in his free time. I just assumed he prowled the night in search of evil until he retired to his lair.

He seemed the type of man who would have a lair rather than a home.

"I read," he explained simply. Which, as usual for him, was no real explanation at all.

"Perhaps Mr. Sawyer owed money to someone dangerous," Aberline theorized. "One of the local crime lords, perhaps. Someone from the High Rip Gang, or the East End Butchers."

"It's possible. If I didn't know better, I'd suspect the *Tsadeq* Syndicate. The Hammer and his assassin are infamous for their escalating brutality." A note of strain harmonized with Croft's usual baritone.

"I would not say that name above a whisper hereabouts," Aberline cautioned. "The Hammer has both devious minions in the East End and powerful friends in Westminster. To speak against him might be the death of your career. Or of you."

Croft puffed out a dubious breath.

"You just said this *pittura infamante* was a Roman or Florentine practice." Aberline deftly changed the subject. "I don't see what it'd have to do with the Hammer. He's a Jew."

"I *know* he's involved in this," Croft insisted, his rumble intensifying to thunderous levels.

"And how do you know that?"

"I make it my business to know all I can about the Hammer. One of these days..." Croft expelled one more lungful of fragrant smoke, letting it carry away the end of his sentence. His hand appeared around the doorframe to crush the glowing end of his cigarette.

Without thinking, I stepped back to avoid his touch. The crunch of the cobblestones beneath my boot heel was louder than I'd expected, and I winced as Croft's hand turned into a fist around the stub of his smoke.

I'd been caught.

I sprang to claim the first word before Croft could accuse me of doing something I ought not to do. I'd found this an effective technique when put on the defensive.

"Do you truly believe the Hammer is responsible for Mr. Sawyer's death?" I blurted the question the moment Croft appeared around the doorframe.

If glares truly contained daggers, I'd have been stabbed as many times as Martha Tabrum—if not more.

He didn't dignify my question with a response. Instead, he motioned to the two men in the coroner's cart and Constable Fanshaw. "Let's cut him down."

The men instantly moved to comply, taking a stretcher and implements from the cart and marching past Croft into the room.

"I'll help," I offered.

Croft's hands caught both my shoulders as I stepped forward, holding me away from his body like something distasteful. "*You* will stay out here until we're finished."

"All right," I conceded. "Under one condition."

"You're hardly in a position to—"

"Tell me *why* you suspect the Hammer," I demanded.

Croft scrutinized me from beneath dark brows. I didn't see the cogs in his mind turning like I could with Aberline. That's what made him so dangerous, I supposed. I could read most people, could tell what they were thinking, and often guess at their next move.

But not Croft.

His motives were as opaque as the Thames in January. He had the occupation of an honorable man and the demeanor of a villain.

I was sure he was going to growl something dismissive when he said, "The Hammer likes to send messages. To feed his infamy."

I stood absolutely still, afraid to breathe lest Croft change his mind about sharing his ruminations.

"He began his empire here in Whitechapel, a Jewish immigrant like so many others, and through violence, terror, and incomparable cunning, he's become the head of one of the most powerful organized criminal syndicates the empire has ever seen."

This wasn't new information because I knew the Hammer.

And he knew me.

"Why would you suspect a powerful, wealthy, Jewish gangster of murdering a poor Catholic in Whitechapel?" I queried, hoping to conceal from Croft just how much his answer meant to me.

"Because his hold on the East End is slipping since he relocated to the Strand. Rival gangs are becoming more prevalent. And bolder. He needs a demonstration of strength. Something to remind the people to fear him, even if it's from afar."

"But message does *this* send?" I gestured toward the door. "And to whom?"

Croft leaned down, his eyes bright and marble-hard in his swarthy features. "That, Miss Mahoney, is what you'll leave to us to find out."

Unsettled by his proximity, I nodded pensively. Rather than focus on the masculine scent of him, I tracked the procession of the coroner's aides as they appeared with no little jostling, and conveyed Mr. Sawyer on the stretcher covered now in a white sheet.

I wondered how they'd gotten him down so quickly. I glanced at Hao Long, who shrugged his own mystification.

I puffed out a beleaguered breath, hoping they hadn't made an even bigger mess. If Aidan were, indeed, paying my bill, I'd have to give him a discount. Two, probably. One for an old friend, and one for God.

Though I'd take a moment to acknowledge just how vast the coffers of the Lord tended to be and remember that you weren't really supposed to charge him for services rendered.

Hardly seemed fair, if you asked me. Blessings didn't pay the bills.

"Do you have reason to believe that Mr. Sawyer had connections to the Syndicate?" I asked and quickly discovered that I'd tested the edge of my limits regarding Inspector Croft's indulgence.

His teeth had barely separated long enough for this unprecedented conversation. They'd now firmly bound together, a muscle ticking just below his temple. It seemed to do that more than was necessary, at least when I was about.

Which begged the question... "Why'd you tell me all that if you didn't want me to know?"

His chin lifted toward the dark street at my back.

43

"Because I didn't want you out searching the night for the Ripper."

"But you said you couldn't rule him out as a suspect."

"All right, my dear." Aberline strode from the room, adjusting his hat and, once again, checking his watch. "The room is yours, I'm sorry to say." He clapped Croft on the back. "Should we share a hackney to the hospital, old boy?"

"Yes, sir," Croft nodded, never taking his eyes from me. "Constable Fanshaw will stay and secure the scene until Miss Mahoney is *quite* finished."

He turned quickly on his heel and led the way toward Baker Street, but the bounder didn't miss the glower I directed at him. I did not wish to be tended like a maiden fresh from the nursery, and well he knew it.

"It's for your own safety." Croft's departing words carried the hint of a smile over his shoulder, though I was sure he was a stranger to the very expression.

"The bloody hell it is," I muttered under my breath. Profanity made me feel loads lighter as I stepped up into the dingy common house. I released the long hiss of breath that prepared every woman for a sticky, disagreeable job and got to work.

Luckily, Constable Fanshaw seemed to have had enough blood for the moment and lingered outside.

Hao Long bent to hold a wide, bladed pan to the floor while I scraped the clotting blood into it with something that resembled a flat broom, *sans* bristles. Once the pan filled, my assistant dumped it into the pail and put it down again to receive more.

Because of the sheer amount of blood, Hao Long filled more than five pans before we uncovered most of the floorboards beneath. On the last sweep, a grating sound accompanied a vibration up my arm, and our eyes met in confusion.

Gathering my skirts, I crouched down and reached into the flat dustpan brimming with crimson sludge. The blood wasn't warm anymore, but neither had it cooled to room temperature as yet. It had the consistency of discolored honey left in the sun.

Something round and hard rolled against my searching fingers. I tried to grasp it, but it escaped. Then I found another and another. Eventually, I was successful in extracting an imperfect sphere the size and shape of a small, freshwater pearl.

Hao Long fetched a glass tube of peroxide and held it out for me to drop the object into.

We both watched in silent fascination as the blood bubbled and dissolved away. The gasp at the sight of what we uncovered rattled in my chest before it escaped.

At the bottom of the beaker, innocuous as you please, sat a single bead, its color distinct and unmistakable. I knew at once that there several more, judging by the grating sound they made on the tin pan. All shaped, pierced, and crafted by the deft hands and primitive tools of an artisan on a distant continent. Ultimately to end up in the leavings of a macabre crime.

Only one man of my acquaintance wore beads of this stark and startling hue. A color darker than the sky but lighter than the sea, shot through with ribbons of gold and black.

"Turquoise," I whispered the foreign word as I'd heard it pronounced only once before. A rare stone, only found in America. And, in my experience, only worn by Aramis Night Horse.

The *Tsadeq* Syndicate's lethal assassin, known as the Blade.

CHAPTER 5

I should *never* have agreed to dispose of those bodies.

Once you did something like that for men like the Hammer and the Blade, the blood stained your hands, too. Not to mention, once you sold your soul to men like them, it was guaranteed that they'd ask you to do it again.

And so they had. Many times over.

I hated that I was a criminal. I despised that desperation and hunger drove me to do something unforgivable. At least, in the eyes of the law.

I'd heard wise men say the past should be left alone, that a person should only look forward. But there were those of us mired in the decisions we'd made and, as it seemed, we'd never stop paying the price for them. My experiences had led me to believe that we were products of our pasts, and though redemption and forgiveness may or may not be offered in the hereafter, I still had to protect my secrets lest I meet God before my time.

That knowledge didn't stop me from frantically searching for any possible way out of the predicament I found myself in as I scurried up Fleet Street until it turned into the Strand. I didn't want to break the law. Not again. But what choice did I have?

I clipped along as quickly as I could, fleeing the dreadful prickles of awareness that'd hunted me since Whitechapel. Something tickled the sensitive threads of muscle along my spine. Invisible, wicked fingers stroked the tender skin of my back through my many layers of clothing. I glanced around often, even ducked into a doorway once to ascertain if someone followed me.

I convinced myself that only memories stalked me through London. Nothing else.

No *one* else.

Very few hansom cabs braved the streets on such a night, and I'd not been able to hail one at this hour. I had the money; I should just acquire my own conveyance and employ a driver willing to work all hours.

It had seemed like too much of a bother until now.

Whores and revelers eyed me with curious suspicion as I swept past them. I couldn't say I blamed them for staring, I knew full well what I looked like. Slight and buxom but too old at nine and twenty to be of much use as a whore in this posh part of town. Aidan had once told me that I was the prettiest girl in all of Ireland, both north and south. But I wasn't a girl anymore.

My mother used to comment on my "endearing" bit of overbite and "adorable" freckles. According to her, both would keep me from true comeliness and thereby protect me from the sin of vanity. She'd been right, I supposed, though she didn't live long enough to see me grown.

To the ladies of the evening, their customers, and the bohemians who owned these hours, I seemed like any genteel spinster with an expensive but sensible wardrobe—and somewhere important to be. They wondered where someone such as I was headed at this time of the morning.

I worried at the turquoise beads in the pocket of my pelisse, letting them glide and roll against my fingers with a surprisingly pleasant rattle. My mood gathered as much gloom as the threatening storm clouds overhead, as alternative options stubbornly refused to present themselves.

I simply couldn't take them to the police. Could I? 4 Whitehall Place, the address of Scotland Yard, loomed scant blocks beyond. Between me and the Metropolitan Police stood the Velvet Glove, the Syndicate's brothel, on the corner of Wych Street and the Strand.

I could have kept walking. I could have found Aberline and Croft and shown them the turquoise beads. They'd know as well as I to whom they might belong. They could follow their own conclusions. Inferences that Inspector Croft had already begun to speculate at.

I thought about Croft. Tenacious and untouchable as he may be around Whitechapel, he was no match for the Hammer. I didn't doubt Croft's strength or capability for violence, but he was only one man. The Hammer wielded an army consisting of not only brutes, rabble-rousers, pimps, game makers, smugglers, and gin peddlers but also policemen and members of parliament.

Not to mention one extremely efficient assassin.

One didn't whisper his name to a shadow where the Hammer didn't hear it. The darkness was his domain, full of his minions.

Sort of like the devil.

Though, if I'd had to take a gamble, I'd wager Lucifer himself is less connected in London than the Hammer.

Which was why I could not take the beads to the police. Someone on the Hammer's payroll might see me at Scotland Yard. And even if they didn't, odds were good that the Hammer would look into the Sawyer murder once suspicion had been laid at his feet. He'd find out I'd been called to the scene. If evidence were uncovered in the blood, chances were, I'd be privy to it.

Turquoise beads were enough to point a finger at Mr. Night Horse, but not enough to hang him. And if the Hammer suspected that I'd known about evidence and didn't warn him, I'd find Mr. Night Horse waiting for *me* in the next shadow.

And then the police would find what was left of *me* come morning.

Or worse, they wouldn't find me at all.

I supposed there was a chance that the Hammer would choose to treat me with pity or apathy and merely inform the police of *my* crimes. He could let them do his killing for him.

Because I'd swing from the gallows as a body snatcher for the deeds he bade me do.

As it so often did, guilt spread like hot tar spilled over my soul, impossible to remove. I'd considered turning myself in upon occasion to face whatever justice would be meted out. I *desired* to be good, to do the right thing. I'd even come close to confessing once or twice, going so far as to set my affairs in order.

In doing so, however, I'd reasoned myself out of doing what was right and did what was practical, instead.

I'd learned that Hao Long's first wife had died some years before and left him with three children. He'd taken a second wife. In the two years I'd known him, every time I saw her, she was in one stage of pregnancy or another. My employee may be a quiet man, but he was apparently a lusty one, as well.

I'd seen the squalor and desperation so many Chinese immigrants found themselves in, trying to scrape by and make a living on the docks or in factories, doing jobs too menial or dangerous for men who considered themselves better. They were paid less and treated worse than unionized Englishmen. It made me proud to say that my enterprise helped to lift Hao Long and his family out of such a situation. Though I feared that if something were to happen to me, his children would again know hunger.

London was in dire need of her innumerable migrant workers to function as the industrial capital of the world, but she wasn't kind to them. It often caused me to wonder why they stayed.

It more often caused me to wonder what they left behind. If the squalid boroughs where they were allowed to live, not to mention the mocking jibes and rank mistrust they were subjected to by Londoners, were more agreeable than their own countries, the world must be incredibly desperate out there...

I thought about that whenever I felt sorry for myself. I was lucky that, with tenacity, dubious scruples, and a strong stomach, I'd been able to carve out a nice living for myself.

Because I looked like *them*. The people who held power. My skin was their skin. My eyes, their eyes. My tongue, more or less, theirs. Though I did speak the old language, as well.

But never in the presence of them. Because then, I'd be different.

And these days—or maybe always—different was dangerous.

Aside from Hao Long, I also needed to consider Aunt Nola. She hadn't left my house on Tite Street since I rescued her from Bethlem Asylum a year ago. If there was a chance I'd be condemned to Hell for my sins, the place they would send poor Aunt Nola would make Hell seem like a holiday.

And I'd commit a mortal sin to avoid that.

Indeed, I already had. Several.

If I were completely honest, however, my motivations could all be boiled down to one. If I were locked away—or hanged—who would be left to pursue Jack the Ripper?

So, I did what I thought I must. I conducted the damning evidence to the Hammer, hoping to ascertain whether or not his assassin had murdered Mr. Sawyer. And if he did, was it with or without the Hammer's consent?

An arm cinched around my waist with bruising force and yanked me into a dark alley between a haberdashery and a deserted café.

I struggled to inhale. To produce a scream that might bring whichever constable was on foot patrol in this district. But the grip crushed my ribs as a gloved hand clamped over my nose and mouth.

My vision alternately swam with violent sparks of light and blotches of darkness as my eyes latched on to a tall, red-brick building little more than half a block away.

The Velvet Glove.

I was only steps from the invisible perimeter of the Hammer's domain. Had I made it maybe three or so more buildings, I'd have been within sight of the many brutes and brigands the Hammer employed to protect himself and his province. *Oh, God.* Whoever had me in his clutches must realize that. Had he predicted my intended destination?

As he dragged me deeper into the alley, I fought to get my feet beneath me. To find purchase. To suck breath into my burning lungs. If my assailant took me beyond the glow of the gas lamps, I'd *never* see the light again. Of this, I was certain.

Doing my best not to flail, I fumbled with the sleeve of my pelisse where I'd sewn a sharp, cylindrical pick, no longer or wider than a pen. A good jab with it had gotten me out of my fair share of scrapes. A small, spring-coiled knife that once belonged to my father was in my pocket, but I didn't have time to reach for it. I cursed at how violently my cold fingers shook with terror, clumsy and stiff.

The hand over my nose and mouth blessedly released, and I gasped in what desperate breath I could, intending to give strength to the primal scream crawling up my throat.

The kiss of a cold blade beneath my chin turned my scream into a whimper.

"Show me your hands." The dark whisper warmed my ear but turned my blood to shards of ice. My every muscle froze, my hand halfway into my sleeve. "By the time you find what you're reaching for, I'll have already drained you."

I flinched as the knife bit into me and lifted my hands to demonstrate their emptiness.

My assailant laughed when he saw how they trembled, and the glee in that laughter made my eyes sting with tears.

My heart shriveled as the heel of my boot dragged out of the reach of the light.

He had me in total darkness. A knife against my neck. I expected, at any moment, the sharp glide of it across the thin skin of my throat. Would it hurt? Would I be sentient for long, struggling to breathe against the warm spill of blood into my lungs?

Through the windows of the darkened haberdashery, the Strand beckoned—no, taunted—past cheery shadows of feathered hats and tasseled frippery. Just out of reach.

Dear God, let this be a robbery.

"My purse hangs at the left side of my belt," I stammered in a labored whisper. "My broach has a sapphire on it, though the pearls are paste, and there is a little gold bracelet beneath my right glove." That would be enough to keep a desperate man in whatever vice he desired for at least a week, maybe more.

"I'm not after your jewelry, Miss Mahoney."

Every part of me tensed with such strain, it ached. He knew my name.

Could it be Jack? Was this how I met my end? My throat slit in a dark alley. Just like Martha Tabrum. Just like Catherine Eddowes, Annie Chapman, Mary Nichols, and Elizabeth Stride. Was I to join their ranks? Another unfortunate woman lost to the clutches of vice and villainy in this, the greatest city in the world.

Only, I was not unfortunate. Not in the way the Ripper victims were. I did sell services, yes, but not sex.

"I do believe I'll take the liberty of calling you Fiona."

Even though it was silly to think so in such a moment, I fully expected the Ripper's words to slither into my ear like a serpentine fiend. Instead, the breathy tone clung to the air in moist, cultured immensity. The pitch was all wrong, closer to alto than baritone, with a slight lisp. This *couldn't* be the Ripper, could it? He sounded like a Nancy, all told.

As it often does, especially for us Irish, my terror turned to fury.

"Who are you?" I demanded.

His sound of delight washed my skin in vicious insects. "You know me, Fiona. You know what I've done."

No, I didn't. He didn't sound familiar in the least.

"I don't care what you've done," I lied. "My only care is for what you're about to do."

"Can you hazard a guess as to what that is?"

My eyes squeezed shut, but the sight of Mary Kelly's final moments presented themselves like a gory portrait, forcing my lids open once more. At least he'd killed her first, so she didn't have to feel her flesh being carved from her bones. If it came to that, I prayed he'd afford me the same mercy.

"Tell me what you want, or get on with it," I hissed, wishing fear didn't shake the strength from my voice as I uttered what may be my last words on this Earth.

"I want to see my deeds through your eyes, Fiona."

"What?"

"I want you to tell me, in precise and illicit detail, what you thought of my work in Whitechapel today."

A spear of renewed terror pierced my guts, and I crumpled a little in spite of myself. My hands instinctively went to my middle.

A sharp pain at my throat did for my posture what no nun at St. Brigit's ever could as the knife nicked my flesh.

"Don't you dare drop your hands!" he hissed.

My hands snapped right back up into his field of vision, and I cringed at the note of panic lacing his voice. It was imperative that I do what he said. If I didn't keep him calm, chances were my throat would be opened from ear to ear.

I frantically searched my mind for the words and panicked when I couldn't produce any. I'd all but allowed Inspectors Croft and Aberline to talk me out of truly believing the Ripper had anything to do with Mr. Sawyer's death. Once Hao Long and I discovered the turquoise beads, I'd credited Mr. Night Horse with the deed almost exclusively.

"Erm," I stalled with a shaky, throaty sound that died when I felt a little trickle of wetness slide into my collar. Blood. I attempted to swallow and failed, which was all right because my mouth was as dry as the piles of sawdust in the mill yards.

"They...they don't think the Ripper is responsible for—"

"That *I*!" He gave me a rough jerk.

"That *you* are responsible for the...for what happened to Frank Sawyer."

"What do *you* think, Fiona?"

It could have been the provocative way he said it, or the fact that I was fairly certain morning would dawn on my corpse, sliced to bits, in that alley. Whichever, it occurred to me that this might be the only time in my life anyone had asked me that question.

My opinion mattered to Jack the Ripper, did it? What *did* I think?

"I don't—*didn't* ultimately suspect you either," I confessed with more confidence than I thought myself capable of in such a moment. "I mean, the other people you...*killed* were women, and posed in a rather lewd sort of way, weren't they? Even though you castrated Mr. Sawyer, you put his trousers back on before you hung him upside down and all. No one could quite make sense of it."

I tended to be a rather terse and quiet individual, not as much as Croft, but more than most. Until my nerves started to rattle. Then people in my direct vicinity looked for just about anything to use as a gag.

I prattled on as I was wont to do. "And you didn't take any of the organs, did you? I mean, you admitted to frying and eating half of Catherine Eddowes' kidney, and you sent the other half to the chairman of the Vigilance Committee. You *always* take something. Why not take from Mr. Sawyer?" The last was posed as more of a curious query than a demand.

The sensation that I was not a part of this moment somehow spurred me, along with a feckless sort of lunacy. I stood in the safety of the gas lamps, watching some other terrified, bespectacled Fiona Mahoney babble nonsense to her nemesis. I even silently screamed at her to shut her idiot mouth before she landed us both in our graves.

She didn't, though.

I didn't.

Everything bubbled out of me in a great, chaotic deluge. My bicarbonate exhilaration mixed with the acidic vinegar of my hatred created a frothy confession that overflowed all reason.

Here he was. Finally.

Jack the *sodding* Ripper. The malevolent killer who'd eluded the finest police force in the entire world for two full years stood right. Behind. Me.

I even told him about the beads, invited him to reach into my bloody pocket should he wish to inspect them.

He didn't.

He didn't move at all, nor did he say anything negative or affirmative. His breathing sped up as I talked, and I occasionally felt a hitch or two in his chest as though I'd revealed something significant.

I thought about other things while I talked. About how badly I needed a wee, and then instantly after that, I dearly hoped Inspector Croft never saw my corpse—though more because of the wee and such than the blood. For some reason, relinquishing control of my bladder and thereby my dignity in front of him seemed like losing a contest I hadn't been aware of until now.

And I hated to lose.

I thought about how I missed the ocean and wanted to see it again. And how I'd intended to take a lover someday but couldn't bring myself to do so. I thought about Aidan, and the cavern in my chest where I kept him opened. How much easier would it be for him to lose me than the other way around? He had the church. He had God. He had his faith and his endless reserves of grace.

I had none of that. I had nothing but dashed hopes, responsibilities, and a creed.

Lex talionis.

The law of revenge.

The Latin phrase reminded me of *pittura infamante*.

I was back to myself again. No longer divided, no longer standing apart in the safety of the light.

I stood in the arms of Jack the Ripper.

I'd joined him in the darkness. I had, in my presence, the man to whom I'd devoted the last two years of my life.

I was suddenly ravenous. A deep, dark void opened inside of me. Not in my stomach, but in my soul. I desired sustenance, but not in the form of food.

I wanted answers. Craved *information*. I yearned for the absolution tendered by the response to the ubiquitous, tedious, but eternally pertinent invocation…

Why?

Why come back after all these years? Why seek me out on the Strand and not in Whitechapel, his preferred hunting grounds? Why kill a man and hang him upside down by one foot? *Pittura infamante?* If I were going to meet my maker, I'd do it with some revelations, so help me, God.

I loosened my jaw to ask him, and what escaped was, "Why Mary? Why did you do what you did to her?"

The questions stunned us both. A gust of his moist, odorless breath disturbed the wisps of fringe at my temple and cooled a warm tear I hadn't realized had escaped down my cheek.

"She wasn't like the others you carved. I'm not saying they deserved it, but you had to know she was different. Why did you take her from me?" I hated that I'd begun crying. My voice tended to thicken to downright raspy when I cried, and there was no hiding the weakness. It didn't stop me, though. Nothing but the swipe of that blade could stop me now.

"I *loved* her. She was all I had left. And you took her. She was the last person I had, the only one who hadn't abandoned me in some way or another. When I was destitute enough to consider working in the factory where my two cousins were killed, she procured me a job here in London. I was going to be a *whore*."

I spat the word at him, though he was still behind me.

"That's right, the very thing you hate. I was to work at one of the West End brothels where I could earn enough in a year to set myself up someplace nice and respectable. Even though she walked the dirty streets of Whitechapel, she wanted better for me. She was *good*. Her soul was good. So, you tell me. Tell me *why* before you send me to Hell."

I was nearly yelling now, and my blood flowed so swiftly in my veins that my skin became unbearably hot from it. I didn't even remember to take care. I'd become my hatred. Had melded with it until it morphed into something tangible that I might wield as righteously as an archangel's sword.

We stood in the darkness together, panting and still for a disquieting moment. I got the distinct impression I'd mystified Jack the Ripper, and a hysterical giggle threatened to belch past the fury burning in my stomach.

After an uncomfortably long while, he said, "At least you never became a whore."

And with one swift movement of his hand, the darkness took me.

CHAPTER 6

I see her stumble through the arched doorway at 13 Miller's Court and I scream her name.

Mary!

She's drunk, as she often was, and she's singing sweetly, as she often did.

She opens the door wider. As wide as it will go. The devil behind her needs all that space to follow, for he brings as much evil with him as that minuscule room will encompass. More so.

When she turns to smile at me, it's so excruciatingly lovely, I'm reminded how sometimes I hated her just as terribly as I loved her.

Aidan kissed her first, you see, and she hadn't been the one to tell me. We were fourteen, and she'd been visiting for the summer from Wales. She'd a new dress, but wouldn't enlighten me as to where she'd acquired it. We both knew it wasn't from her destitute parents.

I didn't press the subject but was acutely aware that my brothers and their mates commented on how fetching she looked in her new sunshine-hued gown.

I studied her, thinking yellow a rather silly color.

And then I noticed what the bodice did to her breasts—breasts I didn't yet have—offering them up proudly like ripe apples, begging for a bite. I noticed her small, even teeth while *stretching my lips along my suddenly more prominent and despised overbite. She'd stopped plaiting her hair and securing it in dowdy ribbons like we did to keep it from disrupting our play. Today, she'd pinned it like some of the pictures we'd fawned over in the society papers.*

Aidan had called round that day, and suddenly, I'd ceased to exist. My brothers, and the boy I loved, heard me plenty yet marked me not at all.

I'd let them all go off somewhere, refusing to leave in a silent and mulish dither. Waiting for them to cajole me out. Aching to be wanted.

They hadn't. I wasn't.

Finn and Flynn had returned much later, sly smiles affixed to their freckled faces. They proudly announced that all three of them had kissed Mary, but only Aidan had been brave enough to use his tongue.

"You probably shouldn't run 'round with Mary anymore, Na-na," Finn cautioned, using the moniker our youngest brother, Fayne, had coined when, at two years old, he'd found Fiona too difficult to pronounce.

"She's becoming the type of girl that'll let just anyone...kiss her...and whatnot," Flynn agreed, a blush deepening his ruddy features.

I furrowed my brow at their identical expressions of sage and manly sincerity, angrier at Aidan than anyone else.

I'd flayed them with my own sharp tongue that day, shrill as a banshee, beating them with their own masculine hypocrisy. I defended Mary, well aware that she wasn't just allowing anyone to kiss her...she was letting my someone kiss her.

And yet, I loved her. I forgave her with no words spoken between us. We understood, as Mary let more men kiss her, that Aidan would not be for her. After a while, I saw who began to pay her for her time. Her kisses. Her...whatnot. I didn't begrudge her the taste any longer.

Even at seventeen, Aidan had been an angel. Who wouldn't want an angel's embrace?

And Mary—ceaselessly pretty Mary—was about to let the devil into her room at 13 Miller's Court.

I had to stop what happened next.

I was running now, my soles are bare on the filthy cobbles just as they had been on the shores of the River Shannon during the days that Mary and I romped through the chilly currents until our feet and lips turned blue.

It takes took me no time to reach the doorway. Seconds, maybe.

But I am still too late.

The devil has gone. Most of Mary remains.

Mary's remains.

A glut of carnage. It's the only way to describe it. Almost surreal in its ubiquity. None of her viscera is left untouched, but. Instead, it is splayed across the white bedclothes with the careful pride of a child showing off a collection of toys. An artful arrangement.

Just so.

Her womb, kidneys, and one breast pillowed the weight of her head. Her face was still all smiles...but only because her high cheeks, suggestive eyebrows, and pert Irish nose ha been carefully removed, while her lips are blanched by several oblique incisions. It is her skull that smiles up at me, relieved of superfluous flesh. A feminine Yorick. A woman of infinite jest... of most excellent fancy. Of a sprightly nature and a quick temper.

In need of validation that only the touch of a man—of many men—could provide.

I find her other breast by her right ankle. Her liver in between her feet.

Her thighs, splayed open in invitation, are missing their skin and fascia. Enough that I can tell her bones are healthy and sturdier than mine. Her intestines stretch along the bed on the right side of her body, her spleen discarded on her left.

She's open from sternum to pubis. The skin taken from her thighs and abdomen draped across the bedside table, not unlike macabre doilies knitted from dust and clay by the hand of God.

Muscle is carved from her ribs, carved away until the Ripper got at what he was looking for.

Her heart. The one thing he stole.

Dr. Phillips says in his report that the deep gashes to her throat were inflicted first, killing her swiftly.

So why, then, are her fingers clenched so tightly?

Mine clenched also, clawing at an unrelenting pain in my throat. An uncomfortable pressure.

Tears? No.

Dread? Perhaps.

Croft.

Croft had wrapped one arm around my waist and the other about my chest, pulling me from the doorway that day. Away from Mary. He'd said I'd been screaming. I didn't remember making a sound. When I fought him, he'd bent the other arm at my throat, effectively immobilizing me by sheer necessity for breath.

I could not feel him now. I could not smell his fragrant tobacco nor hear his thick, exasperated voice.

This someone was above me. I was on the ground. Incense and exotic, aromatic oils cloyed at my senses, beckoning me away from the room I visited in so many nightmares.

No, this was *not* Croft subduing me at the doorway to 13 Miller's Court. This pressure also burned my throat. Burned and stung and...

A mortifying whimper of pain escaped me, and the fingers at my throat tightened.

The heavy lids of deceptively gentle amber-grey eyes met mine as the darkness began to recede.

"Do not move, Fiona." A familiar, accented voice slid into my ear with the ease of a honed blade. "If you do, I shall hurt you irreparably, and neither of us wants that."

He did hurt me then.

The sharp pain in my neck was more a jab than a

slice and did a great deal to clear the dreamy fog from my vision.

I blinked up at the Hammer rapidly, my mind following at a slower pace. The cloudy darkness of the nightmare lingered for longer than I wanted to bear.

Once I realized that his hold on my neck was meant to steady and not to strangle, the tension in my body eased if only enough to allow facts to reveal themselves in no particular order of importance.

I was in a place foreign to me.

Gold had always been something the Hammer dealt in, not decorated with. In my experience, he painted his world in varying shades of red. Crimson wallpaper for the ladies in his employ, wine for his customers, and blood for his enemies.

This cavernous room, foiled in butter-soft arabesque paper contrasted with bold, bronze draperies made me absurdly question if I were even in London anymore. It'd the feel of a country chamber—earthy, spacious, and pleasantly perfumed.

I wanted to look around, but another sharp pain brought more alarming actualities into focus.

I lay on a carpet, sprawled on my back.

The Hammer had cropped his dark hair very close to his head, as though to hide its propensity to curl. Though, why I noted the detail before my own state of undress would likely remain a mystery to me.

Warmth from a fire glowed over the right side of my body, even though I wore no pelisse.

Or blouse.

I gasped and would have covered my breasts, only half-concealed by my corset, if the Hammer's body weren't hunched over my prone form, imprisoning my limbs as well as he could whilst sticking my neck with a needle thrice more to stitch it closed.

"You are fortunate my father was a doctor back in Russia," he informed me blithely, his gaze flickering to mine before focusing on his work. "I learned many things from him. How to slice flesh in the correct way, and how to stitch it back together."

When confronted with a virile, attractive, but unthreatening magnetism such as his, one's immediate response upon meeting the Hammer was often an overwhelming desire to hold him in one's good graces.

Until he quirked a lip and said something like, "You are unfortunate, however, that I have less opportunity to practice stitching than slicing, which is why you must remain still, even if this causes you pain."

It occurred to me, not for the first time, that the Hammer's ever-pleasant expression and illusorily mild, kind eyes had helped him attain unimaginable power.

Where Aidan was beautiful, and Croft brutal, the Hammer's appeal appeared in hints of the exotic, masterfully crafted with the familiar. His skin was just a bit too golden to be strictly Teutonic. His nose a little too prominent. His eyes tilted down, fringed with long, sooty lashes.

In fact, everything about the Hammer was deliciously lengthy. His limbs, his cheekbones, his fingers...

His influence and ruthlessness.

The moniker never made sense to me. The Hammer was an elegant monster. A gentleman gangster. Nothing about him spoke of a propensity to bash or thunder. As far as I knew, he never even wielded his own weapons.

He was much too powerful for that.

"Whoever cut you did so with the intent to frighten you, I think," he observed. "Your assailant missed arteries and trachea. The wound is too low to be deadly, and barely deep enough to have disturbed the delicate muscles of your neck."

His thumb lightly traced said muscles on the unwounded side of my throat.

The cuts had been deep enough to require a few

stitches, so his assessment ingratiated him to me not at all.

"You were found bleeding in Crossland Alley." He glanced away from me. That, in itself, unsettled me. I'd never known the Hammer to flinch. "Were you...otherwise molested?"

Color flushed his cheeks, and a vein pulsed in his forehead near his hairline.

He was asking me if I'd been raped.

"No," I whispered. I'd have known if I were. I'd been told that some women might not notice should the deed be done during a loss of consciousness, but I could scarce believe it.

There was no doubt I would know. At least, in my current condition.

"I did not credit you as a woman with enemies, Fiona. Perhaps I was mistaken?" The prospect obviously caused him more delight than dismay as he finished his last stitch.

I drew on my hard-won stoicism, successfully fending off a wince as he tied the stitched knot and clipped the thread.

"Do you feel you can stand?" He reached down to assist me.

I nodded, testing the muscles of my neck and finding that careful motion didn't cause too much pain, only a strange, warm sting.

I tried my voice next. "You know I have one very *particular* enemy."

The other corner of his mouth joined the first, turning a quirk of his lips into a dubious smile. "Yes, but was it the Ripper who cut your neck?"

"I—I think so."

His gaze sharpened. Suddenly, I wondered how I ever considered it mild.

Or kind.

"Tell me." His command leeched all the warmth

from the room, reminding me of my *dishabille* with a hair-raising shiver.

Crossing my arms over my chest, I whirled around in desperate search of my blouse, noting the fine marble floors, the desk fit for a king, dark leather furniture, and the golden Japanese-style partition behind which any number of things could hide.

"Where are we?" I wondered in the direction of an unfamiliar potted plant. A fern, maybe? "More importantly, where are my clothes?"

"*I* asked *you* a question, Fiona. I am not in the habit of repeating myself."

"And *I'm* not in the habit of telling stories in my undergarments," I remonstrated.

When he stepped toward me, I found that swallowing was more painful than I'd expected.

My ill-concealed fear seemed to appease him, and he merely cupped my bare elbow and led me to the only feminine piece of furniture in the room, a gold velvet settee with remarkably intricate scrollwork.

I glanced at it, at the floor I'd woken up on, and then sharply back up at him before joining him upon it. He had a comfortable chaise, and yet he'd left my unconscious body on the floor?

"You were bleeding," he said by way of explanation, though his strong shoulders lifted in a Gallic shrug. "And this is a priceless, irreplaceable Louis XIIIV antique."

I, on the other hand, was neither priceless nor irreplaceable. Though I wasn't an antique just yet either, I'd thank everyone to note.

Needless to say, I kept my back straight enough to support a Bible on my head, and my thighs quivered with readiness to spring away from him.

"Also, I needed the firelight to see by. My night vision isn't what it once was as a young man, and the stitch work was intricate...and important..." The

Hammer slid his hand from my elbow, up my bare arm, and across my shoulder to graze the flesh beneath his handiwork. "It will not leave too much of a scar, I think."

My breath trembled, and my thoughts scattered.

The Hammer was not a young man, I noticed. Grooves next to his hard mouth, and fine creases branching from his eyes advertised that time was currently having its way with his youth. But his hair remained free of silver, and he carried himself like a gentleman in his prime. He could have been anywhere from a hard-won thirty-five to an age-defying fifty.

I looked away from him, finding a rather queer display case straight ahead the safest target for my gaze.

"Are you feeling like a sacrifice, Fiona?" he asked.

"What?"

"The Shofar." He gestured to the curls and grooves of what appeared to be a ram's horn. "Among many things, it is a symbol to my people of the goat Abraham slaughtered in place of his son, Isaac, to honor God. You are familiar with this, as I understand it is also in your Bible."

I frowned, feeling the skin between my brows pinch together. "I did not realize you were fond of religious iconography." Especially as nothing he did seemed pious in the least.

He shrugged his insouciance, but a current of something deep and dangerous shimmered in the air around him. "It is meaningful to me. It is a reminder of the story of which I am a part."

"Ancestrally, you mean?"

His mouth twisted in a wry wince. "Metaphorically."

"Who are you in the story?" I queried, arrested. "Metaphorically speaking. Are you Abraham or Isaac or...God?"

He gazed at me for a long time before his lithe fingers reached toward my throat. "We are not well enough acquainted for me to answer that question."

"Then tell me this," I said tightly. "What happened to my blouse?"

With a heavy breath, he dropped his hand. "You bled all over the eyelet lace collar. It's completely unsalvageable."

It was my turn to quirk a half-smile at him. "I can get blood out of anything. That's sort of what I'm known for."

He stood, startling me a little, and walked to a covered window across from the settee, pushing the drapes aside to gaze into the night. It astonished me sometimes how tall he was. How, even in his hastily rolled-up shirtsleeves and without a jacket, he cut such a sophisticated profile.

"Your blouse was ripped from your body. It is in tatters and no longer here. Do not ask for it again."

He did not look back at me, and thereby missed the drop of my slack jaw. *Ripped from my body?* Had he done the ripping?

Or had the Ripper?

The word unsettled me a great deal. As did the images it evoked.

I recovered my composure after a pregnant pause. "Where is *here*?" I tried again.

"Why, the Velvet Glove. You've been here before."

"I've never been in this room." I'd been in what I *assumed* was his office on the ground floor, a sumptuous affair done in crimson and crystal from which he lorded over the Syndicate.

This place was a world away from that one.

"I call this chamber *Shiloh*," he murmured, his chin touching his shoulder. "I wonder, was my establishment your destination when you were pulled into the alley in which you were found? Or was your course somewhere more...official?" He gestured out the window.

Possessed an excellent sense of direction. I always know which way is north and, at the moment, it was a little behind me. Which meant, the Hammer's window overlooked the south and east.

Toward Scotland Yard.

I became overwhelmingly aware of how dangerous his question was to me.

"I hoped for an audience alone with you, actually," I hurried to say, remembering my original purpose. "I needed to tell you—"

"As a...purveyor of flesh, you can see why the return of Jack the Ripper would trouble me, especially if he struck not a stone's throw from my establishment." He turned to me with a hard stare, confident that it wasn't necessary to repeat his previous directive.

As I related my frightening encounter in the alleyway, the Hammer strode behind the golden screen and reappeared, carrying a few implements along with a blue and white woolen wrap. The latter he settled around my shoulders before he reclaimed the seat next to me, soaked the corner of an absorbent cloth in fragrant oil, and made to press it against my neck.

Without thinking, I caught his arm. "What is that?"

He glanced at my hand, small enough to barely span the forearm above his wrist.

As did I.

I expected we both considered how he planned to react to the physical challenge, even one as thoughtless and feeble as this.

Every interaction with the Hammer was about power. Sometimes, power a roar. Other times, it was a whisper. With the Hammer, it was a dance, one to which he always knew the steps and forever took the lead. So long as he remained in control, there was less to fear from him.

"I-it hurts to touch," I demurred, relinquishing my

hold on his wrist, and on my own sense of fragility—perhaps a bit more than strictly necessary.

The razor glint in his gaze softened. "Olive oil, lavender, and frankincense." He held the cloth beneath my nose. "Good enough for your Messiah, but not for Fiona?"

I sniffed the cloth and wrinkled my nose at the camphor-like essence but then tilted my head slightly to give him better access.

"It will protect you from infection, and even help with the pain..."

I could sense the warmth of his elegant fingers even through the cloth and, yet again, I shuddered, wondering if the roaring fire in the marble-white hearth was purposely burning up the chamber's available oxygen.

"So tonight, Jack the Ripper followed you from a murder in Whitechapel and dragged you into Crossland Alley, where you proceeded to rebuke him for killing your friend while he had a knife to your throat...and he still let you live?" He summarized my story with what I considered to be inappropriate levity.

"It would *appear* he tried to slit my throat," I needlessly reminded him as he tended to the wound. "And I wouldn't say I *rebuked* him. I just..."

"I would not tolerate one of my girls speaking to me thus."

In a way, I was grateful when he said such things. It reminded me who he was: the man who held the sword above my head. My life depended on his tolerance.

Standing, I pulled the shawl tighter around me. "I am no whore."

"Everyone is a whore, Fiona." I felt rather than heard when he unfolded himself from the settee. He wasn't so much a warmth or an essence behind me, but the absence of either. "We each offer different parts our ourselves for use, do we not? Our sex. Our blades. Our muscles. Our minds. Our time. Our souls."

He might have been right, in a way. I didn't allow myself to contemplate the bleak note beneath his composure, however.

"I've never sold...that."

"We must assume this is why all of your organs remain inside you, and your throat is, for the most part, intact," he speculated.

"A reasonable assumption." I'd be a liar if I claimed the thought hadn't crossed my mind.

"That you are a virgin has likely kept you alive all this time."

Unconsciously, I crossed my legs. "How do you know I'm a virgin?"

That dangerous smile again. Did he borrow it from the devil? "Categorically, I did not...until now."

I blushed and glared and scowled at him.

Mostly blushed.

Pleased with himself, he continued, "What we must wonder, then, is why the Ripper killed this Frank Sawyer, and what he wants with *you*."

A chilling question, that. I contemplated it for a moment, doing my best not to focus on the towering man at my back. What if my visiting a known pimp upset the Ripper enough to strike out at me? Yet, how could he have known the Velvet Glove to be my destination? Had he been watching me? Did he know my habits?

My secrets?

Had he been the one to summon me to the Sawyer murder, only to question me about it later? Had he truly meant for me to survive this night, or had my intended slaughter been interrupted?

Jack the Ripper had been disrupted mid-kill before, on the night of the double murder of Elizabeth Stride and Catherine Eddowes.

"When you found me in the alley, was I alone? Or did someone chase my attacker away?"

"I am told you were alone and unconscious."

"Told?"

"Night Horse found you cataleptic and bleeding. He carried you here, knowing I could treat your wound."

"*Mr. Night Horse*," I gasped, whirling on the Hammer in a fraught panic. "Where is my pelisse? Did he search the pockets? Did he *take* anything?"

The Hammer's sound of mirth was both dark and dry. "Your prejudice is showing, madam. Not all American savages are thieves. Just like not all the Irish are useless, temperamental drunks."

"And not all Jews are money-lending usurers?" I quipped, appreciating the irony in my words every bit as much as I *didn't* appreciate the insinuation in the Hammer's tone regarding my people.

"Do be careful, Fiona." A subtle warning reverberated through the joviality of his voice. "You amuse me, but there are limits to my serenity."

Once again, he disappeared behind the screen to produce my soiled pelisse. Returning it to me, he stood close. Too close. Awaiting the reveal. "What have you in the pocket of your pelisse that frightens you enough to make your tongue so reckless?" He gifted me with a justification for my behavior. I'd be a fool not to take it.

Reaching into the right pocket, I blew out a gusty breath of relief as I produced the tiny spheres of condemnation.

The Hammer made a cup of his hand, and I let the cool stones roll from mine to his.

My knuckles grazed the rough skin of his palm.

"Turquoise?" A husky note underscored his bemusement. "What does this have to do with anything?"

"Doesn't your Mr. Night Horse have several necklaces, bracelets, and other adornments made from these stones?"

"You know he does."

"Have you noticed any missing?"

"My associate's jewelry does not rank high on my list of concerns."

Associate. A gentle word for assassin.

I'd never actually been formally introduced to Aramis Night Horse, but he'd delivered a few corpses to me, along with terse directives from the Syndicate. Even though he never acknowledged my polite gratitude, I always erred on the side of civility during our incredibly brief interactions.

Just in case we should ever meet in a dark alley someday.

Well done, me. It seemed to have garnered enough favor with Night Horse to save my life.

And so, was I now to endanger his? Did I have a choice?

"I found these beads in the puddle of blood beneath Frank Sawyer's exsanguinated corpse," I revealed in a voice low enough for intrigue, even though we were alone. "Any conjecture as to how they came to be there?"

The Hammer inspected the innocuous little rocks in his hand. Such a pretty color. Vibrant, coarse, and foreign in urbane environs such as the Shiloh room. "I thought you said Jack the Ripper claimed Mr. Sawyer's murder in the alley before he rendered you unconscious."

"He did. But he accosted me on my way to deliver these to you."

A grim calculation tightened his features as he regarded me. "You would have accused Mr. Night Horse of the Sawyer murder?"

"It is not my place to accuse anyone," I stated carefully. "But answer me this, do you believe that if Aramis Night Horse had found these upon my person in that alley, I would have made it here alive?"

The Hammer said nothing, his features remaining impassive, but his long fingers closed around the beads until his hand became a fist he dropped to his side.

"How long has Mr. Night Horse been in London?" I ventured quietly.

"Surely, you don't think *he's* Jack the Ripper," he scoffed. "You told me, yourself, your assailant sounded like an invert. Aramis has curious diction, but his voice is masculine, and his accent singular."

I didn't naysay that.

I also didn't say that Aberline had often suspected Jack the Ripper didn't work alone. I didn't note that *the Blade* was partly a moniker coined for the method of murder favored by the assassin. Wet work, some called it. Done by a specific knife, which closely resembled the very dimensions of the weapon used in the Whitechapel murders.

The Hammer assessed me as though unsure whether to catalogue me as loyal or a liability.

I said nothing.

With every part of myself, I wished I'd gone straight home after the Sawyers' and thrown the turquoise beads off the London Bridge.

But then, I'd never have encountered the Ripper. That, in itself, was a double-edged blade.

He was a man I endlessly searched for.

One I hoped never found me in the darkness.

"I brought these to you in case you knew Frank Sawyer. In case you ordered his death and...in case you didn't. I thought maybe Mr. Night Horse acted without your consent."

The air around us changed, and I abruptly knew I was out of danger. My loyalty had been noted.

"Were you acquainted with Frank Sawyer?" I pressed.

"No, I never met the man. Nor did I wish him dead." He seemed to consider something for a moment, then asked, "Fiona, did the inspectors see these beads?"

"No. I was able to keep them from notice," I answered honestly. "But Croft does suspect you might have had a hand in the murder."

His broad forehead furrowed. "Why on earth would he?"

I shook my head, as stymied as he. "Because of the manner in which the corpse was positioned?" I postulated. "Upside down, hanging by one foot, the other tucked behind him. Hands tied."

"*Pittura infamante*," he murmured. "I wonder what it means regarding this Frank Sawyer."

I scowled. Had everyone heard of this *pittura infamante* but me?

"A bit of a mystery, then, how these beads came to be with Mr. Sawyer if he was, indeed, the victim of the Ripper." The Hammer glanced toward the partition.

"You doubt it?"

"I do not doubt your story, my dear. I doubt everyone else in it. The illumination of your disclosures only serves to create more shadows."

I looked away from him then, a dark thrill rising inside of me. "If Jack the Ripper is killing again...maybe, he can be found. Maybe *he* can be killed." I could say this to the Hammer. Unlike Aidan or Croft, he would understand my motivation. He would approve of it. I knew my appreciation of this did little to recommend me to most decent folk.

But it recommended me to the Hammer.

He looked at me, then, for a long time. "Why are you here, Fiona?"

"I already told you—"

"No, why are you *here* in this godless city? Why not fuck away off to America? There are more of you Irish there than are left on your starving island. The Ripper is not there. You would be out of even *my* reach. You have the money, why not go?"

"I have Aunt Nola to look after," I hedged.

"You could lock her in a box and ship her there in five days." He waved off my excuse for exactly what it was.

Malarkey.

I knew how unyielding my eyes were when I looked back at him because my heart was twice as hard. "I have *Mary* to look after."

"Yes. Yes. Your revenge." He went to his desk and leaned upon it, folding one long leg across the other at the ankle. The very picture of a reclining rake. "You know what they say about those who dedicate their lives to revenge?"

"*They* say lots of things." The infamous they. The invisible they. The all-knowing they.

"Dig two graves, Fiona. One for your enemy... And one for yourself."

Once again, I had nothing in way of reply and found myself wishing for an escape. Yet, I didn't want to go back out into the night alone.

Alone, and rather undressed.

"I could ask you the same thing." I redirected the conversation back to his favorite subject: himself. "Jews are faring as well as the Irish in America, by all accounts."

"That won't last," he predicted dryly. "We never fare well anywhere for very long. While Prime Minister Disraeli is still remembered fondly by the Queen, we are more or less safe here. And I have heard that the Irish are gaining power in New York by sheer force of population."

"A boon for the Irish, maybe," I murmured. "But not for the population of people already claiming that land as their home." I thought of Mr. Night Horse and wondered what had brought him here, so far from his native land. America was an incomprehensively large place... but no one seemed to believe it large enough to share with the indigenous peoples.

"Yes, well...they say the land of the free, but they don't mean everyone, do they?"

"Better the chains you know?" I lifted a brow at him.

"Or no chains at all." He opened his arms as though to advertise his liberty.

Pushing away from his desk, he stalked toward me like a cat. His eyes focused on my every ticking muscle, and yet he came at me sideways. A finger traced the coarse wool of the shawl he'd given me, dipping beneath it to skim my bare shoulder. His head dropped below his shoulders toward mine. "Some restraints are velvet."

As was his voice.

My breath became the canary in a cage, sensing the danger and beating wildly in search of escape from the confines of my ribs.

"And some fists are iron." I made certain my reply was as frigid as he was scorching, his body throwing off heat in waves.

He pulled back as though stung. "You fear me, even now."

"Tell me I have no reason to."

He regarded me for a long time. "Sometimes, what we want and what we fear are one and the same."

Before I could retort, a door behind the partition opened and clicked shut as someone entered.

Both of us froze as a whispered congregation was held behind the partition.

Though I'd only heard one set of footsteps enter the Shiloh room. Hadn't I?

The tracks returned from whence they came, and the familiar sounds of the Velvet Glove drifted through the crack in the door before a soft snick shut it out completely.

Before I had a chance to formulate an extrication plan, Aramis Night Horse stepped from behind the screen.

My limbs went cold. Colder. I could no longer feel the fingers that clutched the shawl to me.

Of course. Aramis Night Horse was one with the shadows. He was the Blade, never far from the Hammer's side.

He'd been here the entire time.

He'd heard me accuse him of murder.

"Croft," was all he said, his fathomless eyes never leaving mine.

No, his voice was nothing like I'd heard in the alley. It fit him to precision, dark as midnight, and sleek as a black cat.

His word registered with a jolt of panic. *Oh, God!* Croft couldn't find me at the Velvet Glove. I had no good reason to be here, especially in my current state of undress. This could ruin everything. Were he in a good mood, he'd throw me over his barbaric shoulder and haul me home.

Were he in a bad mood...he'd arrest me.

The Hammer straightened, forgetting me instantly. "Inspector Croft? Here? What does that sanctimonious fuck want at this hour? We know it isn't a whore, opium, a loan, or a good time. The bastard wouldn't know what to do with such things."

I knew it was an absurd moment to laugh, but some truths were both gloomy and amusing.

"Answers." A cold, midnight gaze slid to me, and even with the Hammer by my side, I felt as though I might never be safe again. "About a murder in Whitechapel."

Retrieving his tailored jacket from a hook, the Hammer donned it in a smooth motion and salvaged his cufflinks from the desk.

Gems that size would have paid for my entire house in Chelsea.

"See her home," the Hammer commanded. "I'll deal with Croft."

It took a moment for my dread to register. "But—" I couldn't be alone with the Blade! Chances were I'd never make it home alive.

"See her home *safely*, Night Horse," the Hammer amended as he leveled a speaking glare at the assassin. "And then we have much to discuss, you and I."

CHAPTER 7

It is impossible to express the array of sentiment I experienced whilst alone in a dark and confined space with perhaps the second most unrepentant murderer in London.

The first, of course, being Jack the Ripper.

I had harbored a slight suspicion that Aramis Night Horse and Jack the Ripper were one and the same. But now...I had a sense of the Ripper. A voice. A scent. The memory of his body pressed against me.

The Ripper had those corporeal details of me, as well.

A terrifying thought, that.

Not allowing myself to blink, I stared at the Blade as the Syndicate's luxurious coach swayed on well-oiled springs beneath us.

And he stared right back.

An ashen dawn coaxed the Thames to add silver to the inky swath of ribbon before the light burnished it a dull brown. The moment of beauty was ephemeral, and still, I didn't dare glance away from the assassin before me, even to enjoy what might be my last lovely view before I died.

St. Brendan's bollocks, I inwardly used my father's favorite curse. I'd just been caught tattling—for lack of a better term—on Mr. Night Horse.

I tried not to note the alleys still darkened by shadows as we passed. Nor did I fail to notice the many fantastic places to hide a body short as mine, should one be so inclined. Granted, I generally did the corpse hiding for his operation...but come to think of it, expediency had kept me in the Syndicate's employ rather than anyone else's lack of ability to do the job.

I'd been given to believe that power simply meant you no longer had to hide the bodies yourself.

Ultimate power meant...you didn't have to hide the bodies at all. You could kill people to the sound of applause, and even God would absolve you.

If there were such a thing as God.

If there were such a thing as absolution.

The vice winching about my ribcage released a quarter turn when the carriage veered toward Westminster rather than following the river. Tite Street was a little row of lovely houses tucked beyond Westminster and Belgravia in the charming borough of Chelsea. The quickest route from the Strand was through the city.

I'd never in my life been so happy to pass the grey grandeur of Westminster Abbey.

The wool of my pelisse scoured my bare shoulders through the thin silk lining, a prickly reminder that I was all but naked beneath. I wondered after my blouse.

Shredded, the Hammer had said.

Ripped.

By whom? I wondered. My assailant? The Hammer? Mr. Night Horse?

I peered across at the pillar of ebony and shadow that was my companion, his legs splayed in an alarmingly indelicate manner.

Though an expensive evening jacket stretched over shoulders broad enough to be considered uncouth, nothing about Aramis Night Horse spoke of gentility.

So much of him glinted and shined, even in the pallid light. His inky hair caught in one long braid down his back. The curiously dark fabric of his trousers and fine leather boots. His marble-black eyes. The beaded silver earing dangling from his left lobe.

Turquoise.

A voice of caution whispered to me that it would be most wise to remain in this treacherous, *silent* nether position until we reached my home.

Unfortunately, treacherous silences made me nervous.

And we all knew how I reacted to nerves.

"So, Mr. Night Horse." I summoned what I hoped was a winsome smile, though it felt rather brittle and tight. "I suppose I owe you a debt of gratitude for saving my life." Even as the words spilled into the coach, I winced. Only a rank imbecile would dare to admit owing a man like Night Horse a debt.

One could only imagine how he would choose to collect.

A clever lass would have said, "thank you" and left it there, I thought glumly.

"I did not save your life," he said without inflection.

"Oh. Well. It's only that—that the Hammer alleged you did."

He shook his head, causing the earing to dance. "He said I found you in Crosspoint Alley and took you to him. Had I left you there, you would not have died. Even though it bled, your neck wound was not deep enough to kill you." His accent was American but tinged with an exotic note no less than primeval. It evoked images of jagged mountain peaks and rugged, skyclad people with skin the color of sunbaked sienna.

His eyes burned at me from across the carriage. Two embers of dark coal smoldering within features graced with composure.

I clutched the modest collar of my pelisse tighter.

"Who tore my blouse?" I asked tentatively. "Was it you, the Hammer, or the Ripper?"

When he didn't answer, I made an impatient noise.

"Was it before or after you found me in the alley?" I prodded further.

Silence.

"Do you even know?" I demanded.

"Yes." His voice was as smooth and frigid as a clear Irish stream sluicing over hard stone.

"Well...then answer me." One look at his face caused me to amend my command. "If you please."

"Where I come from, answers are earned through sacrifice."

I tried and failed to swallow the lump of trepidation lodged like a marble in my throat. What kind of sacrifice would a man like Aramis Night Horse demand?

Blood, perhaps.

Mayhap only flesh.

I didn't want to find out. Did I?

"I just...I would like to know if it was the Ripper," I explained honestly. "I deserve that, at least."

"Perhaps," he conceded. "But is it your experience people get what they deserve?"

"No."

He made an infuriating motion with his jaw and eyebrows. One that told me his point had been made and that he would say nothing further on the subject.

It'd been him. Somehow, I knew it with chilling certainty. He'd torn away the high-necked collar. And, for some reason, had kept ripping until the garment was nothing but tatters in his hands.

No image generated by my mind's eye of the occurrence made any semblance of sense.

I'd barely spoken a dozen words to the Blade in as many months, and he'd given me nothing but orders and the occasional corpse. Always staring with those obscure, dark eyes until I made some sort of gesture of understanding. I wasn't proud of the fact, but I often found myself speechless in the company of Mr. Night Horse.

Though, why I couldn't be blessed with that sort of wisdom—or caution—at the moment was beyond the likes of me. Perhaps I was getting used to his company enough for my mortal terror to abate to the aforementioned loquacious unease.

"The Ripper was gone," I deduced. "When you came upon me in the alley?"

"Whoever cut you was gone." A skeptical mien tightened the beautiful skin over high cheekbones sharp enough to etch glass.

Did he not believe my assailant to be Jack?

"Not interrupted by you, then," I clarified, which garnered me a barely perceptible nod.

So, murder—specifically *my* murder—had not been the Ripper's intent during our interaction. What was the significance of that? Why would he want to know what I thought of Mr. Sawyer's demise?

Seized by a sudden chill, I burrowed my hands into the pockets of my pelisse, grazing what was left of the turquoise beads.

I could ponder my terrifying interaction with the Ripper when I was alone and out of danger. Also, after I'd had a few hours' sleep and something to eat. What sat before me now was an opportunity to glean information. I wondered if interrogating Mr. Night Horse was clever or foolish.

Letting this chance slip through my fingers would be pure cowardice.

Better to die a fool than a coward...

I think.

"Did you—know Frank Sawyer?" I ventured.

"You mean, did I kill him?"

"Aye, I was working up to that, I'll grant you."

"Do you think I'd confess to his murder if I had?"

His answer evoked anger in me, which I suspect shocked us both more than a little. If there was one thing I despised, it was a person who answered a question with another question. "It's not as if I don't *know* what it is you do, is it? What you *are*. I've rid the world of enough of your victims to show a bit of good faith. What am I going to do, go to the police? I don't ask these questions to condemn you for Mr. Sawyer's murder. I ask for my own peace of mind. All I want to know is if it was you having a bit of gruesome fun with Mr. Sawyer, or if the Ripper has truly returned to torment London again."

"To torment *you*," he corrected.

I fought the intense urge to squirm beneath his shrewd regard.

"I thought you said he confessed to the deed when he had a blade at your throat."

"Yes, well..." How did I articulate my concerns? Something about that interaction in the alley felt wrong, somehow. And I still wanted to test Croft's theory that Jack hadn't carried out his dastardly deeds alone. The Blade would make a perfect accomplice to the kind of work for which the Ripper was infamous.

Extracting the beads from my pocket, I extended my hand to him. A peace offering of sorts.

"Those do not belong to me." He made no move to take them. "I didn't kill Mr. Sawyer. And neither did the Ripper."

At this, my head snapped up. "How could you possibly know that?"

He gestured to where my thumb fidgeted with the beads. "Where would Jack the Ripper acquire turquoise like that?"

"He could have had them imported from America," I suggested. "I imagine one can buy turquoise at great expense just as we do gems and the like."

"Then why suspect me at all? If the stones are so readily available?"

I scowled. Mostly because he'd made an excellent point. In truth, I had the impression turquoise was *not* so easily obtained. But I could be sorely mistaken. I might make a comfortable living now, but life had taught me that I still had much to learn about the value of things.

"Aren't *you* curious as to the owner of these?" I asked.

"No. I have plenty of turquoise of my own." He parted the open collar of his dark shirt to expose a string of similar beads artfully set in silver. The necklace gleamed against the smooth, hairless amber hue of his chest above a different strand that seemed to have been intricately carved from ivory. Or bone.

"Even though you're a foreigner, you mostly wear English fashion...why not a cravat?" I asked. I thought he'd look rather smart in one, and then his chest wouldn't be on distracting display.

"I don't like cravats," he answered simply.

"Oh..." As far as reasons went, it was a sound one. "But still, if these beads are from—"

"Does it matter to me where someone else's beads came from?"

"It does if they imply that you're a murderer."

"I *am* a murderer." He said it as though reminding a simpleton that the sky was blue or that rain was wet. "My people were not miners or workers of turquoise. Though we traded for it on occasion with people from the south. The gems we found were usually glass or sometimes sapphires. If I'm honest, I'm not fond of the stone."

"Then why wear it?"

He scrutinized me for a long moment before he answered. "It identifies me."

"Oh." To my eternal discomfiture, I sort of ran out

of things to say. Did he mean he identified with the stone? Or that the stone identified him to others?

A safer question leapt into my mind like a startled rabbit. "Do you know of any other Indians? Hereabouts, I mean. Anyone to whom these might belong?"

To say his displeased frown dismayed me would be a gross understatement. "The only Indians I know are from India."

"Right. Well...any other of...*your* people, then."

"All *my* people are dead," he informed me drolly.

I ceased to breathe for a full minute as I gaped at him, doing my best to make sense of the words he'd so blithely strung together to form one of the most lugubrious statements imaginable.

"Certainly not—not *all* of them," I stammered. "I mean, I know a great deal of...*you* have been... killed in the wars..." I faltered, stuck on his revelation. "But, *surely,* some of your people survived. That is to say, *you* did."

I couldn't tell you if it was exhaustion or astonishment causing my witlessness. But, suddenly, I didn't want to know what I knew. For nigh on two years, Aramis Night Horse had been an absolute enigma to me. A sort of preternatural being who melded with the London mists. A primal hunter who'd adapted to urban environs but still capable of some primordial brand of mystic slaughter.

At the moment, he was a man. One who'd lost what I had lost. Maybe on an unimaginable scale.

He regarded me with a touch of pity as though he understood my inner struggle. "Your people. Irish people. They live in tribes."

He posed it both like a question and an assertion, so it took me a bemused moment to reply. "We call them clans, but yes, they do. Or did. That way of life isn't so prevalent anymore."

"My nation is the Niitsitapi. In English, we are

called the Blackfoot. We once numbered as many as the Irish, and our lands were twice as vast. Your tribe—your clan—is the Mahoney Clan." He paused, his eyes shifting to catch an errant thought. "What means Mahoney?"

My Aunt Nola had taught me this when I was young. "In the old language, it was *O'Mathghamhana*, which loosely means *Clan of the Bear*."

My answer seemed to please him as he peeled his shoulders from where they rested against the seat and shifted toward me. "My tribe—my people—were the *Peenaquim*. It means *seen from afar*. There were so many, you could find our village for miles."

"I see," I whispered, and I did. But that didn't stop him from explaining.

"If the Mahoney Clan is...exterminated, there are still Irish, are there not?"

Mutely, I nodded. A lump of emotion lodged in my throat.

"There are still Blackfoot," he said.

But no Peenaquim.

Little did he know that we had more in common than he realized. There were not many Mahoney left, either. For much the same reason. They'd been *exterminated*, to borrow his word.

What had happened to the Peenaquim, I wondered?

I thought of all the reasons the clannish philosophy was fading in my country. Ancient hostilities caused clans to war between themselves. For untold centuries, there was raiding, raping, and many regrettable conflicts. The skirmishes impeded the clans from uniting against foreign invaders. Rudimentary arms gave way to advanced weapons. Unwise leaders signed reckless treaties. Unscrupulous invaders broke those agreements.

And then came the Christians. With a whole new set of troubles.

Their wars still claimed so many.

I didn't want to show Night Horse how his words affected me, but I wasn't convinced I could hide it from him. Especially as I forced my next question through the thickness gathered in my throat. "What happened once your people were...gone? Did you seek sanctuary?"

"No." He picked a tuft of imaginary lint from his suit jacket. "I sought revenge."

The blood seized in my veins. This, I could appreciate. "Did you find it?"

If I thought Aramis Night Horse was intimidating when he frowned, I underestimated what his smile could do to me. It contained a glee only found in nightmares. I could see the blood of his enemies staining his brilliant white teeth as he feasted on the still-beating hearts he tore from their chests.

I could hear their screams as he grinned.

"Did you find other Niit—Niitsit—Blackfeet to take you in?" I asked tremulously.

"Blackfoot," he corrected. "In my tribe, men were makers, shamans, braves, or hunters. I was both a shaman and a hunter before the American army came to claim our land for Montana."

Even as the morning turned from grey to silver, his eyes became impossibly darker. Raptor-like in their intense analysis of my reaction to his tale.

"My village was slaughtered while I was away with a hunting party. All of us hunters became braves upon returning. We painted our faces with the ashes of our loved ones and slipped into the army camp at night." His lashes fluttered with inconceivable memories. "We did things to them that even *your* Jack the Ripper has not yet done."

Every hair on my body lifted painfully as I digested his words.

Not yet. There was no telling what my Jack the Ripper might do.

Was he *my* Jack the Ripper? My personal crusade? Or did Mr. Night Horse mean the word in a broader sense?

Fiona's Jack the Ripper.

London's Jack the Ripper.

England's Jack the Ripper.

The symptom—the personification—of our sensational inhumanity toward women.

A particular kind of woman.

"I survived that night in a very similar way that you survived this one," he continued. "Wounded. Alone. But alive. You asked if I sought sanctuary with another tribe..." He remained silent from one side of Eaton Square Gardens to the other. I let him gather his words. His thoughts.

"I became a killer," he revealed in that neutral way of his. "I began to delight in spilling blood. And did not want to visit that on my people."

My brows drew together. "I see you have no trouble visiting it on mine. Not only do you delight in it, you profit from the spilling of their blood."

He shrugged and smirked. "These are not truly *your* people, are they? You are almost as much an outsider as I am."

"No, I suppose they are not my people," I admitted, as much to myself as to him. When I had previously referred to *my people,* I'd theoretically meant the fair-skinned people of the civilized west. In my subconscious, I considered myself *a part* of them. *Apart* from him. His dark-skinned people. But...I was certainly not English. How strange, that in one category I might be considered one of them. And in another, I was more like him: a clannish pagan ruled by Christian imperialist invaders.

Something to ponder...

"This place," He gestured out the window toward the buildings of brick blocking our view of the sky.

"This machine of steel and stone and light and money, did to your people what it is doing to mine, only much longer ago."

I nodded. Wondering if I was a traitor for being here in London. For loving this glittering, grimy city just as ardently as I had my native Gaelic land.

"We—my people—are still at war," I told him. "With ourselves. And with them." I thrust my chin toward the window. A gesture to encompass all the empire. "The battles are just quieter now. Fewer cannons and more rhetoric. Our battlefields are our neighborhoods, and their warfare is as economic as it ever was violent."

He leveled me with a meaningful look. "And yet you live among your enemies and profit from the spilling of their blood."

The way he gave my words back to me stole every thought from my head, and every remonstration from my tongue.

The knowledge of this lifted a corner of his mouth. "We are not so different. Fiona of the Bear Clan."

Unsettled. Displeased. I muttered, "I wish that was not so."

"There is a charming saying you English have. If wishes were horses..."

"Then beggars would ride."

"We will always be beggars, you and I." A somber note washed away all traces of amusement from his face. "Wishing the past was different. Think of who is gone. Hating who took them from us. Dreaming of vengeance."

"What do you know of my dreams?" Curling my hands into fists, I wrapped my arms tightly around myself, hoping to create a shield against his distressing perceptivity.

"Only that you whisper Mary's name when you sleep. And *his*. Other people call him the Ripper. But to you, in your sleep, he is Jack. He is a man, not a monster."

"He is both," I murmured.

He nodded once. I'd seemingly pleased him again. "The only monster is man."

That Aramis Night Horse knew something I didn't know about myself; that he'd watched me sleep, dreaming of Mary as he conveyed me from Crosspoint Alley, was an intimacy I couldn't face. Not tonight when I shook from exhaustion.

"What were your people like?" I asked the painful question in a gentle voice.

He peered at me oddly. "It is hard to describe a whole people. There are good ones and bad. Weak and strong. Beautiful and..." He slid me a level look. "Monstrous."

"Of course." What a silly thing to ask.

"My people laughed."

It was the last thing I expected him to say. The way his gaze softened as he stared into the past, transfixed me utterly.

For an ephemeral moment, a mélange of emotive manifestations tightened the smooth skin over sharp, high cheekbones. "We hunted and fought and feasted and fucked. But, mostly, we laughed. And we danced."

I could scarce believe it. Here I sat, reminiscing with an assassin. Finding common ground. Sharing stories of loss. I could not decide if this boded well or ill for me.

"The Mahoneys were jolly, as well." I found myself recalling. "We'd gather around a fire with fiddles, flutes, and drums. And we'd drink and dance until our feet ached and screamed at us to stop. I think they could hear us laughing in Scotland, could mark the sounds of our shoes on the ground." My lips melted into a smile, and suddenly his gaze was more alert as he searched my face.

Maybe this was a memory we shared. Bonfires warming the cheeks of those now long gone. Animal skins stretched over frames of wood, driving hearts and feet to fly in tandem. Flute melodies lifting the spirits. The poetry of ancient songs stirring our souls, taught to us by our elders.

The hedonistic worship of the night.

Maybe this was something all clans, all tribes, all *people* once did. Something our souls still ached to do.

"We, neither of us, laugh much anymore," he predicted.

"No, Mr. Night Horse," I whispered tremulously. "In that, you and I are very much alike."

It impressed me how still he sat. He didn't fidget or smoke or examine parts of himself or his surroundings. There was no folding or unfolding of arms. No touching his hair or adjusting his clothing.

Also, he stared at me for an uncomfortably long time until I realized why looking at someone without interruption or respite was considered so rude. After a moment, layers of yourself began to peel away beneath the unrelenting examination. I'd never known how distressing that could feel until just then.

"You see too much death, Fiona," he observed.

I huffed at him, pulling a cloak of indignation around my shoulders to warm the chill beget by loss. "That's rich, coming from the likes of you." I'd grown bolder in his company, in our candid exchange.

"Killing. It is an action on both the part of the killer and the victim. A passing, or a journey. A transition from being here to not being here. Death is a quiet thing. A lonely thing. It is not so much for me to bear. It is not so hard for me to do."

"Isn't it?"

"Those are my moments, Fiona."

I wished he'd stop saying my name like that. So familiar. Almost...tender.

"Your moments are after death. In dealing with the offal that is left behind. The anguish. Or the satisfaction. The vindication. The damnation. The noises of grief, and things that are wet. The smell of fear and blood and shit. The sight of who is left behind, not just the bodies but also the beloveds. Those things are heavy." As was the hand he rested on my shoulder. "They weigh on you. If you are not careful, they might...shackle your spirit to this world when it is your time."

Did the Blade worry for my soul? Like Aidan did? "Are you saying you believe in ghosts?" If he did, how did he feel about creating more than a few of them?

He gave a non-committal shrug, his lethal hand sliding down my arm until it found the beads still cupped in my lap. Lifting one, he examined it in the gathering light. "I believe the dead haunt us, one way or another." He leaned forward, eyes glinting, and his ponderous mouth softer than I'd ever seen it.

For a moment, I feared he meant to touch me. To kiss me or some such ridiculous thing. Instead, he gripped the handle of the door and swung it open, revealing the familiar, tidy, red-brick row houses of Tite Street.

To my astonishment, he caught my jaw with his fingers and lifted my neck, though whether to inspect the Ripper's handiwork or the Hammer's, I could only guess.

"Be careful in the dark," he cautioned. "You've drawn the attention of a killer."

I didn't breathe again until he released me.

He pulled the shadows back around him like a mantle, settling his shoulders against the crimson velvet seat of the coach like a king would his throne.

"Good evening, Mr. Night Horse," I muttered, remembering my manners before I stepped down onto the walk.

"Good morning, Miss Mahoney."

The shadows were, indeed, retracting down the bricks of my home, the sunlight burning away the so-called dangers of the dark.

As the driver snapped the reins across the broad rumps of his team, galvanizing them to trot away, an important query leapt onto my tongue. I took several futile steps toward the carriage, my hand out as though an invisible string could pull it back to me.

To which killer did Mr. Night Horse refer to in his warning? The Hammer? The Ripper?

Or himself?

CHAPTER 8

"Here's what's going to happen next." The voice in my ear reeked of wicked suggestion, almost as much as the man it belonged to reeked of equal parts Irish inebriation and iniquity.

"We two will part ways for the abbreviated time it takes to walk in our front doors, cast off the filth of the night, and then meet in the garden for tea. Whereupon *you*, my darling, are going to confess to me in precise and comprehensive detail *why* you've been dropped at your stoop at dawn *sans* a blouse beneath that blood-stained pelisse like a common tart. And *who* you spent the night with."

I turned to the one man who never failed to bring a genuine smile to my soul. One whom I'd met on innumerable occasions such as this. Both of us staggering home at all hours and exchanging gruesome gossip until we'd settled enough to sleep.

"Jealous?" I taunted.

"Obviously." He held his gloves rather than wore them. The limp, expensive *accoutrement* draped lackadaisically over his palm. In his other hand, he clutched a gaudy walking stick, the bejeweled handle of which he touched to his forehead in greeting. "Except for the bits with the blood."

Everything about him was a little too long. His face, his limbs, his hair. And yet, with charisma and wit as flawless as his porcelain skin, he was perhaps the loveliest man of my acquaintance.

"Pray, how can you tell I don't have a blouse on?" I inspected my own pelisse, modestly buttoned beneath my throat, barely concealing the wound above my clavicle.

"Because I am a master of observation. And you, dear Fiona, are a woman of discrete indulgences. I've noted it is what you wear *beneath* your elegant dark frocks that makes you an intriguing character. You've always a bit of silk ribbon and expensive lace at your throat. Or vibrant combs in your hair."

The series of flamboyant gestures whilst he spoke never ceased to mesmerize me.

"*Why dress up for corpses?* I used to wonder." He tapped his chin dramatically. "Then I realized, a woman does not accessorize unless it matches *something*. Your unmentionables, I'd imagine." He swirled a finger in the direction of my more *unmentionable* parts. "You delight in scandalizing yourself rather than other people. Of holding your naughty secrets close to the skin, as it were." He eyed my black garb as though he could see through it to the butter-gold corset and garters beneath, beribboned with pale green bows and little silk rosebuds.

Both the Hammer and the Blade had seen everything above the waistband of my skirt. Even those scoundrels had had the discretion not to remark upon my intimate attire.

Well, that was Oscar Wilde for you.

Blushing furiously, I pushed the playful playwright toward the stoop next to mine. His entire suit was plush, a rich and extremely velvet trimmed with burgundy silk which matched his cravat. His long cloak must have cost the blood of several minks.

"I'll thank you not to mention my unmentionables on the street, you cad!"

"Very well." He allowed himself to be propelled with his usual conviviality. "Let's discuss them in the garden in a quarter-hour."

"That's not enough time to dress *and* make decent tea."

"Half-past, then."

Releasing him to stumble up his own steps, I checked the watch I kept on the end of a very delicate chain.

If I planned to attend Mr. Sawyer's autopsy by eight o'clock, then I'd missed my window for sleep. "Better make it coffee, I'm dead on my feet."

"*Níl luibh ná leigheas in aghaidh an bháis.*" He yawned half of this in our native tongue and disappeared inside.

I shuddered as I mounted my own stairs, acknowledging the prophetic veracity of his words.

There's no remedy for death.

Maybe not, but coffee came close.

Somewhat refreshed by a cold wash and fresh clothing, I arrived a little late in my cheerful back garden, unhinging the latch so Oscar could let himself in. Hollyhocks, lobelia, and violas lent a perfect fragrance to our cherished—if ill-timed—meals.

An eerie silence settled about me. It was as though all the ambient sounds of the bustling morning had been smothered by an intruder. No larks called, no doves cooed in the eaves. The air became thick and still. Expectant.

I again felt that gaze upon me. The one that seemed to reach through the layers of my clothing—and perhaps even deeper, still. Through the layers of my skin.

The dread I felt was not an abnormal sensation for a woman who more or less lived alone. Especially at night. But I'd never felt it so intensely, and never in the middle of a sunlit morning.

I turned to inspect the fences, crawling with ivy, and the thick hedges providing my little oasis of privacy in such a crowded city.

Could someone conceal themselves in the shadows beyond? Could they be watching me, even now?

Not without alerting my neighbors, surely.

But I didn't know that, did I? The hedges were thick enough to—

The gate banged shut behind me, and I nearly leapt out of my skin.

"What are you looking at?" Oscar squinted toward the hedgerows hiding the wrought iron fence that separated my garden from the one adjacent. He looked fresh as a spring daisy in a cream linen morning suit with a matching brimmed hat and carried with him a tray of sumptuous dark coffee and fresh scones.

"Nothing," I said, rather too brightly. "A shadow caught my eye."

"That doesn't surprise me, you are a woman of the shadows. Of course, they appeal to you."

I couldn't think of a reply to that, so I accepted a linen and draped it across my lap as he arranged our repast.

We preferred to sit in my garden, as Aunt Nola tended to the flora out here as carefully as she did her own neuroses.

"I'll dish the scones," he offered, "whilst *you* dish the dirt."

I measured my words with the concise extents of an alchemist. One did not simply blurt to a well-connected writer that they had met Jack the Ripper in a dark alley unless one wanted to read the story in the papers the next morning. Not that I worried dear Oscar would write the article himself, but I was under no illusion that I was the only confidant with whom he shared gossip.

What was it the Hammer had quoted? Two people could keep a secret if one of them was dead.

It struck me then that I wasn't exactly certain how dangerous my secrets were...to either of us. But Oscar was privy to almost everything about my past, and as far as I knew, he hadn't even whispered of it.

He had secrets of his own.

"I'll tell you mine, if you tell me yours." I borrowed time with banter, one of Oscar's favorite activities. "Just where were *you* reveling last night dressed in such sumptuous garb?"

"The Savoy, darling, where else? I'm tinkering with an idea for a play. It has everything. Obsession, lust, slaughter, you know, all the best parts of the *good book*."

"What's this play called?" I queried, noting that the whites of his eyes were stained a dull pink.

"Salome." He spread his fingers before him as he revealed the name. "She's the perfect jezebel, isn't she?"

I used a linen to remove a smudge from my spectacles. "Wasn't Salome a virgin?"

"Exactly!"

I replaced the spectacles to peer at him curiously. "I don't follow."

"She danced for Herod Antipas, made him want her. Made *everyone* want her. He, in turn, offered her whatever her heart desired. Half of his kingdom."

"Right, I know that bit, I've read the Bible." I made a gesture for him to err on the side of brevity.

"Though she's a virgin, she used sex and treachery to bring about the macabre execution of John the Baptist," he explained solicitously. "She is both virgin and whore." He used his left hand to weigh the virgin, and the right hand, the whore.

We are all of us whores...

"She sold a dance for a death," I whispered.

"And what a bargain." He waggled expressive brows at me.

"They'll never allow it on a London stage in your lifetime," I predicted, as biblical characters were illegal to portray.

"I'll have to write it in Paris, apparently. This city is growing too cold to stay the winter."

I would have believed his insouciance had he met my eyes before producing a cigarette on the end of an elegant ivory holder along with a book of matches.

"Does Constance very much mind that you enjoy the lavish comforts of the Savoy while she remains at home?" I'd noticed of late, a particular distance between the playwright and his perfectly lovely wife. Speculation abounded throughout our bohemian district as to the state of Oscar's affairs.

Not because he had affairs. Everyone hereabouts had affairs. The conjecture wasn't confined to the name of his lover, but to the sex thereof.

"Constance minds Cyril and Vyvyan, and I mind how much noise those adorable miscreants of mine make whilst I'm writing." He blew a puff of smoke into the morning and followed it with a sip of coffee.

We gazed at each other over our cups across the round mosaic table upon which I'd spread an expensive gold lace cloth.

I didn't tell him that I suspected he'd not been *writing* at the Savoy.

And he didn't tell me to mind my own business.

We offered each other closed-lipped smiles and sipped coffee strong enough to strip the need for sleep from our blood.

"Come now, Fiona," he urged, tapping some ash onto the grass and resting his chin in his hand. "You very well know I subsist on absinthe and ado. You must tell me of your latest adventure in all its gruesome glory."

I began with poor Frank Sawyer's ripperesque murder and his lake of blood. I delighted in explaining *pittura infamante* to him as Oscar was ignorant of the antiquated practice. I was relieved to discover I was not the only one.

For such a bombastic man, Oscar was a surprisingly attentive listener and made all of the appropriate noises as I spun the tale of my heart-stopping alleyway encounter with the Ripper into a simple mugging for his benefit. I did, however, loosen my collar to reveal the Hammer's stitches, and was nearly out of coffee when I reached the part of the recounting where I'd been deposited at my doorstep by an infamous American assassin.

Releasing a low whistle, Oscar lit his second cigarette. "I'd call blarney on the entire narrative if it weren't just absurd—nay, *preposterous*—enough to be accurate."

"I wouldn't blame you." I released a sigh, feeling somewhat unburdened by the telling of my misadventures.

"A blouse ripped to shreds by the dusky hands of a handsome savage." Oscar sighed romantically.

"I don't imagine he'd appreciate being called that."

He leaned in to account, "I observed Aramis Night Horse once at the Café Royal, you know. What an intoxicating sight he is."

An inarticulate noise of disbelief squeaked out of my nose. "That's what you're concentrating on? I tell you about a perfectly gory murder, not to mention the fact that my throat was nearly slashed, and all you can think about is who took off my blouse to doctor the wound?"

He slid me a mischievous smile. "To be perfectly fair, darling, we've discussed your gory murders a multitude of times, but I'm unaware that anyone, as yet, has taken off your blouse. You are both a paradox and a prude."

A virgin and a whore. Like Salome.

"You take that back, Oscar Fingal O'Flahertie Wills Wilde!" I shrieked, tossing a linen at him in mock outrage. "I am *no* prude. I'll have you know my fiancé removed my blouse more than once upon a passionate interlude."

"You're referring to the pulchritudinous priest that calls around sometimes?"

"You know I am." I did my best to wither him with my glare.

"Yes, but instead of properly debauching you, he joined a famously celibate order, didn't he? More's the pity. Why do you think that is?"

I poured myself a second cup of coffee. Oscar's wit was most often entertaining, but at times, it came with a cutting price. "Don't be cruel," I admonished. "He broke my heart."

"The heart was made to be broken." He waved his cigarette lavishly. "Everyone knows that. Your tragedy is that you're still in love with a man who is in love with God."

I was in no mood to discuss my tragedy, and so, we sat in silence for a moment, listening to the vibrant sounds of the morning and the commotion of industry filtering in from the river.

"The book of life begins with a man and a woman in a garden, does it not?" Oscar observed dreamily. "It ends with Revelations. I hope we shall be, from now until the end, revealing ourselves in the garden after such adventurous nights."

"Now until the end of what?" I mused.

A world-weary sound escaped him as he motioned to our spacious, tidy houses and lovely gardens. "The end of *this*...whatever this is. Matrimony, civility, prosperity."

Did he mean ours, his, or England's, I wondered?

Troubled, I placed my hand over his. "Is something bothering you, Oscar?"

He shook his head, no, but answered the question in the affirmative. "I've been having dreams lately. Nightmares full of dire warnings and signs...apocalyptic, really. And yet, I can't seem to heed them. To do so would require me to change who I am, and that I cannot bring myself to do."

The hand beneath mine trembled a bit, and I wondered if he was in danger.

Or worse, in love.

"I know this goes against everything we Irish believe," I said, doing my best to offer comfort. "But I've long held dreams are merely the conscience tending to your fears, desires, and memories while you sleep. I dream of my family's death often. Of Mary's. I dream of the Ripper. I think I do because they are so often with me whilst I'm awake."

"You truly think so?" His lively eyes widened with a bit of hope.

"Categorically," I lied. In truth, I hadn't made up my mind about this musing quite yet, but I thought it was something both of us needed to hear. Nightmares had a way of following one into the morning, and neither of us wanted that. "It is not wise to find symbols in everything that one encounters," I told him. "It makes life too full of terrors."

An inspired smile replaced his brooding frown, and he extracted a short pencil and a little diary from the pocket of his vest. "I'm writing that down," he informed me, as he often did. "I may just use that later. Now, let's not dwell on our sorrows whilst we can be entertained by those of others. Tell me more about this Frank Sawyer and his turquoise beads."

At this, I paused. "I never really stopped to consider that the beads might, in fact, be Mr. Sawyer's. I automatically assumed they belonged to the murderer."

"To the Ripper?" He seemed to digest this slowly.

"Yes. But where would a poverty-stricken man like Mr. Sawyer obtain such rare and expensive stones?"

"He could have stolen them, I suppose," Oscar postulated. "Perhaps from the murderer."

It didn't seem likely. "Mr. Sawyer wasn't a thief. He was a hard-working, staunch Catholic with no enemies to speak of."

"Ha!" Oscar swatted his thigh. "Then the murderer is not the Ripper, obviously."

"You can't know that," I argued.

"I can, and I do," he volleyed back. "Frank Sawyer's killer is most *unequivocally* someone of his close acquaintance."

"How do you figure?"

"Because, dear Fiona, if a man has no enemies, then he is almost certainly intensely disliked by his friends."

At this, a laugh erupted from me. From us both. I adored Oscar's observations of humanity. They were unrivaled in their poetry by any philosopher, alienist, or spiritualist I'd ever read.

Also, they were rarely wrong.

Leaning forward, I took a contemplative sip of my coffee, ticking my teeth a few times against the porcelain rim of the cup as I thought. I still couldn't bring myself to reveal that the Ripper—or who *might* be the Ripper—had already confessed to the deed.

"So, if you had to make a wild speculation, who would you say killed him?" I asked.

"Mrs. Sawyer, of course."

I shook my head. "It can't be, the inspectors said she had an alibi."

He lifted a skeptical eyebrow at me. "You underestimate your sex, Fiona, if you assume a woman cannot commit murder without being in the room. Tell me, is Mrs. Sawyer a handsome woman?"

The answer to the question made me squirm. Was it

a sin to tell the truth if that revelation was cruel? "Not...particularly."

"So plain as a peaky nag, then," he surmised.

"I don't know that I would say—"

"Was Mr. Sawyer a handsome man?"

I searched my memory of last night. "There was too much blood to get an accurate sense of his aspect. One dies inverted, and everything sort of...pools in his head."

Wincing, Oscar put down his scone, scrubbing the crumbs off his fingertips with quick, dainty rubs. "I've always hated that word...invert."

It didn't escape me that *invert* was another word for homosexual.

Tapping his chin, he asked, "Where does Mr. Sawyer work?"

"The docks, if I remember correctly."

"Not a place one finds a great deal of women, so he likely met her somewhere else like...a public house or possibly church, seeing as how he was a God-fearing man."

I blinked at him, utterly confused. "Met whom?"

"His mistress, Fiona. Really, do try to keep up."

I seldom could keep up with Oscar, but at the moment, I felt as though he were leading me somewhere ridiculous. I told him so. "You can't know he had a mistress. At this juncture, that's just rank speculation."

"Of course, I can. You only just said he had an ugly wife."

"I said nothing of the sort. I merely admitted she wasn't comely."

"Yes, well, I know you well enough to recognize when you're being kind."

"But what if *he* was unsightly?"

"I'm telling you, an unsightly man may use his wit, charm, and humor to make a woman fall in love with him. An unattractive woman, unfortunately, rarely has the luxury. Men do not use their hearts to fall in love as the fairer sex does, it's why our affection is so easily lost." For a surreal moment, I was unsure if he was going to laugh or weep as he stood and stretched his lithe body, regarding his house as one would an unpleasant conundrum. "Find his Salome, Fiona, and I promise you, the mystery will solve itself."

CHAPTER 9

"**D**id you find the Hanged Man?" My hand froze halfway to my cape as a veiled specter drifted to block my front door.

Aunt Nola often wore a shroud of black lace over her aging features and down her back. It was an utterly macabre practice, but she claimed it assisted her while walking among her spirit guides with ease. Apparently, they recognized her as one of their own. And while I found the idea of spirit guides prosaic and ridiculous...I did acknowledge that she was a living ghost. A shadow of a once vibrant woman who was tied to this one place. She haunted my home. She haunted *me*.

Nola had not left my house since I'd brought her here, aside from venturing into the gardens. And only then, on what we called her "good days."

Today was not likely to be one of them.

"How did you know about the hanged man?" I queried, recovering from my shock. "Surely, it's not in the papers yet."

Black velvet rasped against wine-red muslin as she rustled toward me. "You need to find the killer, Fiona, before he kills again."

Despite my skepticism, her dire words chilled me.

"I do what I can, Aunt Nola, but don't you think finding the killer is the inspectors' job?"

Claw-like fingers clung to my elbow as the smell of incense and mothballs stung my nose. When Aunt Nola spoke, it was like the words were shaken out of her, tumbling from trembling lips with no apparent shape or trajectory. "No, no, no. You already know him. And he knows you. He knows you so, so well." Her eyes were wide and wild behind her veil as she held up the card in her other hand for my inspection. "You—you just need to look him in the eyes. Right in the eyes, Fiona. And ask him *why*. Why did the hanged man deserve to die? What did he do wrong?" She released my elbow to tap the figure on the card several times too many.

"May I?" Reaching out, I took the card from Nola and inspected it thoroughly.

The Hanged Man. I hadn't realized he was part of a tarot deck. On the face of the card, a man hung from a crossed beam by one foot. His other knee bent in a triangle; hands tied behind his back. Exactly like Frank Sawyer, but for one significant difference.

The man in the card seemed alive. Relaxed even. Contemplating his fate rather than fighting it.

Pittura infamante.

This was an interesting development. I wondered if Aberline or Croft had made the connection. Neither of them seemed the type to study the arcane. But then, Inspector Croft had surprised me with a depth of intellect I'd not previously assumed he was burdened with.

"Would you mind, awfully, if I take this card for the day, Aunt Nola? I promise to return it."

"Yes. Yes," she encouraged. "Show the others. See what they see."

I didn't believe Aunt Nola could see the future.

But, sometimes... Sometimes, when I looked into her touched and tortured eyes, I feared I could see *my* future in them. That, maybe, reality would become too intolerable, and I'd begin constructing my own. That the world would seem too big and cruel, and so I'd limit it to whatever four walls I was allowed by the benevolence of a loved one.

Except, besides Nola, all my loved ones were dead or some other form of gone.

And I'd rather die than go to an asylum.

One must do one's best not to go mad, then.

A spurt of sudden tenderness and tolerance warmed my heart toward my father's sister. She looked like him, copper-haired and fair-skinned, plagued with a multitude of freckles. We resembled each other, actually, in both stature and structure. Though her teeth and eyesight were both perfect, whereas mine, were not.

I'd inherited a bit of my mother's darkness. Both literally and figuratively. She'd also been a pale woman, but her hair had been black as midnight, and her eyes blue as cobalt glass.

"A black Irish beauty," my father used to call her.

Grace Mahoney was dramatic and melancholic, whereas my father, Francis, had been light-hearted and quick-tempered. I supposed I was an assortment of all those qualities—with a few more for good measure.

I missed them so terribly...even their not-so-good days.

"You didn't come say 'hello' to Oscar in the garden." This was my gentle way of informing Nola that I was aware she'd likely been listening in as I'd told our neighbor the details of Frank Sawyer's murder, and *she'd* thought to show me *this* specific card.

There was no other way she could have known about the hanged man.

Her eyes shifted, and her movements became erratic and sharp. "My...my guides. They woke me. Told me I-I had to come show you this card before you left. So you could be looking for *him*, explicitly."

I didn't fail to notice that she hadn't addressed my

question. "Looking for whom? The hanged man? I already know where he is. They found a body last night. In fact, I'm on my way to the coroner's office to—"

"No. *No!*" She shook me a little, stunning me silent. Aunt Nola had been many distressing things since I brought her home from the asylum, but never physically confrontational. "*Him.* They said to look for him! In the faces of the killers you already know."

"Think you I'm acquainted with the killer?" I breathed.

"They said you know that he has killed before. He has killed those who did not deserve to die." Tears wobbled in Nola's voice, and I feathered a hand down the veil covering her hair.

Though I didn't acknowledge any veracity to her claims, I couldn't deny her predictions affected me deeply. My hands and feet felt cold and clammy, and my legs were a little less stable than before.

"Do you mean the Ripper, Nola?"

She recoiled from me with a hiss, gesturing wildly. "*I* mean nothing," she wailed. "*They.* They speak through me. I'm naught but their mouthpiece. You've never believed me. You don't acknowledge they're real, even though they're only trying to help you!"

"All right." Afraid she'd do herself a mischief on the banister with her gesticulating, I grabbed her wrists and held them firmly. The Hanged Man card drifted to the herringbone parquet floor as I clutched her fists and brought them to my lips, kissing her knuckles fondly.

"All right," I soothed. "I believe you, Nola. I'm sorry."

I believed she heard them. I believed she wanted to help me.

Regarding me with veiled eyes, her expression both wounded and suspicious, she quieted.

"Will you tell me what...*they* said the Hanged Man means?" I encouraged.

Instantly, she brightened. "I did an entire reading for you. You should come see."

It took every ounce of self-control I possessed to hide my extreme lack of enthusiasm. "I must be going to the hanged man's autopsy just now," I reminded her. "But perhaps you can tell me the meaning of *this* card. And when I return, you can show me the rest, when I have the proper time to digest it."

She listened to the silence for a moment. "Yes. Yes, they find this acceptable."

I found *them* infuriating.

Cautiously, I released her and stooped to retrieve the card.

She huddled near my shoulder, pointing with one gnarled finger. "The obvious meaning is suspension. This is a card of the in-between, you see."

Strange, I'd spoken to Aidan of the in-between just last night. We Celts have always believed that passages from one place to another are both sacred and terrifying. Doorways, gates, bridges. Even dawn and dusk. They are nebulous places where demons and fairies and even the odd deity can lurk. In between one place and another, the veil to the other world is at its most brittle. It is because of our tradition a husband must carry his bride over the threshold.

It protects her from the in-between.

I chewed on this as Nola continued sharing her premonitions about me. "You've been flirting with the in-between for too long. You are not firmly on one side or the other. The Hanged Man is at a crossroads. It's obvious what he's done thus far hasn't worked, and so he must pick a side. Take a path. Or he's vulnerable to all the perils of the Otherworld. To all the demons who reside there. Your reading shows that you're tethered by something—some*one*—whom you may never have. Searching for answers you might never find. If you follow your current path, Fiona, you will always be reaching, and your hands will always be empty."

This, of course, was no great psychic revelation, though I did wonder if I'd somehow underestimated how much of the world, of *me*, Aunt Nola understood. To whom did she refer that tethered me, in particular? Who would remain out of reach? Aidan? Mary?

Possibly Jack?

I chose my next words with great care. "If this card were pulled for someone else, does it have any other connotations? Ones that don't apply to me specifically, I mean?"

She tapped her chin and looked up and to the right, consulting her spirit guides, or more likely, her memory. "Punishment, sometimes. Redemption—no, not that —*atonement*. Your hanged man. He did something. Something for which he must be disciplined."

It was a blessing Nola didn't know just how much punishment poor Mr. Sawyer had been forced to endure.

The lace of her veil gritted against my lips as I kissed her forehead. With a heavy heart, I promised to run her a bath this evening with a bit of lavender and some Epsom salts. Sometimes, if I didn't bathe her, she forgot to do so herself. I'd been at work so often of late, the smell of sweat and mothballs alerted me that she'd waited too long.

Guilt seized me. Maybe I'd need to ask Polly, our maid-of-all-work, if she could take on more days a week than three. Perhaps Nola had regressed enough to need constant care.

With the thought weighing heavily on me, I bid my aunt goodbye and rushed down the block to Royal Hospital Road, where I was sure to find a hansom cab to conduct me to the Royal London Hospital. There, in the basement, Dr. George Bagster Phillips was slicing into Mr. Sawyer's corpse.

CHAPTER 10

If I had to assign Dr. Phillips' examination room a signature scent, it would be *eau de terror*. That is to say, the acrid, chemical, almost metallic mélange of aromas had the precise effect on the olfactory senses as mortal fear did. As sharp and repugnant as a mouthful of nails. There was's something loamy about it, as well. Most likely the result of a moist basement and the distinct threat of decaying flesh.

Doctor Phillips' occupation consisted of racing to keep ahead of decomposition. Of delaying it as long as possible until he might interpret the final signs of life.

He was another of the strange few who profited from the spilling of blood.

I arrived early to the coroner's office, as I knew Aberline would be precisely punctual, and I wanted a chance to converse alone with Dr. Phillips. I thought he might have some insight into the beads I still held in my pocket, and I absolutely couldn't discuss them in front of the inspectors. They'd be confiscated as evidence, and the subsequent outcomes of such a thing all boded ill for me.

The Hammer or the Blade would be instantly notified, if Croft didn't string me up for tampering with his scene first.

Dr. Phillips and I shared a fate, and therefore, we could share indiscretions, as well. There was a black market for corpses, you see, funded by none other than the most esteemed medical colleges in London. Aspiring surgeons and anatomists were in dire need of bodies for dissection, surgical practice, and the articulation of skeletons and the like.

And so, on occasion, I supplied Dr. Phillips with the bodies the Hammer delivered to me, and he outfitted the universities. We split the generous fee.

If I were going to risk breaking the law for the Hammer, I might as well get reimbursed double.

Behind the white screen partitioning the active autopsy from the rest of the cavernous morgue, two men stood over a table, their gestures reminding me of some macabre marionette show. Shadows with scalpels and blustery voices.

"I couldn't more heartily disagree with you, Bond," Dr. Phillips said. "This isn't at all an act of rage brought on by erotic mania. This sort of crime is the product of strategic calculation and the dehumanization of the victim."

Upon noting the masculine conversation, I released a disappointed sigh.

So much for consulting with Dr. Phillips alone.

Subsequently, I suppressed a gag as I'd forgotten to breathe through my mouth. It took several moments of stabilizing myself with the handle of a long drawer used for the storage of bodies to fortify me against an encroaching bout of hysteria for which my sex was often condescended to.

It was as much a mystery to me as anyone how I could stand the natural odors of death, but not the chemical ones.

Or why, every time I visited a morgue, I expected eight tables lined before me instead of one. Sixteen feet tenting sterile white shrouds.

Another memory. Another nightmare superimposed over my reality. The exterminated Mahoney Clan.

And I, the lone survivor.

"Let's not forget, Phillips, that my area of expertise is profiling violent offenders." Dr. Thomas Bond, and Dr. George Phillips conversed in the way of men in their profession, eschewing their titles in private for the sake of brevity, or so I assumed.

"Pish." Dr. Phillip's shadow gestured with his scalpel. "Offender profiling is an infant science not yet old enough to be weaned from its mother. And let *us not forget* that your profile did exactly nothing to aid in the Ripper's apprehension. Why the inspectors summoned you to my hospital—to *my* morgue—is beyond my scope of comprehension."

Bond clasped his hands behind his back. "As is the subtle and complex science of the brain," he muttered.

"Why you—!"

To advertise my presence, I disturbed a tray of metal instruments adjacent to an empty examination table, exclaiming my hasty apologies immediately afterward.

I tried not to smile too broadly as both men popped a head around opposite sides of the white screen. Two of London's preeminent surgeons looking as sheepish as caught-out, quarreling schoolboys.

"What ho, Miss Mahoney?" Dr. Phillips rested a stabilizing finger on the used scalpel in his left hand. "I heard the word *Ripper* whispered over Mr. Sawyer, here, and was certain your shadow would quickly follow."

"You know me well, sir." I bobbed a curtsy, noting that, by all appearances, Dr. Phillips had gotten just about as much sleep as I had. Beneath his surgeon's apron, his vest and shirtsleeves were rumpled, and his cravat askew. The pomade in his hair must have been from last night as it hadn't withstood his hat this morning, the strands jutting in eccentric angles.

Strange, as he was generally such a tidy man, in both action and appearance.

Dr. Thomas Bond, on the other hand, was the picture of a British surgeon. Dapper, crisp and handsome in the way one's father was, clad in a dark, woolen suit, starched collar, and a crimson cravat. With Dr. Phillip's impressive muttonchops and Dr. Bond's dashing mustache, they almost had a full beard between them.

"Dr. Bond." I nodded. "It's been too long."

"Miss Mahoney." He curtly kissed the air above my glove. Some would consider the gesture the height of propriety. Others would consider it an insult. It was impossible to tell how Dr. Bond meant the gesture.

He was another man, aside from Croft, whom I found difficult to properly read.

"How long has it been?" he asked in a voice as cool and smooth as the steel table upon which the corpse of Frank Sawyer was splayed before us.

"Since the Kelly inquest, I believe." Before he could offer a demurral, I reclaimed my hand and maneuvered around the screen. I positioned myself lengthwise along the table where Dr. Phillips was posted at the head, and Dr. Bond at the foot.

"Please, don't let me interrupt your...discussion."

"You know us doctors," Phillips said mildly. "Prefer a good debate to an actual discussion."

I inspected the dishes into which Mr. Sawyer's organs had been separated. His brain, the only organ left inside the body by the killer, had been extracted—presumably by Dr. Phillips—and placed in its own container. It gleamed wetly beneath the Royal Hospital's new electric lights. Like a maze, the brain. A tangle of mysteries. I wondered if we'd ever truly survey enough of it to make a decent map. To comprehend all the journeys one must take through the labyrinthine ripples to find one's self.

"This is highly irregular," Bond observed, though

from what I could tell, he conveyed more curiosity then censure. "Miss Mahoney is neither a nurse nor the police. Should she be privy to all this death and blood?"

"I'm a Post-Mortem Sanitation Specialist, Dr. Bond, I dare say I'm in the business of blood."

"Indeed," he murmured.

Did I detect a note of admiration?

Instead of looking up at him, I pinched the clean edge of the bowl containing the contents of Mr. Sawyer's stomach and tipped it a little, trying to get a good look beneath. Fish, potatoes, and maybe...maybe it had been fish pie, if that was a crust.

"I confess, I was glad to hear tell that you'd landed on your feet, Miss Mahoney," Dr. Bond said.

"What do you mean?" I checked the liver next. A bit larger than I was used to seeing, but nothing out of the ordinary.

"Upon meeting you at Miller's Court on the day we...found Miss Kelly, I assumed you were a...an associate of hers. I feared that you might one day share her fate." The cool inflection of his voice warmed a little. "I was glad to learn that you'd chosen another path, ghastly as it might be at times."

Dr. Bond and Dr. Phillips had both been called to Mary's crime scene. They'd watched me break apart. They'd watched Croft pull me, sobbing and hysterical, away from what was left of my friend.

Disconcerted, I made a non-committal sound and moved on to the kidneys.

"What are you looking for?" Dr. Bond asked.

"Missing parts," Dr. Phillips guessed before I'd drawn a breath to answer. "If memory serves, the kidney was a preferred delicacy of the Ripper."

"Just so," I said. "I took a peek in the basin last night, but it was rather dark. I noted all the organs were present, but I wondered if perhaps a piece was missing from one of them. As the Ripper only took and ate a portion of Catherine Eddowes' kidney, not the entire thing."

"Everything is undamaged and intact." Dr. Phillips motioned with the scalpel between Frank Sawyer's legs. "Whoever gutted this poor lad did so with a deft and precise hand, but was more intent upon making a ghastly example of him than a meal, in my professional opinion."

I had to admit, even to someone as used to death as I, the sight of an unsexed corpse turned the coffee in my stomach to an acid splash against my chest.

Swallowing was no easy feat after that.

"Quite," Dr. Bond agreed. "And upon perusal of your post-mortem report, I'm of the opinion that—"

"What the bloody hell is *she* doing here?" The rough growl announced the arrival of Inspector Croft. He charged around the screen like a Spanish bull, going so far as to stop and glare at me, his nostrils flaring.

I half expected him to paw at the ground, put his head down, and charge.

"I'd admonish you to watch your language in front of a lady, Inspector." Dr. Bond lowered thick, well-kempt brows over his mild eyes.

"That *lady* is looking at a man's spine through his open body cavity, and you're worried *I'll* offend her delicate sensibilities?" Upon noticing the carved-out hollow where Frank Sawyer's sex used to hang, Croft said a few more words I promised myself I'd research later, though I wasn't sure I'd find them in the dictionary.

"Miss Mahoney and I have an arrangement," Dr. Phillips revealed, and, for a moment, my pulse quickened. It wasn't as though I actually thought he would confess to our illegal activities, but, as I said before, Croft's presence put me on edge. I'd always suspected he saw much more than he let on.

I didn't very much think he'd mind seeing me hanged as a body snatcher.

"She often gains additional insight on a case once the police have cleared the scene," Phillips continued. "And, on occasion, I consult with her to ascertain if she found anything in the blood she cleaned up."

"Did you?" Croft demanded of me.

Suddenly, my pockets felt as if they contained bricks rather than beads.

"No," I lied.

Croft turned to Dr. Phillips. "Did you summon her to Frank Sawyer's common house last night?"

Dr. Phillip's soft grey eyes darkened, and he cast me a guilty glance. "As much as I trust Miss Mahoney's skills, I'd not call her to Dorset Street, Inspector. Not after Mary..."

"Interesting." Croft's glare pierced me like a sharp needle, but I refused to look away. "Consultation over, then. You may take your leave, Miss Mahoney."

During the exchange, Aberline had followed Croft around the screen and now finished exchanging handshakes with the doctors. "Oh, do stand down, Croft," he drawled. "I've similarly made use of Miss Mahoney's recollections, and to positive effect. Friends and family of victims tend to watch themselves around inspectors and constables. But they will reveal things in Miss Mahoney's presence wot have more than once provided a break in my case." The inspector took a post next to me, tipping his hat. "The London Metropolitan Police is obliged to you, m'girl."

I smiled at him, but mostly because I found anyone referring to me as *m'girl* at my age rather hilarious. And not a little flattering.

Croft stood across the table, and I was glad, as we'd have struggled to make room for his shoulders should the three of us stand abreast.

I met his scowl with a toothy—er, *toothsome* smile. I prayed my relief wasn't as palpable to everyone else as it was to me.

"Do pardon me, Dr. Phillips, for calling upon Dr. Bond to attend today," Aberline apologized. "Croft and I are fair certain Mr. Sawyer met his end by someone other than the Ripper, but we thought a congregation of a few of us Ripper veterans might create a more definitive picture. And I hoped that maybe we could make use of his profiling skills."

"We were only just discussing theories as to motive," Dr. Phillips gestured to Dr. Bond, with the scalpel he'd yet to relinquish. "Bond, here, only knows how to cry sexual psychosis, whilst I deduce the killer had clinical motives."

"See here! Erotic mania often has more to do with violent rage than actual sexual desire," Dr. Bond defended. "It appears to me that the castration was performed prior to death, and if that isn't sado-sexual, I don't know what is."

"Is that true?" Croft turned to Dr. Phillips, who nodded.

"My examination has led me to the conclusion that the series of events was thus. First, the murderer tied a fully clothed Mr. Sawyer's hands behind his back, as evidenced by the broken capillaries and bruising he presents with on the wrists and ankles here, and here." He motioned to a few red, angry circles that would not have been so visible had the corpse not any blood left in it. "The dislocated shoulder and broken clavicle suggest that the killer hung him by both his hands and his left foot whilst he made quick work with the knife. I can tell you, the killer was left-handed."

"That's why there were no footprints in the blood, other than Agnes Sawyer's," I realized aloud, earning a sour look from Croft. "If he was hung from the low rafter like a pig on a spit, the butchery is easily contained."

"Very good, Miss Mahoney." Dr. Bond pointed at the double gashes in Frank Sawyer's neck, still so prevalent even after Dr. Phillips had tucked his chin down to close the wounds. "Symbolism is very important to this killer, obviously. I'm of the opinion that he knew Mr. Sawyer intimately. This was less a crime of opportunity and more a crime of passion."

"Could the wife have had anything to do with it?" I ventured, thinking of Oscar's Salome theory. "Perhaps he was unfaithful. A mistress, maybe? Or her angry husband?"

"An angle we're considering." Aberline checked his watch. "But Mrs. Sawyer is a broken woman by all accounts. She claims her husband was a right angel. Without him, she's bound for the poor house."

"Guilt can break a person just as easily as grief, I think," I remonstrated.

"You've a rare mind, Miss Mahoney." Dr. Bond examined me as one might a puzzle with a missing piece.

Or a mystery in need of dissection.

"If we could continue?" The look Dr. Phillips leveled at his colleague rivaled that of Croft's in its brutality, but he finished his summation. "The killer must have merely unbuttoned the shirt and vest and pulled the trousers to the knees while the man hung by his hands and foot. Cutting first the..."—he flickered a glance at me before continuing—"the sex organ, then emptying the body cavity into the basin with surgical precision, and lastly, slicing the throat with these two deep, Ripper-like gashes. This accomplished, he redressed the man and cut the ropes from around Mr. Sawyer's hands, letting the rest of the blood drain from the victim's neck and cavity until exsanguinated."

We all stared at poor Mr. Sawyer with renewed appreciation for his ordeal. Croft, Aberline, and Bond had given in to the urge to cross one foot in front of the other, pressing their thighs together sympathetically.

I did my very best not to let my lips twitch. It

wouldn't do to let on how aware I was of the gratitude each man felt for what hung between his legs.

Not that any of this was funny, but laughter was as hysterical a response as tears, and I tended to lean toward one rather than the other. Which, to be honest, was no blessing, especially in my profession.

Tears were much more socially appropriate and acceptable, especially where murder was concerned.

"This further indicates that the murderer is not the Ripper," Croft surmised what we were all thinking. "He always sliced the throats first and conducted his mutilations after his victim had bled out."

I had the very distinct impression that every man in the room made a concerted effort not to look at me.

I didn't mind, as I was certain my expression would have invited speculation. My mind rapidly flung itself from thought to thought like a bee unable to commit in a flower garden.

No one seemed to think the Ripper had killed Frank Sawyer. No one but the Ripper, himself. He'd hissed it in my ear back in Crossland Alley. Hadn't he?

Neither the Hammer nor the Blade believed my assailant was, in fact, who he claimed to be.

Part of me wanted that to be true.

I yearned to confess everything. To blurt to all and sundry what exactly had befallen me the night prior. But then Aberline would ask what I was doing on the Strand at such an hour. Croft would place me in the proximity of the Velvet Glove only moments before he, himself, visited the Hammer.

I risked a glance at him and found him regarding me oddly from beneath the shadows of his sooty lashes.

I could fabricate that I'd been called to work, I supposed, but the canny inspectors would require proof, and I had none. As far as I knew, there were no other violent deaths in London last night save for the one before us.

Drat, I thought glumly before castigating myself for wishing such ill on another for the sake of my own convenience.

A convenient murder. Was there ever such a thing?

"Couldn't it be both?" Croft lifted his bowler hat away from his hair, threaded his fingers into the dark strands, and then replaced the brim low over his forehead.

"Both what?" Dr. Bond asked.

"The motive. Couldn't the killer have carefully calculated this murder and still have been driven to do so by a...what did you call it?" He motioned to Dr. Bond. "An erotic mania."

Both doctors shook their heads. "Calculation and mania do not go hand in hand," Dr. Bond explained.

"Perhaps not." Croft glanced at me again. "But I believe in a patient fury. In fact, I believe quiet fortitude is the most dangerous kind of rage."

Unwilling to ponder his meaning, I extracted the tarot card from my jacket and held the picture over Frank Sawyer's body for all to see. "You probably already considered this, but I wasn't certain if you were aware the tarot deck contains a card with a man positioned just as Mr. Sawyer was. The Hanged Man."

"We were, in fact, not aware." Aberline snatched the card away, inspecting it closely. "Never pegged you for a spiritualist, Miss Mahoney, being a pragmatic Irish woman and all that."

"I'm not. The deck belongs to my aunt."

"Did she tell you what it means, by chance?"

I hesitated. There was the translation Aunt Nola received from her spirit guides, and then there was reality. "She mentioned atonement. Punishment, redemption, that sort of thing. Though, maybe you know someone more knowledgeable about widely accepted card meanings that might offer more insight."

"See, Croft?" Aberline chuffed. "She's a right handy

girl to keep about. This goes hand in hand with your *pittura infamante* theory. Someone meant to punish poor Mr. Sawyer, here. The question is, wot for? Remind me of the crimes the Italians used to string a bounder up by his ankle for."

Croft ran his tongue over his teeth, working a tense jaw to the side. "Small infractions, if you remember. The defamation of an innocent woman, libel, bad debts."

"Like the debts Mr. Sawyer owed to the Hammer?" Aberline said ominously.

My heart leapt into my throat, almost choking my words out of me. "Mr. Sawyer? He knew the Hammer?"

"Can't say he *knew* him, as such." Aberline scratched beneath his top hat. "But he owed him, or rather his Syndicate, some money."

The Hammer, *that bastard*, had lied to me. Not that I should be surprised. He was a notorious criminal, after all. But still, that he'd done so after my show of good faith, knowing what I had riding on the case, certainly demonstrated the trust and esteem in which he held me.

Or the lack thereof.

"That's no business of hers," Croft gritted at Aberline, his eyes flashing with an electric fury of the distinctly *impatient* sort.

Both the doctors and Aberline seemed about to spring to my defense, but I wasn't one to leave such matters to a man. "That's exactly what this is, Inspector Croft," I spat. "My. Business. This is how I make my living. And this sort of information keeps me alive." More than any of them realized. "I'm not hindering your investigation by being here or at the crime scene or anywhere else. Quite the opposite, in fact, as everyone else has pointed out. I aid in the solving of mysteries, and I'm bloody good at it. But what I can't for the life of me figure out is why you're so intent upon acting like a horse's ass!"

His face looked as red as mine felt by the time I'd finished.

His Irish was up, as well.

"Better a horse's ass than a rat," he growled, stalking to a sideboard along the white-tiled wall and snatching Dr. Phillip's morning paper. The twine disintegrated in his hands by the time he reached our speechless circle, and he violently thrust *The London Evening Examiner* at me.

I'd no doubt in my mind he'd have slammed it down on the table for all to see had there not been a stiff corpse to ruin the effect.

GRUESOME MURDER IN WHITECHAPEL! the headline read, with the byline beneath: *THE RIPPER STRIKES AGAIN?*

I took the paper, blinking at it in disbelief. "You think I went to the papers?"

"There are details in that article known to no one but those of us in Frank Sawyer's rooms last night."

"There was any number of people in the Sawyer residence last night," I argued. "Maybe the press got to his wife. Or did you ever consider Constables Hurst and Fanshaw? They aren't possessed of a full wit between them. They were speculating up a storm right in the middle of Dorset Street for any eavesdropper to hear. Then there was the man who drove the coroner's cart and—"

"Let's not forget your priest," Aberline supplied. "Father uh—Fitzgibbon."

"Fitzpatrick," I corrected more sharply than I intended. "And Aidan's not *my* priest. Though he *is* more circumspect than any man in this room!"

"Er—didn't think of that," Aberline muttered conciliatorily. "I imagine you attend mass closer to Chelsea than Whitechapel."

That wasn't what I'd meant. And I should apologize to kind Inspector Aberline for my sharp tongue, but it was in my best interest to let that lie. One day, I might not feel so defensive regarding all things Aidan Fitzpatrick.

Apparently, today was not that day.

"Why do you automatically assume I'm the leak?" I demanded of Croft. "Because I'm a woman, is that it? Because we can't keep our flapping mouths shut?"

He stared at me. Hard. The scars on his knuckles stretching white over the bones as they curled into fists. "It's because I don't trust you." He nodded to the congregation and stormed off, leaving everyone but Mr. Sawyer feeling more than a bit awkward.

"Don't mind 'im, Miss Mahoney," Aberline patted my shoulder in a fatherly gesture, his accent thicker than usual. "he's not slept yet, and who knows the last time he ate? We fellows are cursed with the constitutions of a bear if we're deprived of eight hours, three solids, and afternoon tea. My Emma brings me sandwiches nigh every day at three o'clock. Croft doesn't 'ave no one to do such things for 'im."

"You're very kind, but you don't have to apologize for *his* behavior."

"You're not suspected of providing the press this information. You've been the picture of discretion before," he encouraged. "But...maybe it's safer if you avoid Croft and this case for a bit, yeah? If a devil like the Hammer's involved, who can even imagine what dangers are in store?"

"Who can imagine?" I echoed.

I could. At least, I had a good idea.

"A good find, this." He handed the Hanged Man card back to me. "Could be our key to unlocking the motive. I've a young spiritualist acquaintance, a surgeon, Artie Conan Doyle. Right good 'ead for mystery, that chap. I'll pen him and see what 'e and 'is lot make of this 'anged Man."

I nodded, trying to regain my composure. I hadn't slept, either, or I'd have taken more care to keep Croft from getting beneath my skin and into my Irish blood.

"So, we are agreed we can publicly and categorically refute the Ripper rumors, then," Bond prodded, retrieving his hat and cane. "Just some grisly counterfeiter, or possibly not even that."

"I'd say so." Aberline nodded. "Dr. Phillips?"

"I suppose it's possible the Ripper has escalated his violence by conducting mutilations before death rather than after…" Phillips scrubbed at his sideburns thoughtfully, staring into the distance.

A tense silence followed, but I knew Dr. Phillips well enough to realize that he was merely speculating aloud.

"However," he continued, "until we've one of his ghastly letters or, God forbid, another body, there's really not enough evidence to point in his direction. Is there?"

"Something upon which we finally agree." Dr. Bond plunked his top hat onto his head and bowed. "Good day, Inspector, Doctor, Miss Mahoney." His bow to me was the deepest, and his grey eyes became even more opaque as they captured mine. "I expect we'll meet again."

And then, we were three.

"I'll have my full autopsy report delivered to you by courier this afternoon," Phillips said to Aberline.

"Obliged, Doctor." Aberline tipped his hat and chucked me under the chin like one would a disconsolate child. "Chin up, Miss Mahoney. Get some rest."

I nodded again, speechless, as he sauntered out. A certain shame sort of stole my words. It wasn't difficult to lie to a blowhard like Croft. But to a good man like

Aberline, keeping secrets in my pockets felt unnaturally heavy.

"Speaking of organs, you wouldn't happen to have any extra livers on short notice, would you? Preferably a bit necrotic." Dr. Phillips asked me. "Westminster Hospital is having a Hepatology lecture for surgeons, and I'd like to give that bounder Bond a what for in front of his chief of surgery."

"I'm sorry?" I blinked over at him, feeling especially bleary now, and doing my best to calm my racing thoughts long enough to process his change of subject.

He studied me for a brief moment, his expression brimming with a knowledge of me that I obviously didn't possess. Setting down the scalpel, he took up a curved needle and some thick, black thread. "Don't you let that bully inspector get to you," he advised, pulling the open flaps of Frank Sawyer's middle together. "Were you on the playground at school, he'd be tugging on your braids and flicking bugs into your hair."

I chewed on that thought for a strange moment. The hardest thing for me to picture, I found, was Inspector Grayson Croft as a little boy. He seemed like the sort of man crafted, fully formed, from stone and steel by some forgotten god of the north. It just didn't seem as if he'd ever been cuddled by an indulgent granny or tugged the braids of some poor schoolmate he fancied—

My skin went cold all over.

"What do you think, does it seem possible?" the doctor prodded.

"Hardly!" I gasped. "You're not suggesting Inspector Croft fancies me, are you?"

"About the livers." He leveled me with a droll look before carefully placing the first stitch into the pale, dead flesh.

"I-I'll have to look into it." The paper clutched in my hands distracted me. "How many would you need?"

I unfolded the paper to read the article, my heart climbing into my throat. It was all here. Every single detail of the Sawyer murder. The castration, the disembowelment, the fact that none of the organs were missing. The reporter made a few wild conjectures, that there might have been a letter the police were hiding for the sake of avoiding hysteria. But the facts were absolute.

The murder wasn't but ten hours ago. How many people were even privy to this information by now?

"About seven, I should think."

"Seven?"

"Livers, Fiona. Livers."

"Right. Yes." I checked the name of the journalist at the bottom of the article.

Thaddeus Comstock. I knew the name. He'd made quite the career covering the Whitechapel murders. If Jack the Ripper was the worst thing that had ever happened to Mary Kelly, he was the best thing for the unscrupulous Mr. Comstock.

"I will see what I can do," I promised. "If you'll excuse me, Dr. Phillips, I'm late for an appointment."

"I need them by Thursday, if you're able," he called after me as I retreated. "I'll even provide the ice!"

I hoped there was enough ice for Thaddeus Comstock.

Because I was going to kill him.

CHAPTER 11

Just as I realized I'd forgotten to consult with Dr. Phillips regarding the turquoise beads, a rough hand snaked from behind the hospital gate, jerking me toward the shadow of the stone wall.

"What the devil?" I screeched, drawing the attention of a few wary passersby.

"Not the devil," Croft rumbled. "Just me."

"Little better than," I spat. "Release me at once." As imperious as I sounded, I glanced around for Aberline should I require rescuing. He was nowhere to be seen along the wide, cobbled streets in front of the Royal London Hospital.

Bugger.

Croft held me fast by one arm, but he leaned against the yellow stone wall, the picture of a man at ease. The way his shoulders rested appeared as though he propped up the heavy stone, rather than the other way around.

What must it be like, I wondered, to have shoulders as strong as a ballast? One might live their entire lives without fear of collapse buttressed by a strength such as his.

If they could stand his presence so long.

"You lied to me," he accused.

I balled both of my fists to keep from fidgeting and stared him straight in the eyes.

"*A guilty man looks down,*" my father had once told me.

"You don't deny it?" Croft's face tightened over brutal bones as he released a heavy sigh. I'd disappointed him.

Not that it mattered.

"I'm not inclined to dignify your accusation with a response." Of course, I wasn't going to admit that I'd lied to him, especially when I wasn't clear to which lie he referred. Only an idiot incriminates herself, especially without additional information.

My stomach flopped upside down, and my heart shrank several sizes as he studied me through the slits of his eyelids.

"During the Kelly inquest, you told me your father was an Irish garda. You swore under oath."

It wasn't a lie and was easily proven. I didn't know whether to be relieved or terrified.

I settled on outraged.

Was Inspector Croft investigating me? After all this time?

"I never lied." *About that.* "My father was a member of the Irish police."

"He is no longer."

"So?" I challenged.

"You claimed your family remains in Dublin."

"They do."

"You mentioned your brothers, all Mahoneys, were named Fallon, Finnigan, Flynn, Farrin, Fitzwilliam, and Fayne."

I tried not to be impressed that he'd remembered them all. My dear, beloved brothers.

"Indeed." As much agony as their names brought upon me, I fought a little giddiness, as well. It wasn't often I had the opportunity to exploit the monosyllabic portion of the conversation with Croft.

See how he liked it, for once.

"There is no record of a Frank and Grace Mahoney living in Dublin. Neither could I find your brothers. They don't have employment records, residences, licenses, travel papers... Not that the bloody Garda were much help, even to a fellow officer."

"You're not a fellow officer to them, are you? You're a representative of the enemy. Why should they give you information about one of their own?"

He released me then. Testing the limits of his shoulder seams as he crossed his arms over his chest. "Are we at war, you and I? Are we enemies?"

We certainly weren't allies. But perhaps that was as much my fault as it was his.

"I didn't lie to you when I testified that my family remains in Dublin, Inspector. I never said they *lived* there."

"Remains." Beneath his swarthy complexion, he flushed an ashen shade. "I didn't check death certificates," he realized aloud. "I didn't request the bloody cemetery records."

He'd have found my entire family if he had.

And they were bloody.

So. Much. Blood.

"You're...alone." His gaze became softer than I'd ever seen it, his expression touched with pity—something I hadn't thought him capable of.

"I'm alive." My voice, on the other hand, was hard. Harder than I'd ever heard it. My bones felt forged of steel, though the heart beneath them seemed as fragile as glass.

I welcomed his pity even less than I wanted his suspicion.

"What happened to them?" he whispered.

"That's none of your concern." While I backed away

from him, my brittle vulnerability threw up pikes of protection in hopes he'd skewer himself before breaching my well-built fortifications. "Their murders are not your case. They've been explained."

But not avenged. Does anyone in this world really get justice?

"I think *you're* the mystery that needs solving, Fiona Mahoney." He looked as if he might reach for me again. Like maybe this time his touch would neither restrain nor repel me.

Wouldn't that be a first?

God. He wasn't about to...console me, was he? I could handle Croft's antipathy. I'd come to expect it. But what the hell would I do with his kindness?

It might melt the fortifications I'd erected, leaving my glass heart even more vulnerable.

Hastily, I retreated several steps until I almost slipped off the curb and into the gutter of Whitechapel Road. "You want to solve a mystery, Inspector? Find Frank Sawyer's murderer. Better yet, apprehend Jack the Ripper," I challenged. "But don't waste your time trying to figure me out. You won't like what you discover."

As exhausted as I was, I stormed off in the opposite direction of home, searching for a place that might provide me with some semblance of sanctuary.

And perhaps a few answers.

～❦

To SEE a sweet-faced child in Aidan Fitzpatrick's arms unstitched me. The unexpected ache buckled my knees and clenched feminine muscles with which no man was familiar.

Aidan could have been. I'd have given myself to him.

He stood tall and straight by the front pew of St.

Michael's Cathedral, the wee girl clinging to him like a burr, her legs around his trunk, and her arms clasped at his nape. His large hand cupped her head over a dingy bonnet beneath which wisps of flaxen hair escaped.

Would our children have been fair-haired or red? Dark-eyed or green? Would our boys have been tall as a Greek statue, like Aiden? Or stout and sturdy like my da?

How needless to ask questions to which I'd never know the answers. How utterly weak I was.

Sinful, even.

Dipping my fingers into the holy water, I crossed myself and touched a knee to the floor. Rising, I pressed a kiss to my knuckle, letting my fingers linger at my lips as I observed.

Silent tears leaked from the child's red-rimmed eyes.

Aidan conducted a whispered conclave with a stooped-shouldered woman. The distressed girl's mother, I assumed.

What tragedy does the unfortunate girl mourn? I wondered. Something as simple as a skinned knee? Or as complicated as a broken heart?

Those young eyes held an ageless kind of pain as they found me. Though I'd put the girl at maybe six or seven, I found no innocence in her gaze.

A broken heart, then.

I tried not to consider all she might have suffered. A cruel father? Maybe an absent one. Poverty. Hunger. Disease. Loss...?

Such heavy burdens Aidan must sometimes carry, ministering to such heavy, weary souls.

Touched, I wriggled a few fingers in a tentative wave at the child, putting all the pathetic cheer I was capable of summoning into my smile.

She turned her head away, burying her solemn little face against Aidan's neck.

My shoulders fell. Perhaps it was for the best I remained childless. Children found me far too honest to be charming. And besides, I had no granddad or *móraí* for them. No uncles to tease them, or cousins to make mischief with. There was no music left in me for dancing. No Mahoneys to dance with. No lullabies for comfort.

What sort of mother would I make?

What right had I to create life when my only business was death?

Aidan glanced across the chapel. Noting my inelegant loitering by the holy water, he nodded toward a bench beneath the stained-glass window on the far wall.

I tiptoed to the seat, knowing he'd join me once he finished comforting the afflicted.

In so many Catholic cathedrals as ancient as this one, a lack of windows and a preponderance of heavy stone filtered daylight into a sonorous gloom.

I appreciated St. Michael's for its luminescence. Time inched toward noonday, and celestial pillars of sunlight from the many kaleidoscopic windows felt as comforting as God's love.

The velvet-cushioned bench encircled one of the many white columns supporting the arch of the chapel. I perched facing a window, soaking in the light, basking in its warmth.

The glow through the painted panes was soft. Because reverence is soft. Because worship should be soft. Not fanatical, like it tended to be back home.

I listened to the whispers echoing off the stones. Even conversation sounded like prayer in a cathedral. The reverberations fractured the words, so I could not make them out, but the woman came across a bit desperate. Frightened, even.

Aidan's level lilt became a solemn, reassuring tune. I rested my head on the column behind me and did my best not to let the whispers lull me to sleep.

I must have drifted because Aidan was suddenly beside me, his hand on my shoulder.

"You always did like to nap in the sunlight," he remembered fondly. "Even as a little girl."

His lean hips swathed in a cassock with a black sash were at eye level, I realized, as I blinked awake. Quickly, I looked up to where the sunlight turned his golden hair into an angelic halo.

"Still afraid of the dark, Fiona?"

"Still." Always.

"Did you come to collect your fee for the Sawyer house?" Stepping out of the light, he sat beside me. I didn't answer him as the image in the windowpane arrested my attention for a heart-stopping moment.

A bearded man with a golden halo, swathed in red robes, hung from a cross.

Upside down.

Gasping, I fumbled in my pocket for the tarot card, gripping it with trembling hands as I studied the similarities. *Of course. Saint Peter.*

"What's this?" Aidan asked mildly.

"Aunt Nola showed me a card from her tarot deck. It's called the Hanged Man. Look at how he's positioned. And look at St. Peter in the window."

"Just like Frank Sawyer," Aiden realized aloud.

"Exactly!" I did my best to connect the significance with my sleep-deprived mind. "Remind me why St. Peter was martyred thus."

"He is thought to be the only other apostle of Christ who was crucified. But, because he thrice denied that Jesus was the Messiah, he felt unworthy to be martyred in the same fashion. He requested to be crucified inverted to signify his shame."

There was that word again. Invert.

"Strange, then, that the Pope sits on the throne of St. Peter, if he was so unworthy. Hardly seems right, does it?"

Aidan tweaked my arm. "Are you here to blaspheme the Holy Father, Fiona? Because it's been a long night for me, as well, and I don't have the constitution to argue theology with a heretic like you."

I waved the card at him, undaunted by his half-hearted ire. "Aunt Nola mentioned that the card signifies atonement. Repentance. Redemption, maybe. There could be some sort of connection here. This was Mr. Sawyer's parish, after all. Can you think of anything or any*one* who's been specifically interested in this window? Or St. Peter in general?"

Aidan took the card, glancing between it and the window. "Poor mad Aunt Nola," he murmured. "Does she still fancy that she's a mouthpiece for the dead?"

A defensive ire grew heavy in my chest. "How is it, that if you claim to be the mouthpiece of God, you are holy and revered—greater than kings and queens. But claim to be in touch with the departed, and you're insane?"

A winsome dimple appeared in Aiden's cheek. "There is only one disembodied voice you're allowed to hear, I'm afraid. Two, if you count the devil. I don't make the rules."

I rolled my eyes, refusing to be charmed.

"What else did Nola say about the Hanged Man?" he asked.

"She said it's a card of suspension. Of the in-between. That it could also mean a crossroads perhaps. Being paralyzed by indecision, not knowing which path to take."

Suddenly, he looked very serious. "You know what the crossroads is, Fi. Canonically, I mean. It's the last stop before Hell. You'll only find demons there, fiends looking to make a bargain for your soul."

Maybe that's where I was. Because sitting there, staring at Aidan, all I felt was wicked. None of the righteous paths appealed to me. And perhaps I'd have made a deal with the devil to change what was between us.

"How is Agnes Sawyer?" I asked, grasping on to distraction with both hands.

My question seemed to please him. "She's still in shock. But she's surrounded by loved ones and will pull through this with faith and heart. She'll have the little one to comfort her, God willing."

"Is it possible her child doesn't belong to Mr. Sawyer? Or that Mr. Sawyer had a lover? You were their confessor, the absolver of their sins. Maybe infidelity is the reason for—"

His smile crumpled into a grimace of disgust. "Oh, Fiona, don't go searching for fire where there is no smoke." His eyes shifted to scan the chapel, presumably to make certain we were still alone.

"There may be smoke," I said defensively. "Look!" I produced the turquoise beads from my pocket.

He squinted. "Where did you find those?"

"In Mr. Sawyer's blood."

"You think they belonged to Mrs. Sawyer?"

"I think they belong to the killer. But I'm not sure what to do with them. They could be dangerous to me."

Brows only slightly darker than his lambent hair pulled low over his eyes. "Dangerous how?"

"It's complicated." I sighed, swirling a finger in the pool of smooth stones. "I just need to consider what to do next."

He nudged my shoulder with his. "So, you came to me for advice?"

"Not exactly," I muttered. "You'd only counsel me to do the right thing."

"Probably. And am I to take it you already know what that is?"

"I know the easy thing and the hard thing." *And the dangerous thing,* I added silently.

"Nothing that matters is easy." He glanced at St. Peter. "If I've learned anything, it's that."

"But must everything be so complicated?" I groused. "I'm so mired in these details, I can't step back and see the picture they form. I feel as if there's an arrow pointing somewhere, at someone, I just...don't have a sense of the direction."

"The devil, as they say, is in the details." Aiden plucked a bead out of my cupped hand, inspecting it in the light of the colored glass. "Maybe you need a fresh pair of eyes. Tell me what you're struggling with."

Where to start? "I shouldn't even be involved in all of this, should I? Frank Sawyer's murder, I mean?"

"Then, why are you?" He shrugged.

"Because someone called me there. Because I found these beads, and I thought they belonged to Aramis Night Horse because of the American's connection to turquoise. But, on my way to deliver them to..." Did I want to tell him just who I was delivering them to? Probably not. "Well, I was accosted by a man claiming to be Jack the Ripper."

"Holy God, Fiona! Are you all right? Did he hurt you?" He dropped the bead onto the tiles of the floor where it rolled under a pew, instantly forgotten.

"Not really. I mean, he cut my neck a little, but it's nothing."

His pale skin blanched an unnatural, ghostly shade, blotches of red creeping up his neck from beneath the collar. "Cut your neck—a *little*?" he echoed breathlessly before pawing at my lace collar. "Let me see."

I'd never in a million years pictured Aidan Fitzpatrick undoing my blouse again, and yet, here we were. He only released enough buttons beneath my chin to reveal the bandage at my nape. He peeled it back and made a sound I'd never heard before.

I hissed as his fingers tested the flesh next to the wound. "Whoever stitched this did a decent job," he remarked. "But it wasn't done at hospital or in a doctor's surgery."

I was so distracted by his face so close to mine, by the scent of incense and forbidden fruit, the truth sort of just—slipped out. "Courtesy of the Hammer, if you believe it. I was found in an alley behind the Velvet Glove, unconscious. The Hammer nursed me in his private chamber. The Shiloh room, he calls it. Did you know his father was a doctor?" Oh, dear, I must have been nervous. Too much information spilled out of me, unbidden.

"I know very little about the Hammer." Aiden's voice remained measured, careful, though his expression was anything but. "I'm amazed that *you're* acquainted with him. That his hands were on you."

"I wouldn't call us anything so friendly as acquaintances," I hedged. I mean, he'd seen me half-naked, but that hardly counted since blood was involved. "Both he and Mr. Night Horse forswore any knowledge of Mr. Sawyer. And Aramis Night Horse similarly denied that the beads belonged to him." I hoped to distract Aidan from the part where the Hammer's hands were on me with the details of the mystery.

I could admit, his displeasure ignited a tiny spark of warmth within me.

He paused in rebuttoning my blouse to cast me another look of disbelief. "You interrogated the Hammer and his Blade about these? Are you mad?"

"I didn't *interrogate* them. I simply asked a few questions."

His frown deepened to a scowl. "Let's go back to the part where Jack the Ripper *cut* you in an *alley*."

"I'm not certain he was the Ripper," I confessed. "I found out from Inspector Croft at Frank Sawyer's autopsy this morning that Mr. Sawyer owed the Hammer a great deal of money. So, the Hammer and the Blade *clearly* lied to me. They're such obvious suspects."

"For Mr. Sawyer's murder, or for being the Ripper?" Aiden clarified.

"Both. But, the man in the alley claimed to be the Ripper, whispered it right in my ear."

Aidan crossed himself. Cursed. Then repeated the gesture.

"There's no need to worry." I rushed to soothe his increasing distress. "None of the experts believe Mr. Sawyer's murderer was the Ripper. But perhaps Mr. Sawyer's murderer and my assailant are one and the same. You see, everything I mentioned to the man in the alley who claimed to be Jack the Ripper wound up in *The London Evening Examiner*. An exposé written by a journalist named Thaddeus Comstock."

He stroked his chin thoughtfully. "I recall that none of the inspectors at the scene believed Jack the Ripper truly responsible for Mr. Sawyer's murder. Especially Inspector Croft."

I made a vague gesture. "I wasn't convinced one way or the other, but I see now the murder was all wrong. The Ripper always slashed throats first, and mutilated corpses after. He posed all the victims the same. Not to mention his tendency to take gruesome prizes. And they were all women, weren't they? *Prostitutes*." I whispered the word, as Jesus Christ was just over there, staring down at me from his cross.

"I wish you were never called to that scene, Fi. I'm just glad you're all right." He took my free hand in his, and we sat silently for a moment as he thoughtfully digested what I'd revealed.

After a pensive moment, I started, struck by an idea. "Do you remember, after Mary...died, the police suspected the Ripper might be some mad, sadistic journalist creating his own sensational headlines?"

Gasping, he gripped my arm. "That's right. They even arrested a few newspapermen during the blitz, didn't they?"

"I'll have to ask Aberline if Comstock was among them." I leapt to my feet.

"Fi, this is not irrefutable evidence. They arrested over eighty people that year, and were forced to let all of them go."

"Sure, but it's a place to start." I was in the middle of dropping the turquoise beads back into my pocket when Aidan firmly dragged me back down to the seat.

"I do *not* want you chasing this Comstock fellow on your own, Fi. It's neither smart nor safe. What did the inspectors say about your attack? Could you not send them after Comstock?"

Puffing out both cheeks, I slumped guiltily back against the pillar. "I...didn't tell them."

"Why ever not? Have you gone all but mad?"

I stared at him long and hard. I wasn't often afraid of the secrets damning my soul...but I didn't want to fall from Aidan's grace. Taking a deep breath, I adopted my most penitent look. "Bless me, Father, for I have sinned..."

"Oh, Lord, Fiona!" He put his head in his hands, scrubbing at his face.

"After Mary, I was hungry and destitute. I'd only just rescued Nola and had no true place for us to live and so...I did a favor for the Hammer."

His hands dropped to hang between his knees as he glared at the tiles at our feet. "A...sexual favor?"

"No!"

"Thank God," he breathed.

"But, maybe worse. And most definitely illegal."

"Did you murder someone for him?" At this point, the shock and inflection had drained from his voice, turning it flat as day-old champagne.

"Of course, not. But should I bring the beads to Scotland Yard, Croft could use them as fuel for his crusade against the Hammer. And...my crimes might be discovered should he dig too deeply."

Finally, Aiden turned to me. He bore the look of a disappointed father that I didn't at all appreciate, but it was in no way my place to say so. "What's the worst that could happen should you be found out? How serious was your crime?"

I was already in for a penny... Might as well spend the pound. "If my secrets are discovered, either the Hammer kills me for it, or...the Crown does."

"Jesus, Mary, and Joseph!"

"I didn't know what I was doing! Nor did I understand the severity of the punishment for my delinquency at the time."

"Ignorance is not innocence, Fi!" he said from between clenched teeth.

"Don't preach to me, Aidan Fitzpatrick." The look I gave him could have withered entire fields of wildflowers. "You may be a priest, but you're no angel. I know your sins."

"You don't know the half of them." He lowered his eyes. "I am compelled to ask; did you repent for this favor?"

I winced. "Not...as of yet, but I fully intend to." I rushed to add before he could say anything else, "Why, you could absolve me right now, couldn't you?"

"Fiona," he groaned. *Drat.* His head was back in his hands again.

"What was I supposed to do?" I huffed. "I was alone in the world. I was desperate. Broken. It was either that or prostitution."

His head whipped up, and he speared me with a level glare. "You could have come to me."

Tears stung the back of my nose and seared my eyes. I suddenly wished to be anywhere else. To be confessing any other truths. "No. I couldn't. I couldn't look at you yet without my heart being torn from my chest. I couldn't ask for the help or protection a *husband* should give. You'd forsaken me, Aidan. Everyone had forsaken me." Annoyed with my own emotion, I dashed an escaped tear from my cheekbone before he could find it there.

His features softened. "God has not forsaken you, and neither will I."

"Maybe I've forsaken him," I said in a churlish if wobbly voice. "And as for you, it's not the same, is it? I can't rely on you. Not like that."

Gently, he took both of my hands in his, his touch rousing a gentle memory sweeter than the last day of childhood. "Will you forgive me someday, Fi? As a soldier, I was an angry and violent boy... Being a priest allows me the grace of a penitent man. I *tried* to come to you when I returned from fighting, but all I could do was remember the ghastly things I'd done on the battlefield. I feared God might not recognize me. That I'd fallen so far from grace, I'd do nothing but drag you down with me."

I threaded my fingers through his. I was not God. I did not need to forgive. Not yet. But I still loved him. And hated him. "Memories make for powerful ghosts..." I whispered.

He nodded. "And some people deserve to be haunted."

"Reminiscences haunt me, too." Another tear fell, but I didn't want to drag my hands from his to do anything about it. "Memories of you and Finn and Flynn. Of Mary and me. Of you and me. Of Mary and *him*. I don't sleep, but they torment me."

"Could you not let them go, Fiona?" The earnest expression on his face erased a few of his years. "Some memories are best buried with the dead. Only then can you make brighter ones."

I shook my head adamantly. "Don't you think I've *tried*? No matter how deep I bury them, still they rise. With a vengeance, they rise. I do not think my ghosts will let me rest until there is justice."

He interrupted the trajectory of my tear with his knuckle. The air between us warmed with grace and sympathy as he nodded. "There is always a reckoning. I learned there always comes a time when you stop and turn around and face the adversary who chases you. If you take a stand against evil, good *does* win. Everyone gets their justice before God."

A caustic sound escaped me. "I wish I had what you have. I wish I had faith...in anything. A person. God. In an outcome. My own choices."

His exhalation was just as acrimonious. "Faith isn't always a comfort. Sometimes, it's a burden. But I have faith in your goodness, Fi. That you'll do the right thing. You *are* at a crossroads, and you need to decide. Go to the authorities. Confess. Have faith that justice will be done in your favor."

Perhaps he was right. Maybe it was time I faced my demons, regardless of the outcome. "I wish...I wish you'd have let me try to make you happy." More tears welled as I cast my gaze about the room. I hated this hallowed, hollow place. Hated that he'd chosen it over me.

"There are days I wish that, as well," he murmured. "But there is no choice we can undo by wishing."

He was the second man to tell me that today.

If wishes were horses...

"Did you love me?" It was a pathetic question asked in a pitiful whisper.

"Oh, Fiona." The lips Aiden pressed against my temple were anything but ecumenical. His hand on my back drifted to my waist. "My feelings for you cannot be reduced to a single word. *You* are my only temptation."

"Did you *love* me?" I demanded, lifting my hands to curl in his cassock.

Palms bracketed my face as though I were in the way of their meeting for prayer. With searching, tender eyes, he mapped the topography of my features. "Of course, I loved you, Fi. I *love* you still. I pray to God for you every night...but—" His voice broke as his eyes snagged on my lips.

"But?" I breathed.

His grip on me tightened, moved, his fingers threading into the hair behind my ears. "There's still a dread that lurks in my heart," he confessed through his teeth. "A fear that I'd sit down with the devil if you asked it of me."

I didn't know if I lifted my mouth to his, or if he lowered his lips to mine. All I knew, was that the kiss was both an invocation and a benediction. It contained all desires both conceivable and impossible. Sacred and profane. It awakened a hope inside me that was instantly crushed when he ripped his mouth away as though fighting a powerful adhesive.

"I can't," he panted, surging to his feet and shoving his fingers through his tidy hair. "We can't."

Every part of me felt bruised. My lips. My heart. "I-I'm sorry," I stammered, gaining my feet. "I'm sorry. I'm tired, was distraught. I didn't mean—"

He shrank from my outstretched hand as though I carried the plague. "It's best if I...I don't see you for a while."

"Don't say that," I begged.

Giving me his back, he said over his shoulder, "Take those beads to Croft or Aberline, Fiona. Unburden your conscience. Confess. Repent. Atone. As *I* must now." He left me then, alone with the savior looking down upon me.

I knew the tilt of his head was supposed to appear merciful and compassionate. But all I saw was vicious pity on the shiny, lacquered features of the Lord. A sort of gloating wistfulness. As if he really, *truly* regretted that things had turned out the way they had and would do something if only he could get down from that deuced inconvenient cross.

I escaped the chapel as fast as I could, conceding the day's battle for Aidan's heart to the one being who could offer him what I could not.

Forgiveness.

CHAPTER 12

Nothing interrupts a good confession like a murder.

At half-past nine in the morning, I'd been at H Division on Leman Street, marking the rise of Croft's temper across his desk as I divulged the details of my encounter in Crossland Alley.

Now, at quarter past ten, I held a handkerchief dabbed with lavender and rose water to my nose, wishing Katherine Riley hadn't been slaughtered quite so close to a roaring fire in yet another poorly ventilated room in Whitechapel.

It shouldn't have caused me a vague sense of relief that her throat had been twice slashed on a carpet—a rather expensive one I noted. But after the tedious hours and sheer amount of chemicals it had taken to scour Frank Sawyer's blood from untreated wood, I couldn't help but appreciate that her cleanup should be a snap by comparison.

Unlike the Sawyers', Katherine Riley's rooms were in a proper tenement, dissected into a parlor, a great room, a kitchen complete with cookstove, and a separate bedroom with the toilet facilities inside the house.

In Whitechapel, this was luxury.

Croft and Aberline had sufficiently recovered from

their initial astonishment at the horrific familiarity of the victim's placement and were now surveying her domicile for clues. There was a certain frenetic quality to their investigation. Something borne, I gathered, of a traumatic catastrophe revisited. The sense of security that the Ripper had become a failure of their past had been torn away from them. With the murder of Katherine Riley, he'd become a closed book reopened. The case file had long since been taken from their hands and given to someone closer to the top.

To become another man's failure.

Even for men with whom the dreadful had become routine, I didn't think they expected to see the likes of *him* again.

Yet, here she was. A woman of a certain age. A particular class.

Met with a specific, remarkable demise that, this time, had no apparent variances from the canonical Ripper murders.

What had been her profession? She'd been too old to make such a nice living as a prostitute, even I knew that.

Her throat was opened by two very deliberate, efficient slices. Her legs lifted and parted at the knees. Her middle skillfully cut from thorax to pubis. This time, the organs had been left inside the cavity. At least, several of them appeared to be visible through the narrow gash.

As Dr. Phillips began his crime scene examination and report, I stood unobtrusively in the corner by a faded velvet chair that might have been expensive during the Regency. I occupied myself by counting the stab wounds on her chest and torso. Most of which were marked by vibrant red against the cream of her linen apron still tied behind her body yet sliced down the front along with her dress.

I'd reached forty before conversation interrupted the tally.

"How long has she been dead, you wager?" Aberline asked Dr. Phillips, who currently checked her rigidity by testing the flexibility of her elbows and wrists.

Phillips was much more himself today than he'd been two mornings prior at the Sawyer autopsy. His thick, brown hair, liberally threaded with silver, was carefully styled, his beard trimmed and neat. He wore sleeve covers similar to the ones I used as he dictated post-mortem report notes to his assistant coroner, a sprightly medical student by the name of Nelson.

"It has to be three days, doesn't it?" I offered. "It's my experience that it takes at least that long for rigor mortis to pass. And, unlike Mr. Sawyer, her corpse is *not* fresh." I motioned to Katherine Riley's limp wrists and the ease with which her joints moved.

"Very good, dear," Dr. Phillips praised. "But environmental factors are key. The stifling heat of this room could have sped up the process, and the ashes in the fireplace are not yet completely cold, though they're safe to touch now." He motioned to the cavernous fireplace with the syringe Nelson handed to him before he plunged the needle into her eye, testing the vitreous humors. "Her corneal fluids are quite cloudy. Lividity is not as advanced as I would expect for seventy-two hours. My estimation of her death would be a day and a half. Two, at most."

Nelson took vigorous notes in shorthand.

"She could have been murdered at the very moment we were all attending the autopsy." Crouching, Aberline retrieved the white ashes from the fireplace, testing them between his thumb and forefinger. "The killer must have remained with her for a time, then. Kept the fire going."

I'd spent a great deal of time catching up on my sleep. So much so, that the autopsy felt like yesterday rather than two mornings prior. "The Ripper's never been known to keep vigil before," I remarked. "Even with Mary, he couldn't have stayed more than a few hours between when she was last seen alive and when her body was discovered." And he'd had to have been working on her almost that entire time.

I was proud of myself for being here. For not allowing the twisted mélange of tormented and excited emotions to manifest themselves in front of these men. I didn't let them see how much Mary's name still affected me.

I couldn't let on that I could feel the Ripper with me, with us, in this room. His evil lingered, much like the sickly-sweet smell of death would cling like an unwanted ghost to this dwelling for days. Maybe longer.

It seemed ludicrous, didn't it? To sense a presence so acutely? To feel his pleasure at the blood, at the deed. To absorb his rage. At whom, I wondered? At this poor victim? At someone with enough audacity to claim the Ripper's hard-won infamy as his own?

I kept that lunacy to myself.

Well done, me.

"You make an excellent point, Miss Mahoney. Our biggest mystery regarding Miss Riley here is to ascertain if she is, indeed, a Ripper victim." Aberline brushed ashes off his hands and stood, looking as grim as I'd ever seen him. "I find myself certain there is a link between this butchery and the Sawyer murder. Perhaps the deeds were not committed by the same odious hand. But we have to consider that Ms. Riley is the Ripper's brutal answer to a copycat killer."

Croft returned from the kitchen with several knives from the butcher block. He accepted an evidence bag from Nelson and placed them inside. "At the moment, the biggest mystery to me is why Miss Mahoney is allowed at this scene instead of being relegated behind the police constable line with the rest of the curious civilians." He glared at me, gesturing to the door where a line of police constables already held back an anxious crowd.

"If you remember, you expressly forbade me to seek out Thaddeus Comstock on my own," I said as if that were sufficient explanation.

"If *you* remember, I forbade you to follow me here, as well."

"Just so." I made a production of gathering my skirts and readjusting my reticule and parasol. "In that case, I'm off to the offices of *The London Evening Examiner*. Good morning, gentlemen. I'll give Mr. Comstock your regards."

I expected to make it five steps before Croft stopped me. I only managed three before his hand bit into my arm, anchoring me to his side.

"I suppose I'll stay right here, then," I snapped tartly. "Though I'd take it as a kindness if you'd make up your mind."

Croft's mouth opened, promising a remark every bit as thunderous as his expression, but Dr. Phillips beat him to it.

"Thaddeus Comstock? The idiot who imagines himself a journalist?" Phillips frowned at the masculine hand currently gripping my arm.

"The very same." I tossed the ringlets I'd arranged to spill down my bodice back over my shoulder. I'd hoped they'd hit Croft in the face, but I didn't dare turn to look.

"That self-proclaimed Ripper expert has barely enough grasp of the Queen's English to thread together a coherent thought." Disgusted, Dr. Phillips stood with a great deal of ease and grace for a man of his age, pinning me with a narrow-eyed glare of his own. "Pray tell, why ever would you seek out *his* odious company?"

"Because there's a chance he might *be* Jack the Ripper." I left that proclamation hanging in the air for a moment like a shimmering mist so each of the gathered investigators could process the implications. Turning to Croft, I poked at his chest. The joints of my finger crumpled unexpectedly against the muscle beneath his vest. I shook my hand, undeterred. "Now we can ascertain where he was yesterday. Maybe he celebrated his terrible Sawyer article by conducting this bit of savagery."

Phillips accepted a towel from the ever solicitous Nelson and began to clean blood and such from his fingers before peeling the sleeve covers away. His eyebrows dropped in bewildered increments. "Other than Comstock's uncanny knowledge of the Sawyer scene, which you already pointed out could have been obtained in a variety of ways, why would he make a viable Ripper suspect?"

Croft's grip tightened. "Fiona, don't—"

"Because I believe he got the information for his article when he dragged me into a dark alley, put a knife to my throat, and interrogated me about the Sawyer scene, all the while insisting that he was Jack the Ripper."

"Good God, Miss Mahoney. How distressing," Aberline gasped. "Are you convinced it's him?"

"That's why I want to go visit him," I declared. "To find out."

"Did he harm you?" Dr. Phillips asked, his eyes owlish behind his spectacles.

"I'm almost entirely unscathed." I held my free arm out to advertise my wellbeing.

This morning, I'd donned what I considered my most flattering dress, a mahogany silk blouse with dark lace at the collar and sleeves that almost matched my hair. A fitted vest of crushed velvet in a lighter hue paired with the intricate pleats, drapes, and tassels of my skirt, shot through with pinstripes of dark, lush gold. I'd dressed thusly in hopes Croft would feel less like stretching the neck of a comely woman than a dowdy one. Though, judging by the murderous glint in his eye as he glared at me now, I had the feeling my efforts were for naught.

"Why didn't you inform us of your ordeal at the autopsy?" Aberline's mustache drooped, conveying equal parts concern and effrontery.

"Why, indeed?" Croft finally released me to cross skeptical arms over his intimidating chest.

I stared at him for longer than an honest woman would, my guilt pulling hot blood to my ears with all the speed and noise of a steam engine at full tilt.

Because I cannot trust the police with my secrets. Because, sometimes, I fear the Hammer every bit as much as I feared the Ripper. Because, should I fall, I would topple everyone who stands on my shoulders, dear Dr. Phillips included.

"Because I...wanted to be certain the man who accosted me was Jack, and I am not yet convinced."

Croft snorted. "Because you wanted to do something foolish, like go after him yourself."

Also, that.

Dr. Phillips stationed himself on the other side of me, patting my shoulder indulgently. "Come now, we credit Miss Mahoney with a great deal more intelligence than all that."

They did?

"I never saw my assailant's face," I explained. "But his voice was excruciatingly distinctive. I'll never forget the effeminate lisp, the waspish cadence. I wanted a chance to identify him lest I bring you yet another useless clue."

"You of all people know the importance of reporting a crime directly," Croft snarled. "Crossland Alley is a stone's throw away from Scotland Yard. I can't imagine why you'd hesitate to run to us immediately. In fact, I can't imagine why you were on the

Strand at that hour in the first place. Just what are you hiding?"

"Did he threaten you?" Dr. Phillips settled a gentle arm around my shoulders, simultaneously digging a finger into a sensitive spot below my ribs and causing me to gasp and reflexively crumple forward. He caught me deftly like a father would a distraught child. He tsked and tutted solicitously as I turned my face against his chest in a false gesture of distress. "There, there, my dear. How brave you are. Did he warn you not to go to the police?"

"He—he did." I grasped the lifeline he offered with both hands. "He said anyone I told would be in danger." The catch in my throat was more from a sort of marvelous amusement than wretchedness. Just as Croft had cornered me, the genius doctor had rescued us both. It was not in my nature to play the damsel, but one did what they must.

All thoughts of confession planted by Aidan had dissipated the moment poor Katherine Riley's body was found. She was a stark reminder of why I must be allowed to continue to be who I am.

To do what I do.

If Jack was back, then I *must* be free to search for him.

There was little doubt that I was the lesser of the two evils. Why should I hang, and he continue to terrorize all of London?

I relaxed into Dr. Phillip's hold incrementally. For a man who'd likely lived a half-century, he was surprisingly solid. He smelled of pomade and formaldehyde and strong lye soap. Not exactly a fatherly smell, but oddly comforting nonetheless.

The scent of preservation.

In lieu of a family—and in the absence of a beloved father—Dr. Phillips had become more than just an ally.

Or merely a business associate. He'd become something of a friend.

Aberline, as well.

And, I supposed I didn't want Croft to come to any harm, either. At least, most days.

"I can't, in good conscience, stomach the idea of risking any of your lives." I looked up into Dr. Phillip's benevolent features, wondering if he understood how honest I was in that moment.

"That's fucking ridiculous!" Croft exploded, his face reddening. "I can *protect* you. That is, *we,* the London Metropolitan Police, are perfectly capable of protecting ourselves. And you."

"Language, Inspector Croft, I implore you," Phillips admonished.

"You don't have jurisdiction over me. I don't reside in your borough." I pushed away from Phillips, leveling Croft with a sharp look. "And I cannot say I know how safe I'd feel even if I did." I pointed at Katherine Riley, not able to bring myself to look down at what remained of her now.

A vein had begun to pulse in Croft's temple, and his shoulders bunched up to his ears. Wordlessly, he turned into what I assumed was the bedroom and began to slam about in there.

I'd been cruel. I'd questioned his ability to do his job, to be a man, and all in front of his colleagues.

Regardless of how I felt about Croft, I wasn't proud of what I'd said.

Aberline diplomatically interceded. "What Croft is trying—and failing—to convey, is that there is more safety in knowledge than ignorance. The more you trust us, the better we can help. We hoped you understood that by now."

"I do understand, Inspector." My regret was conveyed in earnest, and I hoped that he could see that. "I never want to cry wolf."

Cry Ripper?

"Yes, well..." Aberline checked his watch, and I tried to contain an aching fondness for him. "I'm going to assemble some constables to span the neighborhood and gather what information we can about Ms. Riley, here." He regarded me as one would a particularly troublesome puzzle. Or a volatile one. "Best you stay with the good doctor, Miss Mahoney. At least until the press clears out. It wouldn't do to have you photographed where you ought not to be, I'm sorry to say."

"If you think that's best, Inspector." I feigned contrite obedience. I'd positioned myself inside the house in hopes of that precise outcome.

Sighing, he glanced into the bedroom and then back out to the street. "I'll talk to the landlord about your services and fees and send an errand boy to fetch your Chinaman, shall I?"

I bit back a sly smirk. "I'd be obliged if you would."

"You'd just insist on cleaning it up, regardless," he muttered on his way into the humid afternoon. "Better to keep it aboveboard."

"Nelson," Dr. Phillips addressed his assistant by his given name. "Be a good lad and check the kitchen, the bedroom, and the facilities for any objects which might be responsible for these puncture wounds, would you?"

The young man balked. "Isn't that the inspectors' job? We already have the kitchen knives."

"Do the inspectors have the proper training and precise medical knowledge to identify this very specific style of instrument and how it might penetrate flesh?" Phillips impatiently gestured to the copious wounds.

Nelson appeared unsure. "Likely not."

"Likely. Not."

Scurrying to the bedroom, Nelson seemed as reticent as I would be to share an enclosed space with a surly Inspector Croft.

"This is why I prefer to work alone." I sensed more

than saw Dr. Phillip's invitation to join him as he dug into his medical bag and crouched over the corpse.

Using two instruments, he eased Katherine Riley's middle open. "I suppose I only need six livers now," he remarked in a register meant only for me.

"You're going to use Ms. Riley's?"

He nudged at it, the generally pink organ slightly dark and discolored in some places. In others, a whitish film clung to the outside and seemed to be eating away at it. "It is a bit necrotic. She was a heavy drinker at one time, I can tell you that much. And there's some obvious hepatic damage I'm certain was caused by a venereal disease. Though, I'll not know which until I get her on the table. Hepatitis, maybe."

"You could consult Dr. Bond," I suggested wickedly. "I hear he specializes somewhat in venereal diseases."

"He most certainly does." Sarcasm oozed from him as thick and toxic as blood. "In more ways than you know."

"Look at her face," I whispered. "How ghastly." The Ripper had left it alone, and still, the memory of it would raise chill bumps on my flesh for a long time to come.

Katherine Riley hadn't been a young woman, and her loose skin had pulled the thin, wrinkled lips away from a pair of false teeth. Ivory, it seemed. Another luxury. Her lids were likewise unnaturally wide, though her eyeballs had begun to dry and shrivel.

Phillips paused in his perusal of her insides. "She looks as though she's seen a ghost, doesn't she?"

"Do you believe in ghosts, Dr. Phillips?" I'd credited him with more sense, but one never knew the spectrum of another's relationship with the hereafter.

His instruments made wet sounds as he worked, stirring smells that sent me in search of my scented handkerchief. "I believe that people are haunted by many things. But not the dead."

"Do you think her soul is in a better place? Heaven maybe, or Hell?"

"What nonsense is this?" He threw an impatient look at me over his shoulder.

"I'm just curious as to your views regarding such things. A man in the company of so much death must have a great deal of time to ponder it."

He returned to his work, sliding his instruments down the open seam of Ms. Riley's body as he spoke. "I think Heaven and Hell are aspects of one's self. They are both very limiting if you think about it. Both places from which there is no escape. That being said, I am possessed of an open and scientific mind. Should someone provide me irrefutable proof of the hereafter, I'll take myself to confession and prostrate my soul before God. Until then, I'll retain the opinion that people turn to the occult when they have not the intellectual nor the emotional fortitude for the scientific method."

"You're saying you think religious people are either lazy or willfully ignorant?"

"I'm saying I think it is a great deal easier to believe in a benevolent father figure than to consider that we are all supplicants to the chaotic and rather ruthless whims of both nature and time."

"Oh." I couldn't think of anything else to say. He wasn't wrong. Hadn't I bestowed that very assignation upon him only moments ago when he sheltered me from Croft's ire? A benevolent father figure. Someone upon whose mercy I could rely.

"On the other side of benevolence, I suppose it's hard for us to imagine that there's no justice to be found for people like Katherine Riley," I postulated.

"That's assuming she's deserving of justice," he muttered.

"What do you mean? Do you know something about her?"

"No, nothing." He shook his head adamantly, and

THE BUSINESS OF BLOOD

the wan afternoon light glinted off a small patch of thinning hair on the back of his pate that was usually covered by his hat.

The whims of nature and time.

"I'm merely posing the question. What if St. Peter is, in fact, not up there tracking your sins for judgment day? What if vengeance doesn't belong to the Lord, as the good book claims, but to us? Does that make life more precious, or less? Does it alter the significance of existence?"

I wasn't sure. "It certainly makes death seem more tragic."

"Does it?" Setting his speculum down, he scratched at the back of his head as though my gaze had caused an itch. "Depends on the death, I suppose."

Didn't it just?

"We need to find out if Katherine Riley had a child," Croft announced from beneath the arch of the bedroom door. He brandished a small baby bottle with a rubber feeding tube and two tiny, hand-stitched booties. "If so, it's been taken."

Dr. Phillips made a speculative sound. "Impossible to tell just now, Inspector," he said ominously. "Her womb has been taken, as well."

CHAPTER 13

Even I was allowed to join in the search for the missing child. We tore the place apart—the attic, the basement, the roof, the window wells. The pathetic garden out back. For all our efforts, we uncovered a worn baby blanket, a wooden rattle, and a few other tiny garments. One a little boy's jumper, and the other seemed to be a christening dress.

The search fanned out after that.

Neighbors reported that they'd heard a baby in Ms. Riley's home, but not regularly. They'd assumed she tended a child, or perhaps that she had grandchildren close by.

For as close as residents seemed to be in such crowded neighborhoods, no one knew much about Katherine Riley. She was pleasant, kind, and kept mostly to herself.

Maybe she was part of what my father used to call "the forgotten ones." The lonesome aging sort with no one to shoulder their filial duties. Often isolated and neglected, especially in these communities of the underfunded and the overworked.

My father used to look after these people in our neighborhood. He was forever sending my brothers on shopping errands, or conscripting them to lift trunks,

162

move furniture, or take our leftovers to Widow So-and-So.

Even I'd learned advanced reading at a three o'clock appointment every Wednesday with a mostly blind and completely childless septuagenarian professor named Donegal O'Dowd. My father had called him a "confirmed bachelor," but now that I thought about it, he might have shared a few tendencies with Oscar Wilde.

And I didn't mean their affinity for poetry.

I'd been inconsolable when poor Mr. O'Dowd passed on when I was sixteen. I still owned a book of Shakespearean sonnets he'd lent me. It was one of my most carefully guarded treasures, and yet I'd never taken the time to truly read it.

Strange, how you forgot to think about those people until moments like this.

I hoped Professor O'Dowd wasn't lonely anymore... wherever he was.

Croft now paced behind the orderlies, who carried the remains of Katherine Riley out the narrow door. I won't tell you what they to keep her contents from spilling. Needless to say, they stepped lightly and most certainly dreaded being jostled by the crowd.

"Where are you off to?" I asked Croft, aware he'd become like a hound *en pointe*. He had a colorful paper clutched in his fist, and I would stake my life that he considered it a lead.

"*That* is no business of yours."

Inspired, I plucked the paper out of his hand.

It was an advertisement for a recent fundraiser for unwed mothers, unfortunate children, and orphans held at a local diocese some three weeks prior. Katherine Riley had been one of the patrons and organizers of the event.

Just wonderful. I tracked the stretcher draped with its white sheet as they loaded it into the coroner's cart and pulled away with a sharp crack of the reins. She'd been a saint with a soft spot for women and children in desperate situations. What a bloody shame.

What a terrible loss.

Croft snatched the flier back. "It seems we both have work to do." Plunking his hat low on his head, he squared his shoulders in preparation to part the gathering throng. "Good afternoon, Miss Mahoney." With those words, he shoved into the crowd, which seemed to part for him as the Red Sea had for Moses.

I muttered a few of the words I'd learned from him.

An embarrassed cough beside me alerted me to Inspector Aberline's presence.

"Pardon my profanity." I made room for him in the doorway. "That man gets my Irish up like no other."

"You're not alone in that." He traced Croft's trajectory for a moment with a knowing smile as he broke from the thinning crowd and marched toward Whitechapel Road. "Do you know what his problem is?"

"You're insinuating he only has the one?" I knew I was being unkind, but it was not even noon and already turning out to be a very trying day—the blame belonging in no small part to Croft.

Aberline's mustache twitched in amusement. "Look there. Croft is the kind of man what walks in straight lines. London has no straight lines. Just twists and turns and labyrinthine corridors behind which any danger could lurk. For men like him, the vagaries of fate are untenable. It is difficult for them to navigate the chasms between what should be, and what is.

He spent some of his formative years as an underground ironworker. Chipping away at the stone until it gave beneath his will, shaping it with rough hands, sharp tools, and brute strength into something he could use. He attacks his cases—his life—in a very similar way."

"With all the subtlety of a pickaxe?"

"Sometimes." Aberline chuckled. "Does make for an excellent detective, though he does his best work in the field."

I could see that. He'd seemed like a caged beast in his office this morning. A vicious dog needing to be let out.

Aberline glanced at me with frank speculation. "Do you like him?"

"Not generally."

"No, I mean, do you *like* him?" He nudged me with his elbow. "Fiery women tend to take to Croft. They enjoy his indifference. Relish the chase. They like what happens when he lets them catch him." Aberline winked before waggling his bushy eyebrows at me.

"I doubt that," I said drolly but cut my grimace short when I marked Aberline's expression. It would not do to seem bitter. Or interested. "My heart is not free to like anyone."

"Pity." At that, he turned back to Dr. Phillips, dismissing all notions of romance for only slightly more gruesome subjects. "We've gathered that Katherine Riley was, once upon a time, a prostitute who went by the name of Roxy the Doxy."

I pressed my lips together, clamping them with my teeth. No matter how ridiculous the moniker was, now was not the time to be amused.

Not whilst gathered around her blood.

"She was popular with sailors and dock workers," Aberline continued as he consulted his pocket notepad. "Apparently, there was even a song."

"I'd give my last shilling to hear it," Nelson remarked, earning him reproving glares from his superiors.

"By all accounts, she gave up that profession a decade ago. These days, either no one knows what she does for a living—what she *did*—or no one is willing to tell." With a frustrated sound, Aberline took up his suit coat and hat. "The landlord's agreed to your fee, Miss Mahoney. I'll join the bobbies whilst you tend to the house, here. This calls for some good old-fashioned footwork."

"It really could be him, couldn't it, Inspector?" I asked, staring at the blood-soaked carpet and cold, white ashes in the fireplace.

Ashes to ashes. Dust to dust.

Aberline paused at the door as we both turned to mark Hao Long's patient progress with my cart through the hastily dispersing crowd.

People tended to lose interest once the body had been taken away. In mere moments, one would hardly be able to tell this street from any other crowded thoroughfare in Whitechapel.

Exhaustion and anxiety pinched the lines at the corners of the inspector's eyes and lips, turning them a stark, aggressive white. "I'm afraid so." Aberline shook his head, his shoulders heavy with regret. "Just when I thought the nightmare was long over. It's been my greatest fear, you know? The return of the Ripper."

"I know. Mine, too." As I watched him leave, I swore he'd shrunk three inches in as many days.

Dr. Phillips was next to scuttle to the door, anxious to take his leave. "Well, Miss Mahoney. Must be going. Death waits for no man."

"Nor woman," I volleyed back.

He shook my hand like he would a respected male colleague, and somehow, it meant more to me than any kiss brushed against my knuckle, bow, or courtesy I'd ever received. "He'd wait for you, I'd wager. I think he likes you. He'd take his time with you."

"He certainly keeps me in business."

"Well, we can always count on him for that." Phillips touched his hat. "Dying is the only thing people do with any regularity."

I went to extract my hand from his, but he held fast,

boring into me with his ice-blue gaze. "Miss Mahoney... I want you to be careful out there until we sort all this out. I am very distressed by your encounter in that alley."

His concern melted me. "That is kind, Doctor. But I'm not the Ripper's type, nor am I a denizen of Whitechapel. I am not afraid."

"Yes, you are," he argued gently but with alert perception. "And you should be."

I hesitated, supremely uncomfortable under his observant eye. He was right, of course. I was not fearless, but I could be brave.

"Don't misunderstand me," he rushed to correct any sense of undue impudence. "You possess good instincts. Fear is wisdom in the face of danger. Intuition is merely the brain assimilating actualities faster than the conscious mind can process. Just...step lightly, Miss Mahoney. For my peace of mind, if nothing else."

"I will," I promised, impulsively planting a kiss on his bristly cheek.

An ear-splitting shriek shattered our fond moment as a petite, harried woman carrying an infant swaddled in a patched shawl limped up the walk toward us. The commotion, courtesy of the little creature in her arms, was enough to set the local stray dogs to barking.

"Wot's going on?" She blinked up at us from watery, dark eyes, sensing the increased police presence. "Is Miss Riley in there?" She tried to peek around us, desperately rocking from one foot to the other. "I need to tell 'er I changed me mind. That I cannot do this anymore. I 'aven't got all the money, but I can pay 'alf now."

"What's your name, child?" Dr. Phillips seemed more likely to retreat back into the odiferous house than deal with a hysterical woman.

"Mary. Mary Jean McBride." She greedily eyed my dress and Dr. Phillip's smart, tailored suit and expensive silk cravat. "Do you be one of 'er couples?"

Dr. Phillips met my wide-eyed gaze with a look, his expression as aghast as mine. *Couples?* He was almost twice my age. More likely to be my father than my husband. Though, I supposed wealthy men took young wives with alarming frequency these days.

Tears streamed down the woman's grimy face as she both leaned toward us *and* clutched the squalling child tighter to her. "Do you want a li'il girl? This is Teagan, but you can call 'er wot you like. She's usually a right angel, perfect li'il fing. She's just so 'ungry. I dried up after a week an I can't afford the powdered stuff."

Dr. Phillips held up his hands as though to protect himself from the baby. "I'm sorry, miss, but we're not—"

"I know. I know. Ms. Riley told me most childless couples want a boy. But think of 'ow sweet she'd be, take'n care of you when you're old. And keep'n your young missus comp'ny when you're gone. She's got all 'er fingers, she does. And toes. And look, er hair might be red as yours one day." She uncovered a tuft of copper matted to the little thing's head. "No one would even know you din't squirt her out yourself." The woman—girl, as I deduced she could be no older than twenty—sobbed uncontrollably now, shoving the increasingly distraught child toward us.

"Take 'er, please! You seem like such nice folks. Dandy an proper. She's even 'alf Irish, like you, missus. She won't survive one night where I'm go'n. The work'ouse in'nt no place for 'er."

Dumbfounded, I actually took the child from her, only because I feared the poor girl would collapse, which she did. Crumpled to her knees right there in the walkway, a skinny pile of bones and rags.

I turned to a gawking constable and sent him after Aberline. He'd want to hear this.

A glowering Hao Long darted up to me, reaching for

the baby, scowling with all the disapproval of a thousand ancestral grandparents.

Gratefully, I passed the babe to the perpetual father, and he produced a curious amber-colored shard from the pocket of his silk tunic. The moment it touched the child's lips, she quieted, emitting slimy suckling noises.

Dr. Phillips and I looked on in stark amazement. What had he given her? Some sort of hardened sugar, I hoped. Or maybe honey. Whatever it was, I could have kissed him for it.

Now for the wails of the mother. I smoothed my skirts beneath me, perching on the stoop as I rested a hand on the young woman's shoulder. "You were bringing your daughter to Katherine Riley so she could place her with a childless couple?"

"I got 'er name from Jane Prentice wot sews in the factory. She got 'erself in trouble but couldn't take care of it because she's Catholic, so she brought 'er boy 'ere. Said Ms. Riley put 'im with a well-to-do miller's family in Southwark."

"Does she perform this service for a lot of women who...find themselves in trouble?" I asked.

"I'm not like 'em. I gots morals," she insisted, misreading the reason for my inquiry. "I was a married woman, respectable like." Blowing her nose on a dingy handkerchief, she eyed Hao Long with open suspicion bordering on hostility. "Who's 'e? What's 'e gonna do with 'er?"

"He is my employee and father to many children of his own. Your daughter's quite safe."

The woman nodded, trying desperately to compose herself, but she didn't let Hao Long out of her sight. Whatever desperate circumstances had driven her to seek placement for her child, she did it out of love for little Teagan.

"You want 'er?" Mary's dark eyes shone with a mother's desperate, consuming adoration. "Look at 'er now.

She's so easy to love. 'Ardly makes a peep if she's fed, see? I think you two live even more west than South-wark. Might could send 'er to school. Teach 'er 'ow to speak proper like. Give 'er a 'ome, yeah?" She hadn't stopped nodding the entire time.

"Mary?" I asked. "Where is Teagan's father?"

It took her so long to reply, I wondered if she con-cocted a lie. "My Joseph, 'e died last week in an accident at the docks." She crumpled again, curling in over her middle as she dug into an apron pocket with filthy, trembling fingers. "I 'ave 'is last wages an' me weddin' ring to give to Ms. Riley to place Teagan for me. But they're yours, if you want to cut 'er out of the deal."

So, Katherine Riley had been taking infants from desperate or unwed mothers and placing them with well-to-do childless couples. Acting as a sort of unoffi-cial adoption agency. That certainly explained the sparse child accoutrements we'd found. And the lack of a child for them to belong to.

If both the mothers and the couples paid her, then her luxuries made a great deal more sense. The expen-sive carpet. The ivory teeth. The comfortable rooms.

What she'd been doing for a living wasn't at all legal, but neither was whoring.

Besides, who was I to judge? I was sometimes little better than a grave robber.

"I'm sorry to tell you this, Mary." I rubbed her back as she wrestled with hiccupping breaths. "But we are not a married couple, and therefore, cannot take in your child."

"Oh." She eyed me with a little more alert interest now. "I-I thought you kissed 'im."

"Only because he's a dear friend and associate of mine." I looked up at him. "This is Dr. George Bagster Phillips, surgeon and coroner. We are here because Katherine Riley died under suspicious circumstances this morning."

Suspicious circumstances. Possibly the grossest under-statement I'd ever uttered.

"Oh." Mary absorbed the information, then put her face back in her hands. "Oh, no. What'll I do now?"

I can't say why I did what I did next. Maybe it was because her name was Mary Jean. Perhaps because she was pretty, young, and had dark, soulful eyes, and a stubborn jaw.

Just like Mary Jeanette Kelly.

"Can you work, Mary?" I prompted.

She blinked up at me, wiping her eyes with her sleeve. "I can't lift much for a while…" She blushed as she shyly avoided Dr. Phillip's gaze. "I only 'ad 'er a fortnight ago, see. I in't healed up yet."

Cupping her palm in mine, I emptied the contents of my purse into her hand. "I want you to take this, along with your husband's earnings, and find Teagan a nurse. Get a room nearby for a week where you can rest and eat. After that, if you've not found a better situation, call 'round at 38 Tite Street in Chelsea. I live with my eccentric aunt, who is in need of care and companionship, maybe four days a week. Do you think you could do that?"

She stared at the coins as though she didn't believe they sat in her hand. "I—I ain't never been no lady's maid, missus."

"We're only in need of a maid-of-all-work. Someone to make sure she's taking care of herself. That she's properly fed and bathed, and the house is tidy. Possibly to run a few errands here and there."

Her gaze darted back to her new daughter. "I don't 'ave no one to look after Teagan."

"You can bring her, if you wish. So long as she stays on the first floor." I'd need somewhere to sleep away from baby noises at strange hours. "I think it would bring Aunt Nola some cheer to have a child to entertain her."

"She in'nt one of them dangerous looneys, if you pardon me asking, missus?"

"It's miss," I corrected her. "Miss Fiona Mahoney. And the worst you can expect from Aunt Nola is that she'll assign you and poor Teagan a few spirit guides. She helped raise me a long time ago after my mother died."

Clasping my hands in her strong, callused grip, she pressed a tearful kiss to my gloves. "Bless you," she sobbed. "Bless you."

I helped her up, motioning to Hao Long to return the baby to her. She snatched Teagan away, though she stood passively as my enigmatic assistant placed the little amber pacifier into her hands and bowed before striding to the cart.

I'd never been more grateful to him than I was at that moment.

The constable returned with Aberline, who led Mrs. McBride and her baby away for questioning. I was happy to release them into his care. He'd likely offer her Leman Street's warm, bitter tea and sandwiches from his own lunch pail as he'd once done for me. Then, gently, he'd convince her to give him information on Katherine Riley.

"Are you certain about her?" Dr. Phillips asked. "She'll likely steal from you soon as work for you."

"You'd have said that about me once upon a day," I chided gently. "I was in this very position when first we met if you remember, sobbing and penniless on the ground in Whitechapel, nothing but a shilling and a broken heart to my name."

"I knew you were different. I always have."

"That's very kind of you." I could sense more than hear that Hao Long had patiently taken up residence behind me.

"I'll leave you to it," Dr. Phillips touched his hat

once more. "Good afternoon, Miss Mahoney. Don't forget about the livers."

"I won't." I smiled, though the thought of approaching the Hammer for work was more repugnant now than it had been these past months.

Sighing, I steeled myself for the job ahead, anticipating maggots beneath the carpet, which I'd have to take straight to the incinerator. That would certainly cut into my profits.

I turned to Hao Long. "Please tell me you brought—"

He held up my black over-frock and sleeve covers.

"Thank you." I slipped the frock over my dress and stood as he tied it behind me. I'd have to tip him handily for today. He'd earned it.

No need to change clothing, I thought. The scent of death already clung to the fibers of what I was wearing.

And, luckily, I was the only person of my acquaintance who knew how to get rid of it.

CHAPTER 14

The next morning, I set out to discover whether or not Thaddeus Comstock was the man who'd cut my throat.

If I visited him during office hours at *The London Evening Examiner*, the likelihood of his accosting me was dramatically reduced. I but had to hear his voice. Then I could elect what to do next. Go to the police?

Or take a darker path.

I was, as yet, undecided.

I'd never forget that voice in the darkness. As soft against my ear as his blade was hard against my neck.

Damn him for making me afraid. Shadows were hard enough to search for in the dark. How dare he become one more shade of mine.

I was further disgruntled to find Croft's shoulders supporting the weight of the Reinhold Building on Brompton Road, guarding the entrance to the *Examiner*.

I shouldn't have worn my aubergine frock with the violet cuffs and braiding at the bodice. It was one of my smarter dresses and boasted enough layers for a day that promised rain. However, it matched a dark hue in Croft's cobalt paisley cravat and the pinstripes of his dark wool suit. It would appear to passersby that we complemented each other. And wasn't that laughable?

Oil and water, that was Croft and me. Two negatively charged magnets repelling each other by the very nature of physical law.

I wasn't the only one who noticed that he didn't at all integrate into the bustling streets this far west in London. He stood much too rigid, too wary and frank in his observations of other people. Here in Knightsbridge, as in Chelsea, Westminster, and Belgravia, people nodded politely to each other in the unlikely event that their eyes met. Most went so far as to offer a well-meaning felicitation.

Croft analyzed those passersby who dared notice him with unrepentant scrutiny. A great deal of them offered a cautious, "Good day." If they were women—which most of them were, I noticed with a frown—he had the decency to reward them with a barely congenial nod.

He drew deeply on his cigarette as he marked my approach, then picked a sliver of dried tobacco off his tongue before flicking both onto the pavestones.

"What are *you* doing here?" I allowed my irascibility at his presence to color my question with temper. It took everything I had not to brandish the umbrella hooked over my forearm at him like a cutlass.

En garde, Inspector Croft.

"Waiting for you," he answered, infuriatingly unperturbed. "I knew you'd be foolish enough to contact Comstock on your own but shrewd enough to do so in public."

Shrewd. That may be the nicest thing he'd ever called me.

"I hope you weren't waiting for long." I swept past him and stood by the door to the Reinhold building, pausing to let him open it for me. It was half-past eleven, and business hours had begun some time ago. He could have been standing there for ages. I hoped his feet hurt.

He wore no hat today, and I prayed the pregnant clouds soon birthed a mighty storm. I'd not mind one bit if Mother Nature decided he should spend the afternoon wet and cold and miserable.

"Not long at all," he assured me, sweeping the heavy door open with a mock gallant gesture. "I'm aware of the hours you keep, so I visited Comstock's home first. When I didn't find him there, I figured he'd already gone to work. And that you would be nipping at his heels like an angry lapdog who thinks herself bigger and a great deal fiercer than she actually is." His northern brogue was more apparent in the West End, somehow, than in Whitechapel. Perhaps because Londoners spoke so crisply here, and his unhurried patois commanded more presence among the starched, hassled voices of higher-born or better-educated men.

It took a great deal of will not to let my frustration show. How did he know what hours I kept? Until very recently, I'd barely stepped foot in his borough unless I had to.

I wanted to snap at him, but I didn't relish the comparison to the aforementioned lapdog. Instead, I decided to mine him for information. "How did your meeting with the Diocese go? Did you find out anything helpful about Katherine Riley?"

"Your priest was there," he said evenly.

"He's not my—wait." I put up a hand. "What did he say?"

"That's confidential."

"No, it isn't," I protested. "All I'd have to do is ask Aidan what he told you, and I'd have every detail you do. Why not save me the trouble?"

"When have we *ever* saved each other trouble?"

I whirled on him, nearly dropping my umbrella. "We could, you know. As they've mentioned, Aberline and Phillips and every other officer of my acquaintance finds me most solicitous. Helpful, even. Why not you, I wonder? Why do you have to insist that our relationship remain so acrimonious?" By the time I'd finished dressing him down, my face was inches from his.

He reached his hand out to the wainscoting in the tight hallway as though he might rip it away from the wall.

He didn't, though. He merely gestured for me to accompany him.

We climbed the winding stairs to the third floor, where the offices of *The London Evening Examiner* resided. Croft took one step to two of mine, and I quickly became winded by my determination to keep up with him.

I'd be damned if I let him into the offices first to control the interaction with Comstock.

"You let me do the talking," he ordered as we passed through the etched-glass doors and into the sanctum of the fourth estate. "All you need do is listen and confirm whether or not he is the man who accosted you in Crossland Alley that night."

I'd. Be. Damned.

"How about *you* let *me* do the talking?" I sniped back, louder now that I had the clack of Smith Premier typewriters and masculine conversation to compete with. "He has a lot to answer for, and I know exactly what to say." I'd been practicing all morning.

"Dammit, woman. For once, would you—?"

"May I help you with something?" A rather studious-looking clerk approached us with a cautious but friendly expression. We adjusted our spectacles at the exact same time, though he could look down his patrician nose at me due to his height advantage.

"Yes, thank you. I'm Miss Fiona Mahoney, how do you d—?"

"We're here for Thaddeus Comstock," Croft interrupted without the requisite pretext or pleasantries. "Which office belongs to him?"

"Do you...have an appointment?" Alert now, the clerk glanced toward a specific closed door indistinguishable from a line of them along the back wall.

Comstock's office, I guessed. "I'm afraid we don't have an appointment, but I'm certain he—"

"I'm Detective Inspector Grayson Croft, Criminal Investigations Division of the London Metropolitan Police. I don't need an appointment." He thrust his badge beneath the clerk's nose. "I'm here on a murder inquest and will speak to Mr. Comstock now."

He turned toward the unmarked door, having made the same assumption I did about who worked behind it.

The clerk fell into step with Croft, forcing me to walk along the lone isle behind them, lest my thighs bang into any of the several desks crammed into the wide room. I might as well have not been there for all the attention the men paid me. "H Division? What's a Whitechapel inspector doing in Knightsbridge? Care to comment on the Sawyer murder? Or on the rumors that another Ripper victim was found in the Bilkington tenements yesterday?"

So, not a clerk, then, I surmised. Just a poorly kempt journalist with dreary taste in suits.

"That's not your article, is it?" I chimed in, narrowly avoiding a collision with a distracted man deciphering messy notes. "Mr. Comstock is the one who broke the story, and our business is with him."

The man glanced back at me as if just remembering I existed. As if I weren't the only female in the room, let alone the solitary individual draped in something other than black or beige. "And who are you again, darling?" He took my measure from the top of my violet velvet hat to the ivory handle of my umbrella, then down to the lace on my dainty Berk & Kessler boots, making it expressly clear how unimpressed he was by me. "Scotland Yard doesn't employ women, and you're too posh for a Whitechapel street doxy."

Croft's face was suddenly mere inches from the startled journalist. "Piss. *Off.*"

"See here!" the man blustered. "I'm Mr. Stanley Leventhorpe, the associate editor of the crime beat here at *The London Evening Examiner*. Thaddeus Comstock is my subordinate, and anything he's published has been read and edited by me. So, in essence, his stories are my stories."

Blimey. I couldn't have been more wrong in my initial estimation of Mr. Leventhorpe. Not only was he not a clerk, or even a journalist, he was an editor. And possessed of big enough stones—as my father called them—to stand up to a glowering Grayson Croft.

Say what you will about the press, they were often very brave. Or reckless.

"What did I just say?" Croft inched closer. Were Leventhorpe a woman, one would surmise that as close as Croft's nose was to his, they were about to kiss. However, anyone with eyes could see that the editor was in imminent danger of learning just how hardheaded Grayson Croft could be.

As he squared off with Mr. Leventhorpe, I sidled past them both and let myself into Thaddeus Comstock's office.

"You won't find him in there, miss," Leventhorpe called after me. "He's yet to come into the office today."

"He's not at home, either." Croft followed me into the dim square box that passed for a star reporter's office at *The London Evening Examiner*. He opened the heavy damask drapes, revealing an untidy mahogany desk that took up half the meager office, and a beleaguered leather chair. No other furniture ornamented the room, certainly nothing that invited one to stay. No art adorned the walls, but several plaques, diplomas, and trophies were strewn on and about the desk as though Comstock had only just taken possession of this office and meant to set it to rights at any moment.

"Must be in the field." Leventhorpe made a valiant effort to protect the chaos of Comstock's desk from Inspector Croft's curiosity. But alas, he was swept aside with as much ease as the damask drapes. "You are not privy to that. Everything in this office is privileged information protected by the integrity of the free press."

"Since when did the press have integrity?" A humorless scoff escaped Croft's throat as he scanned a handwritten list. "In my experience, you lot are the most unscrupulous of rabble-rousers, who are regularly bought at great expense and with astounding regularity." He tossed the list onto the desk and retrieved a letter to which the seal had been broken. "The free press. Don't make me laugh."

I tried to remember if I'd ever heard Croft laugh and came up with an absolute blank.

I did my best to distract the sputtering, red-faced editor with questions of my own. "When was the last time you were in contact with Mr. Comstock?" I found a gas lamp and lit it when I noted Croft squinting in the pallid light provided by the window.

Leventhorpe leveled me a distasteful look, obviously considering whether or not he felt beholden to answer a woman's inquiries.

"It would behoove you to not make *me* repeat the question," Croft threatened without looking up.

"Two mornings ago. After he turned in his article."

Croft glanced over at me. "Do you know where he was the night prior? At say, four a.m.?"

"At home asleep, I would assume. Like I was. What's this about? Just who is this woman?" He eyed us both suspiciously.

I avoided the question. I'd already introduced myself, and if he couldn't remember, that wasn't my concern. "What can you tell me about Mr. Comstock's... um...vernacular?"

Leventhorpe's eyes became narrow slits of distemper. "I don't intuit your meaning."

He gathered every bit of my meaning, it was all over his priggish face. "Would you say his dialect is rather..." Feminine, anemic, waspy... "Does he have a lisp?"

"What a ridiculous question."

"Perhaps, but I'd like the answer."

Scowling, the editor crossed defensive arms over his chest. "It's not a lisp, per se, it's more like a—oh, I don't know—a serpentine pattern of speech. A sign of sophistication, I'd say. Half the nobility is affected, utilizing a similar dialect." He plucked one of Comstock's plaques out of my hands, a trophy for excellence of some kind or another.

Afflicted was a more apropos word than affected, especially where the aristocracy was concerned.

"This is empty," I tapped on a rectangular glass case with pronged pillars upon which something should be displayed. "What goes in it?"

"A bayonet, if you must know. From the Crimea."

"Do you know where it is?" Croft met my eyes once more. Some believed Martha Tabrum to have been stabbed over and over with just such a weapon.

"How long has it been missing from this case?" Croft set down the papers and drifted toward it.

"Why ever would I know that?" The editor's brows drew together. "Just what are you looking for?"

"You may see yourself out, Mr. Leventhorpe." Croft held the door open for him.

"You-you cannot dismiss me from my own—"

"If I have to tell you to piss off one more time, I'll take you to Leman Street for questioning."

Off he pissed.

"I'd give my eyeteeth for that bayonet," Croft grumbled once we were alone.

"You're not alone in that." The first few drops of rain plunked against the window as I joined Croft back at the desk and leafed through a few papers, bills, article notes, and a heavily used datebook. I checked the journal. Comstock was supposed to meet someone here in his office today. A half hour ago. Someone with the initials of DRP. The letter had been traced with an idle pen a number of times and thrice underlined.

He'd missed his very important appointment.

Just then, a bothersome thought struck me. "Don't you find it odd that Comstock, a self-proclaimed Ripper aficionado—"

"Was nowhere to be found near Katherine Riley's murder scene?" Croft finished my thought to the letter, as though he'd plucked it out of my head.

"I unexpectedly find myself more worried for him than for myself. He's missed two days of work and a clearly important meeting this morning with the mysterious DRP. Also, Katherine Riley's murder was reported by five papers, *The London Evening Examiner,* not among them. Are you quite certain he wasn't at home? What if he…couldn't come to the door?"

"He wasn't there." Croft looked down over my shoulder, and a strange, heady awareness of him lifted the fine hairs all over my body. This is what Grayson Croft inflicted upon me. Ire and goose pimples.

At my raised eyebrow, he said, "His door was unlocked."

"Was it, now?" I turned the page of the datebook back to the night of Frank Sawyer's murder.

And found nothing. He'd no appointments on that night, social or otherwise.

"I'll have to ask that loathsome Leventhorpe if he knows who DRP is," Croft lamented. "Comstock's script doesn't match the Ripper's. Though I suppose that could easily be altered." Croft reached past me to pluck a folded piece of paper from the crease of the datebook. His chest brushed my shoulder, and the aroma I always associated with Croft coiled through my senses. Clove cigarettes. Clean linens. And...something else. My nose twitched. Something like sharp vanilla. Was Croft wearing cologne?

"What did you find?" I wanted to put the desk between us, but it was all I could do to inch to the right and turn to face him.

From behind dark lashes, his eyes scanned the document. Quickly at first, then snagging on a word here. Rereading a phrase there. Before long, the paper began to crumple beneath the increasing compression of his grip.

"Dash it, Croft. What *is* it?"

He finally looked up as though he'd made an important discovery. "You weren't lying. About what happened in Crossland Alley."

I couldn't tell you what my expression was in that moment. Somewhere between incensed and astonished I would guess. "You thought I *lied* about being accosted by a man claiming to be Jack the Ripper? That I cut my *own* throat? Why the bleeding hell would I do something like that? Just who do you think I—?"

His hand clamped over my mouth with a hiss. "Not. Here." Just as I opened my lips to bite him, he shoved the paper in front of me, and my mouth remained open for a multitude of reasons.

FM: *Near Wych. Armed. Unconscious. Prostitute? Possible JR association?*
FS: *Castrated. Disemboweled. Redressed. No organs taken. Hanged. JtR or imitation?*
MK: *Childhood friend. Different than other victims. Research history. FM: Lovers?*

MOISTURE CAUSED my lips to cling to Croft's skin as he finally pulled his hand away. I shook with anger, Croft's slight all but forgotten beneath this new outrage. Here was proof Comstock had been my assailant. I was obviously FM. Crossland Alley was off Wych Street, where I'd been found unconscious by Aramis Night Horse.

"He thought I was a *prostitute*?" It's unclear if I whispered this or shrieked it. Perhaps both. "Well, he's obviously possessed of the journalistic ability of an illiterate guttersnipe."

"That's the detail you selected for emphasis?" Croft lifted a caustic eyebrow.

"He underlined it." I stabbed the word with my finger. "*Twice*!"

That blasted dimple appeared in his cheek again, the one that only materialized when he was laughing at me internally. "Didn't you relocate to London for that very vocational purpose?"

I'd only confessed that to Aberline whilst giving my statement at H Division after Mary's murder. And then again to Comstock when I thought the moment might just be my last.

So...how did Croft know? Had he read Aberline's report? My statement? Why would he have done that?

"I changed my mind, obviously." I glared an Arctic blast in his direction.

"Is it worth it?"

"Pardon?" I wasn't certain I'd heard him correctly.

"Most people would argue what you chose as a profession is a great deal more unpleasant than that of a whore."

"Most people are imbeciles."

He cocked his head to the side, regarding me intently. "So, in your opinion, blood and death are preferable to sex?"

I wouldn't know, but I'd die a thousand times before admitting it to Croft.

I hissed an irate breath through my throat. "There are two reasons I won't dignify that question with a response. First is that the query is vulgar and discourteous. Second, because I believe the answer should be evident by which profession I ultimately chose."

"Fair enough."

My fingers itched to claw the dark glint of salacious speculation from his eyes. If I didn't know better, I'd think he was mentally placing me in some alternate reality. One in which I'd made the opposite choice.

Did Croft ever pay for pleasure?

I snuffed the offending question like a match, lest it start a fire I couldn't put out. "If we could focus on these ludicrous notes, please." I made to snatch the paper from him, wishing I could rip it into shreds.

His fingers tightened as I clutched at it, and the thin paper slipped right through my gloves. At least I'd succeeded in wiping whatever ridiculous thoughts he'd harbored from showing on his features.

Argh. Men.

"The initials are especially significant." He pointed to each with a square finger, returning to the task at hand. "FM. Fiona Mahoney, of course. FS, Frank Sawyer. MK, Mary Kelly. But look here. JR and JtR. Why do you think he made a distinction? Was it a mistake, or a coincidence? Do you know anyone else with the initials JR?"

I took a moment to flip through my very limited list of connections. "None that I can think of. And what a bog-licking blighter that he should even speculate that I'd be linked with such evil as Jack the Ripper. Why would he suppose any such thing?"

"That's an excellent question." He ran his finger down the paper to caress one word near the bottom of the note.

Lovers.

"Were you and Mary...?" He let the word draw out as his cavernous voice darkened. Lowered. As though the thought of Mary and I carrying on didn't revolt him.

Quite the opposite.

"No, you rank pervert, and if you ever say different, I'll blast you for libel." This time, I really did put the desk between us. "I told Comstock I loved Mary, not that I was *in love* with her. She was my friend. My only friend at the time. That's the extent of it."

He held his hands up as though the finger I jabbed at him were the dangerous end of a pistol. "All right. Stand down. I believe you."

"Do you? Do you believe me, Inspector? It's about bloody time!" I hoped the ice in my glare frosted his nethers as I turned and stomped out of Comstock's office.

The clacking of typewriters froze as I stormed away, clutching my umbrella like a cudgel. I dared not meet the stunned gazes of any number of newspapermen, lest they take the opportunity to question me.

Croft caught up with me two flights down, but I couldn't stand to look at him, so I didn't acknowledge his presence.

Once I escaped onto Brompton Road, I didn't find any hansom cabs in my immediate vicinity. I wrenched my umbrella open, determined to walk the several blocks back to Tite Street. My temper was so swelter-ing, I was sure the rain would simply steam off me.

"Miss Mahoney, where are you going?" Croft demanded.

Home sounded like too tolerable an answer. "That's none of your business, Inspector."

"It's raining. Let me at least hail you a—"

"While your powers of deduction are astounding, I'm also aware of the weather, and I came prepared." I pulled my umbrella low over my hat, knowing the edges would poke him in the neck should he attempt to come any closer.

"Dammit, Fiona—"

"You may call me Miss Mahoney, I've not given you

leave to be so familiar, sir." I sniffed my prim disdain, hoping to drive him off with what he would consider obnoxious female behavior. "If you'll excuse me."

"You have to admit, your claim of surviving a Ripper attack was more than a little—"

"I have to admit nothing, as we found I'm neither a suspect nor a victim. Good day, Inspector."

"But you *are* a victim. Comstock did accost you, held a knife to your throat. He cut you and knocked you unconscious." His temper seemed to build, as well, as he listed the atrocities performed against my person. "His notes prove that, don't they? And now we don't know where he is. Don't you realize—?"

"Perhaps you should use your astonishing deductive skills to find *him*, then, and leave me in peace." I could hear Croft—feel him—pacing behind me in the rain, looking for a place safe from my umbrella whilst dodging the rest of midday foot traffic.

"I'm trying to protect you, woman. You could be grateful rather than giving me grief."

"What would you know about grief?" I scoffed.

"More than you think!"

I chewed on his dark response the entire time it took Brompton Street to turn into Fuller, where I promptly veered down Elystan Road toward the Thames.

Who did Croft mourn? Who did he grieve? What suffering had he endured? Enough to turn him *insuffer-able*, that was for certain.

I listened to his heavy footfalls as he trailed me like a faithful sentinel. Somehow, I managed to retain my ire, even though my lesser instincts pitied him for the very thing I'd wished upon him only hours prior.

He was probably wet, and cold, and miserable. Not that it was my fault. I wasn't responsible for the rain, for his absence of foresight *or* lack of umbrella, nor had I invited him to escort me home.

And yet...

"I...should have believed you." The words were stilted, as though he fought to keep them inside.

I paused. Lifting my umbrella high enough to glance back at him in order to ascertain if I'd heard him correctly.

I would have caught him under the chin had he inferior reflexes.

"Pardon?"

His eyes glittered hard and bright as gems against the grey afternoon. His midnight hair clung to his scalp in slick gathers as rain sluiced from his jaw to the collar of his shirt. "My profession doesn't lend itself to trust or confidence. I'm trained to be wary of extraordinary stories."

I confess I found his reticence to meet my eyes endearing. He was such an unflinching man. Except, it seemed, when blundering his way through an admission of fault.

"I'd forgotten, Miss Mahoney, that you are an extraordinary woman, with a tendency to experience extraordinary things."

I was also a woman cursed with an intense sense of stubborn pride, and a bevy of Irish brothers, so I immediately recognized the moment for what it was. An apology.

We stood in the rain for several uncertain moments. Each of us, I was quite sure wishing Croft hadn't humbled himself enough to melt my disdain.

Something about a penitent, almost forlorn gleam in a hard man's eyes unstitched me. I lifted my umbrella, silently inviting him to join me. He ducked beneath and relieved me of the burden, sheltering us both.

People regarded Croft differently with me by his side. Gentlemen nodded and met his forthright stare with a sense of congeniality. The more unsettled he became by this, the more delighted I found myself. He was not a man inclined to give his trust. Did he have *anyone* in his life upon which he relied? Or who relied upon him? He'd been a part of the most defining moment of my life, and yet, I didn't even know which borough he resided in. I'd always assumed he lived in Whitechapel, but on an inspector's salary with no wife or family to support, he could afford someplace grander.

"What made you decide to work for the Metropolitan Police, Inspector Croft?"

He looked at me as though I'd grown horns and asked for his soul.

"It's just a friendly question." I sighed. "Pardon me for attempting to be amiable. I'd forgotten for a moment in whose company I found myself."

He heaved a sigh of his own before answering. "It was steady work, and I fit the requirements."

"Which are?" Lord, I hoped the revelation wasn't too taxing.

"I was tall and fit enough. Young enough. Strong enough."

I rolled my eyes, my good nature toward him quickly evaporating. "Stubborn enough? Offensive enough? Relentless enough?"

"*That's* how I became an inspector."

Had he just attempted humor? Merry and unexpected laughter bubbled into my throat, and even *his* eyes and mouth crinkled at the corners.

Oh, I thought. *There he is*.

Grayson Croft, the boy. I had to recant what I'd supposed earlier about being unable to picture him as a child. I could see it now. Transposing a face round and smooth over what had become square and grizzled. His hair would have been wild instead of slicked down. But his eyes, his emerald orbs would be just as they were on that Chelsea road. Pleased. Surprised. Quirked with a smile and not a smile.

"Do you enjoy what you do?" I ventured.

"I'm good at what I do."

I nudged him with my elbow in mock exasperation. "You *never* answer my questions."

That dimple again, deep as I'd ever seen it. "I always answer your questions, just not with the responses you desire."

"Well, it's infuriating all the same," I huffed.

"My profession..." He paused for a hesitant moment, choosing his words carefully. "My life is like most men's, I expect. Sometimes I do what I want to do. The rest of the time, I do what I have to."

I doubted most men were trained as he was. To suspect and distrust every extraordinary thing. "What are you doing right now? What you want, or what you have to?"

Now, *there* was a question he didn't answer.

I tucked my arm into his for the sole purpose of increasing his discomfort. "I know you don't want to hear this, Inspector. But we're more alike than you think."

"How so? Because we're both consumed by the pursuit of retributive justice?"

"Actually, yes." I'd not at all expected him to be so completely correct.

The cross into inner Chelsea is abrupt. The gentry becomes more threadbare. The manners and diction learned from a university rather than a governess. Street vendors plied their wares to doctors, solicitors, writers, and students as they disembarked from cabs and trains to retire to their comfortable, if a bit more modest, addresses.

On the corner of King's Road and Radnor Walk, a woman approached us with bundles of fresh flowers. She was drenched with rain, shivering, and pathetically thin.

"Buy a Posey for your missus?"

She'd startled me a bit, and I took longer to reply than I would have had I been walking alone.

"I've a bunch 'ere of lilies of the valley. 'Twould match 'er fine dress." The desperate woman shook dripping flowers at us.

"How much?" Croft asked.

"A ha'penny."

"I'll give you a shilling to get out of the storm." He dropped the coin into her hand, but only took one flower.

Her eyes rounded to positively owlish proportions. "What a lovely man you 'ave," she praised me. "Never seen a more 'andsome couple in me life. May the Lord bless you with long lives an' many children."

Here is where Croft met the end of his patience. "Find somewhere dry," he ordered with a strange sort of terse gentility. If I didn't know better, I'd have thought him shy.

She curtsied as though the Queen, herself, had given her a command, and scurried back to her cart.

"Mrs. Croft." The inspector smirked, offering me the flower.

Stymied and more than a bit wobbly, I took it, in spite of myself. We continued in pensive silence. "You didn't correct her," I admonished as we turned onto Tite Street.

"Neither did you."

Damn his propensity for relevant arguments.

"Aberline mentioned you were not married," I said. "Do you have a sweetheart?"

All conviviality disappeared from his features as though it had never been. "I did have, once."

"No longer?"

"It became readily apparent that she didn't have the constitution to tolerate a vocation such as mine. You understand." He reached in his jacket for his cigarettes, then seemed to change his mind.

"That I do," I commiserated. "The long hours. The late nights. The dangerous nature of the work." The blood on your hands, and the blood in your nightmares.

I tried to picture Croft down on one knee. Courting a woman. I might as well have tried to peek into the afterlife. It was something that could not be imagined, only experienced.

"What about you?" His elbow nudged me back. "You don't want a husband to care for you?"

I made the most unladylike sound I'd ever made in public. "It is my observation, Inspector, that husbands rarely *care* for their wives. At least, not for very long."

"Is that so? Did your father not care for your mother?"

"She passed on before I was old enough to note what kind of relationship they endured."

He inspected me curiously. "So, if husbands do not care for their wives, what *do* they do, in your experience?"

"Men dominate women, or they rely upon them, use them for pleasure, for a dowry, for a family, for society. In the lower classes, men take wives to fulfill what vocations can be hired out to a wealthier rank. For example, a cook, a maid, a nurse, a companion...a prostitute. Women can be many things. Still, they are generally the *caretakers* of their families, not taken care of *by* them."

Croft's dark brows drew together in a troubled scowl. "Certainly, it's only fair for a woman to help the man who protects her and provides for her."

"Oh, certainly," I agreed. "If that's the contract one makes. But I provide for myself. I am responsible for the care of no one else, save Aunt Nola."

"But...don't you ever get tired of working so hard?"

"Don't you?"

"Sometimes," he confessed. "But—"

"But you're a man?"

His frown turned into a glower. "That's not what I

was going to say."

"Wasn't it?"

He looked down.

I continued. "My time is my own. My money. My property. My *will* is also my own." I ticked all of these off on my silk-clad fingers. "If I were to marry, I'd have to give that all up. Could you do that, Inspector?"

"No." He regarded me like a circus oddity for an uncomfortably long time. "But what I was *going* to ask, is if you ever become lonely."

I blinked. Several times. Suddenly, I was very aware of the flex of his arm beneath my hand. "I am rarely alone, Inspector Croft," I hedged. "My ghosts provide constant company. And until I put them to rest, I have no room to spare in my life or in my heart."

"I understand."

"Do you?"

He was silent until we reached my stoop, where he turned to face me, bringing the umbrella low over our heads. It created a strange world. Just the two of us, the patter of rain, the lily of the valley he pressed into my hand, and his new cologne. "I understand that the dead make for cold companions. Do you have someone to provide you with...heat?"

I leaned back as much as the umbrella would allow. "Heat?"

"There must be balance in all things. Certainly, your memories—your vengeance—can consume your heart for now...but, surely, it isn't enough to fill the cold, empty places in your life. In your bed."

Abruptly, my knees lost their starch. "You assume much, Inspector."

"I know more about you than you think." His mouth became a hard, alluring threat, hovering above mine.

"Blood on the streets," a disembodied voice sang.

Heat flooding to my ears, I ducked away from Croft

to see Nola standing in the archway of my door, dressed in enough black lace to meet the Pope or mourn the dead.

"They're gutted," she informed Croft. "Why aren't you there?"

"Aunt Nola?" I rushed forward, leaving my umbrella with Croft. "What do you mean?"

"Who is gutted?" Croft demanded.

"They're at parliament. Didn't you hear them?" She regarded us as though *we* were the senseless ones. "So angry. They're throwing things. They'll kill each other. You'll have to wash the organs off the pavestones."

"Aunt Nola, where did you hear this?" She never left the house, and an active riot wouldn't have made it into the newspapers just yet. "Did Oscar tell you something?"

She speared me with eyes as sharp as jade daggers. My father's eyes. My eyes. "*You know who* is there."

"Who?" Croft asked.

She regarded him oddly. "Why, Jack, of course."

Croft pressed the handle of the umbrella into my palm, eyeing both of us as though we were venomous serpents who might strike at any time. "I'd better be off."

Because of how Nola had just found us, I couldn't bring myself to meet his gaze. Had Inspector Grayson Croft just offered to warm my bed?

We didn't even like each other. Did we?

"Good day, Inspector." I dismissed him as I herded Aunt Nola back inside.

"Take care, Miss Mahoney." His civil words were delivered with the immensity of a threat. "Until Comstock is found. I'm not convinced you're safe."

What an absurd thing to say. I watched him from beneath my umbrella until he hailed a hansom at the end of the block.

No one was safe. Not in London. Not anywhere.

CHAPTER 15

T he devil wrote you a letter.

Aunt Nola's whisper echoed off the white and silver marble of my entryway and followed me into the dark wood of the more expansive foyer, fracturing into a thousand ephemeral warnings.

I'd barely had time to stow my umbrella in the wrought iron stand before she shoved the little note into my hand.

I stared down at the sealed paper through spectacles spattered with rain, struggling to swallow—to breathe —amidst the strangling pressure in my throat.

Nola paced before me, her feet only ever touching the dark squares on the floor.

Only the dark squares or it would be a dreadful day. "Don't you think the paper reeks of brimstone? Wouldn't the devil write in blood?"

"It's not blood. It's red ink." This, I already knew. I tested the weight of the note, no more than a feather. I sensed the immensity of it, as vast as a destiny.

The devil wrote me a letter.

During the Autumn of Terror, there had been many letters. Some sent to the police. Others to the press. *Hundreds*. Written by those who *would be* him. Who admired what he did but never had the nerve, the will, the brutality, the hatred, the... true evil to carry out the deeds of Jack the Ripper.

Only a few letters had been truly notable. One had accompanied part of a human kidney, delivered to George Lusk. Lusk was the chairman of the East End Vigilance Committee, a rather militia-like organization of neighbors formed in Whitechapel after the police had proven their inability to stop the Ripper from killing.

The committee proved as futile as the police in preventing the last two Ripper murders. And, it seemed, the various writers of the Ripper letters enjoyed taunting the Vigilance Committee every bit as much as they did Scotland Yard.

Catherine Eddowes *had* been missing a kidney, among other organs. But, ultimately, there was no way to tell if the kidney delivered to George Lusk belonged to her. Only that it was human.

It could have come from anybody.

Any. Body.

Then there was what we all called the *Dear Boss* letter, in which Jack the Ripper had titled himself. He'd signed it:

Yours truly, Jack the Ripper
Don't mind me giving the trade a name.

HE'D BEEN KNOWN ONLY as the Whitechapel Murderer before then.

The penmanship and prose of the *Dear Boss* letter didn't match that of the letter sent to Mr. Lusk.

But the ink had matched.

Red ink. Identical to that of the letter I now held in my trembling hand.

The missive bearing my name.

Nola laid her fingers on my cuff. "I couldn't give it to you in front of him."

She meant Croft, of course, and I applauded her for her foresight. "Thank you, Nola, that was very well done of you."

"Burn it," she urged. "You should send it back from whence it came."

From Hell.

Nothing in the world could stop me from reading this letter.

Just as soon as I summoned the courage to break the seal.

"Aunt Nola? Did this come by courier or post?"

"I couldn't say. Whoever left it slipped it through the mail slot when I was in my sitting room."

I wobbled across the foyer to the staircase and lowered myself with the help of the mahogany banister. Nola went to the gas lamp at the bottom of the stairs, by way of the dark squares, and loosened the wick, providing light to read by on such a stormy day.

I took off my gloves and wiped my damp palms on my skirts before running tentative fingers across the red wax seal. A strange line was the only impression in the wax. A sword, maybe. A blade?

With a bracing breath, I broke the seal and unfolded the letter. The first sentence spread brittle tendrils of ice through every extremity.

And then it got worse.

Dearest Fiona,

I've been watching you since that day. You know the one. The one that haunts us both. The day I made Miss Kelly my masterpiece. You've been looking for me, haven't you? You see me in the blood of every corpse. You erase me every time you clean. What would you like to do to me, I wonder? What mess could we make together? You are so clever, but I begin to fear you are not clever enough. Still so innocent. So provincial. And yet unlike the coarse, violent drunkards who populate your island. Unlike the drunken whores in the East End. I'd hoped you'd absolve me of these new Whitechapel murders by now. I

*shan't abide plagiarism; the very thought gives me fits. I've
sharpened my knife again. I might have to go to work.*

   Yours truly,
   Jack the Ripper

A NOTE: *to find the killer, look to his victims. They are chosen
because they are the same. Like mine. Good luck.*

I SCANNED the letter a million times, dissecting each
sentence. The prose. The pacing. The penmanship. So
achingly similar to the ones I'd pored over countless
times when Aberline allowed me into the records room.

Jack the Ripper considered himself an artist. A
painter of masterpieces. One whose technique sometimes evolved. But his preferred hue remained the
same.

Red. Always red.

And his canvas a woman who sold her body.

I couldn't feel the tears until they dripped onto the
paper. I didn't realize I'd ceased breathing until I
screamed in a gulp of air and sobbed it back out again.
The band clamped about my ribs threatened to squeeze
the life out of me. To paralyze my lungs forever. To trap
my heart in its cage while it threw itself at the bars like
a panicked bird, only to collapse with exhaustion.

The letter drifted to the floor. I didn't hear it land. I
couldn't hear a thing but the ocean in my ears.

It settled on a dark square. Thank God.

I reached for it, but my fingers were too cold and
stiff to move, my elbows had become rusted hinges. My
face burned. I was on fire. And heavy, unwieldy like my
tongue.

Was I going to die? Had there been something on
the paper, in the ink? Poison, perhaps?

A strong, bony hand shoved my head toward my knees.

"Close your eyes and breathe." I hadn't heard Aunt Nola sound so completely sane in ten years.

I couldn't close my eyes. I could only stare at the letter through vision blurred by vertigo and tears.

Dearest Fiona...

Did he think me dear? Dearest?

Did Jack the Ripper...*like* me? Did he know me?

Did I know him?

My stomach rolled dangerously, and I gripped the hand Nola slipped through mine hard enough to crush her fingers, but she made no protestation.

"He's been watching me." I gulped breaths like a fish drowning in the air. "How? How could he be close enough to—? Who? Who could possibly—? A-and when? How often does he watch—? From where? From *where*?"

"Peace, Fiona," Nola crooned as she rubbed tender little circles on my back. "Peace, child." She rested her head on my heaving shoulders and sang *Mo Gille Mear* in the sweetest tones I'd heard since my father died. She made it to the third refrain before I could breathe normally again, soothed by the echoes of the clear Irish words fractured and sent back to me by my foyer.

I closed my eyes.

The darkness transported me home, where the air was scented with frost and barley and the River Shannon. Though the cottages were cozy and warm, we sat outside in the cold around a fire made of peat and rowan branches. My father did his best to belt out *Mo Gille Mear* with greater gusto than Father Seamus. Their tenors rang through Limerick with a harmonious rapture deepened by whisky and brightened by Robert O'Toole's accordion, and Thomas McBride's drum.

I could see him, my jolly da, red-faced and smiling,

petting my hair as those of us gathered for the evening joined in the chorus.

I opened my eyes, and all the green grandeur disappeared, replaced by wreathed marble embellishments inlaid into dark wood. My house was grand. Grander than anything my father had been able to afford. I lived here because I'd taken one look at the Irish crystal chandelier throwing prisms onto the pale green paper interrupted by mahogany wainscoting and had fallen in love.

To be clear, I'd fallen in love with Aidan when he snuck me into the library at Trinity College. The dark wood in the house at Tite Street was precisely the same color, the banisters carved with the very likeness of the one I'd leaned against when he kissed me, surrounded by all those lovely books.

I still wore his ring on my right hand.

What a maudlin fool I'd turned out to be. I'd filled this house with lovely furnishings and handsome decorations.

Yet it was still so empty.

I'd give anything to be back in the modest Mahoney home, curled on my bed in the closet partitioned as a bedroom for me—the only girl—back behind the kitchen. The cookstove had warmed the east wall, and I'd press my hands to it in the morning when mother made breakfast.

How was it I could live in the largest city in the world and feel so utterly alone?

I had Nola with me, but one could rarely call her present. Even so, her song meant so much. She'd given me a gift.

She'd given me a memory. Something to cling to. To pull me back from the edge.

Stronger now, I reached for the letter, glad when my limbs proved capable of obeying me.

What would you like to do to me? the Ripper wondered.

I wondered, as well. I wondered all the time. In the beginning, it had been an obsession. A comfort. Pondering the dastardly things I'd do to Jack.

Did that make me a monster, too?

"That song was a favorite of Da's." I squeezed Nola's hand, and she lifted her head from my shoulder.

"I know. I sang it for him when we were little." She patted me indulgently as if I were the looney one.

And perhaps, I was.

I glanced around the foyer, wishing I possessed a sense of divine direction, real or imagined. "Aunt Nola... does—does Da ever...does he ever talk to you?" Lord, I needed my head examined.

"No." Releasing a sad sigh, she gave my hand another regretful squeeze. "He's moved on. They all have."

Of course, they had.

"But I know what he'd tell you to do with that letter."

I blinked at her. "You do?"

"I know what killed your father, Fiona."

At that, even my ability to blink disappeared. The death of my father, of my brothers, had never been solved. But it had always been explained in one concise sentence.

They died in the Troubles.

They'd died as soldiers on the losing side of a war, and no one investigated the deaths of soldiers as murders. But they *were* murdered. Down to young Fayne at merely thirteen.

"We Mahoneys are a fierce and scarce lot." Nola sat up tall like a sage, making certain to maintain my attention. "Your father tried to fight an entire war by himself, and it got them all killed. Do you understand?"

I didn't need to blink as tears moistened my eyes once again. "I don't understand." I never had.

"Your father would tell you not to fight this war against the Ripper alone, Fiona. If you do, the outcome will undoubtedly be the same. You are clever, but *he* is evil, and to beat the devil, you have to play his game. I don't think you can. You're too innocent. You're too...good."

Was I good?

Stunned, I stared at Nola for a long time. She spoke with clarity. Conviction. With the strength and wisdom of the woman I'd known her to be at my age. Her hands didn't tremble now. Her voice didn't shake.

"Who do I go to?" I asked, gripping onto her moment of sanity like a drowning man would a rope. "I don't know who to trust."

"Your father would tell you to go to the police."

He would, but my father *was* the police, not a criminal.

"Not the one who brought you home," she clarified. "The..." She made a gesture at the side of her face, imitating muttonchops.

"Aberline?"

"Him, you can trust."

She'd been introduced to Aberline maybe twice. He'd come to fetch me on occasion to hire me for a job. He also conducted me home safely after I'd completed one. In truth, I thought Nola might be a bit sweet on him.

"This is his war, too," she remarked with a pointed expression.

She was not wrong about that. Aberline had been a foot soldier since the very beginning, searching dark alleys and vast shadows for the Ripper when other men dared not leave their lofty offices. The search still consumed him. It was something we had in common.

I checked the watch on my broach. If I hurried to Scotland Yard, I'd be there in time for tea.

Standing, I folded the letter carefully, fitting the broken halves of the seal back together. "We can have supper together when I return, would you like that?"

Nola nodded and then held her hand out to stop me as I made to fetch my umbrella once again. "The dark squares, *please*!"

Of course. The dark squares.

How could I forget?

CHAPTER 16

By the time the mob tipped my cab over, I was too terrified to be angry at the driver anymore.

Too often, a woman's word of caution was patently unheeded by a cocksure man. Because of this, I found myself crumpled against the inside door of my coach, which now rested on the cobbles.

I'd been uneasy when we'd passed the small groups of livid men with union signs. The last time the Labourer's Union and the Fair Traders clashed in Hyde Park, there'd been casualties.

That had been four years ago, at least. Before I'd come to London.

As we clopped along, I'd spotted signs for the Social Democratic Federation and marked the strong presence of the Irish National League.

When the poor stormed the West End *en masse*, nothing good came of it.

And when the Irish wore their colors, even in this age of advanced enlightenment and ceasefire treaties, there could be no doubt they were going to war.

I'd unlatched the window and called into the diminishing rain, "Mightn't we take the long way to Scotland Yard? I sense trouble."

"Naw. Just a few rabble-rousers on their way to

Trafalgar Square, miss," the cabby had tutted at me. "In'nt that where you Irish riot these days? We'll stay along the river and be perfectly safe unless you want to join your countrymen."

When a crowd became a mob, their violence was indiscriminate. I had no desire to be anywhere near such an occurrence.

"I'd rather we just turn around and go back to Chelsea," I'd pressed. "I'm not political, and I fear that this could quickly become dangerous."

"No easy feat in these cramped streets," he'd snapped. "If you want to go back, get out and walk."

I'd been too frightened to leave the safety of the carriage at the time, but now I wished with every bone in my body that I had done so when I'd had the chance.

A murderous energy had vibrated in ocean-like ripples through the humanity in the streets, and the closer we clattered toward the House of Lords, the thicker the throng became. They bumped the carriage at first, like a shark testing a fisherman's dory. Then they pounded on it, shouting the vilest threats.

I could hear the panicked screams of the horse, and the curses and warnings of the driver as he swung his whip, hoping to dislodge the hangers-on.

Of all the days for one of Aunt Nola's outlandish predictions to be accurate.

Despite my misgivings about divinity, I'd closed my eyes and whispered a silent prayer of the *dear-God-please-let-me-survive-this* variety.

The next time I'd peeked out the window, they'd been dragging the driver away and working at unlatching the horse from the carriage.

Where are the police? I'd frantically wondered as the coach had begun rocking with the violence of an Atlantic sea gale.

A rock the size of my fist broke through the left window. It would have landed in my lap had I not scrambled onto the seat, using my bent legs as shock coils, stabilizing myself as best I could with my arms outstretched, braced against the walls.

Once the carriage tipped to the left, the fall seemed to take an eternity. Long enough for me to clutch at the plush seat covers.

The impact with the ground threw me forward, and I cried out in pain as my hip landed hard on the door handle. Glass crunched beneath my weight.

I looked up as a canopy of mutinous faces and hands grasped at the door, which had now become the ceiling. Daylight dappled through their fingers until enough of them swarmed the coach to hide the golden spires of parliament from view.

They were going to get into the cab. And once they did, they'd tear me apart.

Desperate, I searched for a weapon. I had my knife, my pick, and my umbrella. None of which would save me from a violent horde.

Still, I took my blade from my pocket, opened it, and held it at the ready. In my left hand, I grasped my umbrella, preparing to poke out a few eyes if I had to.

The window cracked beneath the weight of so much force, giving me just enough time to open my umbrella before the glass shattered. Shadows of shards slid off the thick fabric, ripping it in places.

Better it than my flesh.

A victorious roar echoed through the mob as my umbrella was torn from my grip and disappeared.

When they couldn't fit through the window, someone managed to pry the door open.

Hands were on me. Clawing. Lifting. And whatever made me human, a person, fled before an animalian fear so electrifying, rage billowed in to fill the spaces reason had deserted.

A sharp ringing in my ears drowned out the cacophony of their obscene words. My vision blurred, then sharpened. All I could see was my knife. How bright it glinted among their rough and often dirty fingers.

I took a few of those fingers with my blade. Several, in fact, before someone managed to drag me from the coach.

They called me a whore. They called me a cunt. They called me worse than that, and with no reason. I'd barely marked them.

The blade was like a part of me I'd never learned how to use. A claw that had been retracted until this moment. Whenever it found purchase in flesh, I snarled with a sense of triumph. When blood erupted from a wound, my own sang with glorious ferocity.

I was no longer a lady. A woman. Or Fiona. I was a wild thing.

Perhaps a killer.

I knew not who I cut or where.

I expected to be stabbed, myself, at any moment. Or bludgeoned, punched, kicked, trampled. But when I was finally dragged into the crowd, the sheer press of humanity was both my protector and my enslaver.

I sank into that ocean of bodies. Gulping for air with lungs left no room to inflate. My fingers became talons, clutching my knife, considering whether I could angle it to use against myself.

Despair crushed my throat like a boot heel.

The report of a gunshot echoed from the west, along the river, and a reprise of startled screams created the chorus, followed by a verse of more explosions to the south.

As if of one mind, the throng surged north, toward Westminster Abbey. I was powerless to do anything but ride the motion like a wave, lest I be trampled.

Another shot broke through the discord. This one right next to me, in the middle of it all.

The devastating pressure of bodies against me

abated as though it had never been. I stood and inhaled air greedily as people screamed and scrambled like rats from a matron's broom.

An arm clamped around me from behind. Still a creature of instinct, I stabbed at it. A hand gripped my wrist, popping my fingers open with embarrassingly little pressure against the tendons. My knife clattered to the cobbles.

I'd thought if anyone might rescue me, it would be Inspector Croft. The gunfire surely belonged to the police, didn't it?

But I could not smell clove smoke and sharp vanilla.

And the color of the hand was all wrong. Too dark.

My wiry struggles proved feeble to the preternatural strength of Aramis Night Horse.

I sagged against him, not knowing whether to be comforted or distressed. My body, apparently, chose relief.

The sounds of pain, of violence, drew my notice, and I looked over to see the Hammer using the butt of his pistol to break a man's jaw.

Hammer, indeed.

He bared his teeth in an eerie, deceptively calm smile. "Do come along, Fiona." He beckoned to me as one might invite a friend into his house.

Night Horse's shoulder became my bulwark against a sea of bodies, and I was happy to tuck myself against his smooth, solid frame. To bury my cheek in his loose hair and let him half-drag, half-carry me along. I liked to think my feet helped, but I couldn't be sure.

As the crowd surged north, the Hammer cleared a path toward Great College Street by way of punishing brutality.

He was the sort of man crowds parted for.

Had I been religious, I'd have said he was the sort of man the *seas* parted for.

In that moment, he was my savior, and I would have worshiped him thusly.

After breaking a few bones, he pointed his pistol at anyone who should happen to venture too close, and luckily, the mob was now wary of stray bullets.

The crowd thinned at Great College Street, and the Hammer fell into step beside us. "They'll herd the blighters back to the East End. We'll press this way until we're safe."

"Who will herd them? The police?"

A laugh, rich as warm cream, was discordant in such chaos. "The police? You think those imbeciles could organize themselves against such a mob so quickly?" His hazel eyes danced at me. "No, darling, the Tsadeq Syndicate will restore order, here. The mob of unions and gangs must be reminded that the city is mine, after all."

Even in my shaken state, his grandiosity amazed me.

"Butchers," Aramis warned. "To your left." He thrust me to his right and used his body as a shield.

Night Horse snatched one by the throat in mid-run, used his momentum to jerk the poor sod back, and snapped his neck with a good wrench on his necktie.

"That,"—he motioned to the broken man on the ground—"is why I don't like cravats."

Duly noted.

Pressing anxious fingers against my own still-healing throat, I looked away from the body in time to witness the upward arc of the curved blade clutched between the Hammer's fingers. It caught the man running at him with his cudgel raised, right below the navel.

It only took a few swift, merciless jerks. Then the Hammer stepped back in time to avoid the brute's innards splattering against his expensive shoes.

"The city is *mine*," he informed the doomed assailant exactly as he had us only seconds prior. I don't think the man marked the reminder. He was too busy gawking at his own guts.

He fell to his knees, and by the time his face hit the earth, life had deserted his eyes.

The Hammer spat on the ground next to him. "They won't forget after today."

Nola had been right yet again.

They would be washing organs from the pavestones.

CHAPTER 17

As dazed as I found myself, I'd not failed to notice how expertly the Hammer had gutted his adversary. He'd opened the stomach cavity with that short, curved blade, without perforating the intestines.

So far as I could distinguish, anyway.

As Aidan had pointed out, the act took a certain kind of knowledge. Talent.

Practice.

Could he have done Frank Sawyer thus, and so quickly?

I remained shielded by Night Horse's shoulders long after it was necessary. Partly because I didn't trust my legs. And partly because I felt he understood the animal I had become. He understood it better than I did. He was someone with the morality of a wolf, or a fox, or an owl.

He was someone with claws. Blades.

He didn't wear much for such a chilly, rainy day, I dimly realized. Trousers, boots, and a vest with no shirt beneath it.

I wondered where his jacket was before he settled it around my shoulders.

I clung to his umber arms, taking comfort in the strength I found there.

I couldn't tell you how long we walked or how many turns we took. Only when I was unable to clearly read the street signs did I realize I'd lost my spectacles somewhere in the fracas.

We eventually ducked beneath a doorway arched into a stone garden wall, where I was allowed to catch my breath.

"Are you hurt?" Aramis removed his jacket from around my shoulders and performed a cursory physical examination that, on any other day, would have left me feeling more than a little molested.

"I-I don't think so." Over my clothing, his questing fingers found a few tender bruises or abrasions. A great deal of blood stained my torn pelisse. He inspected it roughly, shoving the sleeves up my wrists in search of the wounds.

"It's not mine," I whispered, more to myself than him, I think. "The blood isn't mine."

"Do be careful, Night Horse, she's a tendency to sever the fingers of men she does not want touching her." Though his tone was light, the Hammer watched our exchange with displeased speculation.

I pictured the detached digits that likely still rested in the up-ended coach and shuddered. I'd had to disassemble a few bodies in my day, mostly thanks to the Hammer and Mr. Night Horse, but not someone still alive and bleeding. I'd never get used to the feeling of blade against bone.

At least, I hoped I wouldn't.

Shame brimmed into heat in my cheeks as I contemplated the violence, the permanency of what I'd done. To be without fingers...I couldn't imagine such a thing. "I-I didn't mean to—I didn't want to..."

"Don't apologize. It was well done, Fiona. If a fraction of my generals were half so as fierce as you, I'd be twice as powerful."

I gawked at him dumbly, this man who had an army all his own.

The empire bowed to a great queen, an empress, but London had a king, as well. And it was wise to show him the respect he claimed as his due, lest I incur his wrath.

"Thank you," I murmured, feeling the gratitude down to my bones, which, because of these two men, were all still intact. "Thank you." My second articulation at Night Horse wobbled as my entire body seized with uncontrollable shivers.

All three of us perked to the distant pitch of police whistles pealing above the chaos we'd escaped.

The Hammer thrust his chin back toward the fray. "Make certain all is as it should be," he instructed the Blade. "We do not want police casualties. It will change the conversations of the public and the press."

I was certain the Blade's hesitation was imagined, at first. He increased the pressure of his hold on my arms from barely perceptible to almost painful.

At my flinch, the Hammer said, "Not to worry, I'll see Fiona to safety."

I didn't realize I'd been clinging to the assassin until he pulled away from me. My fingernails had bitten little half-moon crescents into his bare arm and accidentally tangled into the long, loose, ebony hair spilling over his biceps. He only glanced at me when the strands caught and pulled at my fingers. An unholy darkness glinted in his eyes.

"Take off your pelisse." My head whipped around at the Hammer's gentle command.

My hands trembled too much to be effectual, so he undid the oversized buttons with deft and steady fingers. "This is becoming a distressing pastime, Fiona. Ridding you of bloodstained clothing."

I made a sound somewhere between a giggle and a sob, causing the brackets around his mouth to deepen fondly. As far as I could tell, my violet blouse had escaped the gruesome stains I might never be able to lift from the wool of my pelisse, and I inspected my plum skirt and wide belt with its golden arabesque buckle for evidence of the carnage.

Finding none, I sighed in relief.

Looking up, I noted that Night Horse had vanished.

"Follow me." As always with the Hammer, his invitation was more a command. He took Night Horse's place as my protector and propeller, his arm around my shoulders, bearing the weight my knees refused to support. He provided a taller, leaner, more well-dressed escort than his exotic cohort, and I certainly felt less conspicuous in his company.

Around the corner, we found a passably quiet reprieve from the bedlam, a cul-de-sac of shops hunkered in an alley crowded with colorful signs and shingles. They hung at jaunty angles from beams between buildings preserved from the days of the Tudor dynasty. The façades had once been white, but the pall of time had painted them many colors of faded, exposing some of the brick through cracks.

There was a certain charm to the place. The cobblestones boasted memories of the treads of men and women I'd read about in history books.

"We can take our respite here until the streets are quieter." The Hammer swept his hand toward a small café door halfway down the alley, above which hung a black shingle, concealing more than it advertised.

"The Morning Star?" I read aloud. "Isn't that a reference to the devil?"

The Hammer replied with a cheeky wink. "Not to us."

Us?

As we ducked inside—well, the Hammer ducked, I

fit through the door just fine—I observed the almost exclusively masculine crowd. They dressed in dark, somber colors; most grew heavy, impressive beards; and some were adorned with the unmistakable ringlets by their ears.

Oh, *us*. The Hammer's people. The *chosen* ones. The Jews.

Without my spectacles, their faces were mostly indistinguishable, but wariness and displeasure were more often sensed than displayed.

I was not welcome here.

"Let us drink and wait for the crowds and police to disperse, shall we?" He nudged me forward, toward the back wall.

"I-I don't really drink." I offered a mild protest around a voice still infuriatingly unsteady.

"An Irish woman who doesn't drink? Have you ever heard of such a thing?" When I didn't respond to his ribald teasing, he sobered. "Come now, Fiona, just something to calm your nerves."

My nerves. I didn't think they'd ever be calm again. Perhaps it was best I searched for courage of the liquid variety. "Very well, just the one."

I'd never felt so conspicuous as when he directed me through the candle-lit restaurant and coffeehouse. I'd have thought such a dim, windowless place would be gloomy. But I found the contrast of white walls and dark wood painted with candlelight downright cozy. In all, The Morning Star was a great deal less rowdy than the cafes in which you'd find the students, artists, and young philosophers locked in sprightly discussion in Chelsea or along the Strand.

Men here spoke in sonorous tones. Respectful, even when impassioned. Their conversations most often carried on in a guttural but lyrical language I understood to be Hebrew. I could not imagine anything so different from my own native Gaelic. Nor so similar-sounding in the back of the throat.

Men eyed me with rank speculation as we passed. I could tell some of them liked the Hammer, and some of them were disgusted by him, but they all cast their eyes down and issued respectful nods as he passed.

A few greeted, "*Shalom Aleichem.*"

He always answered back, "*Aleichem shalom.*"

His were not a people, I gathered, where a blanket greeting to a room would do. I couldn't imagine a regular tipping into the place with a rote, "*Oi, mates!*" and receiving anything back but censorious glances.

The Morning Star was larger than I'd guessed, and partitioned by a few railings, screens, and decorative columns to attempt to give every table the illusion of privacy. We claimed a spot in a rear nook of the café away from the only windows by the door. The Hammer positioned himself with his back to the wall.

I sat across from him but could not be still. Little tremors and twitches erupted in strange parts of me. My upper thigh. My eyebrow. My shoulder. My muscles zinged and twinged with the last vestiges of primitive instinct and mortal fear.

I wondered if I'd ever relax again.

Squinting, I traced a lovely tapestry woven with a symbol I'd never seen before, hanging behind the Hammer's head. I longed for the extra pair of spectacles I kept back at home.

The Hammer ordered in Hebrew from a hovering, anxious waiter, who served us generous glasses of garnet-hued wine and dark, salted bread accompanied by a dish of thick liquid as smooth and gold as honey.

"We prefer olive oil to butter," the Hammer explained.

"You've never had Irish butter, then." I eyed the dish with more than a little incredulity, not believing him for a minute. How could anyone prefer anything to butter?

"Have *you* ever tasted olive oil?"

"No," I conceded.

An ewer and bowl were brought to our table, and we each washed our hands. I wasn't sure about the Hammer, but I was unspeakably grateful for the low light in the café. Perhaps the waiter wouldn't notice the traces of blood.

If he did, he gave no indication.

Once we were alone again, the Hammer broke the bread, dipped a small piece into the olive oil, and passed it to me.

The last thing I felt like doing was eating, but I took it, remembering my manners.

"Everything tastes better to someone who just escaped the clutches of death, or someone who is about to surrender to it." This was the Hammer's idea of frivolous conversation? He observed me candidly as I popped the warm morsel into my mouth, and whatever expression I made pleased him enough to warrant a smile.

He wasn't wrong. I'd rarely tasted better in my life. I should note here that I wasn't about to give up my position on the superiority of Irish butter. Still, a good olive oil was now a welcome addition to my palate.

Awareness returned to me in warm, sluggish increments. A melancholy tune filtered from around a wall in a dark corner I could not see.

Now that we'd settled in, conversation resumed throughout the café with a muted, almost reverent hum. Strong coffee scented the air, but we were offered none.

The Hammer rested his fingers around his glass and lifted it toward me. "*L'chaim*. To life."

I touched my rim to his, trying—and failing—to hide my trembling. "*Sláinte*. To health."

I was not a great appreciator of wine, but what I held was unlike any vintage I'd ever tasted. Both dry *and* sweet. Earthy and velvety. It left syrupy rivers clinging to the edges of my glass as well as on my tongue.

An appreciative breath slid over the temperate warmth of the alcohol in my throat as some of the ache in my stomach relented. I sipped at first, but before I realized what I'd done, my glass was empty, and the Hammer signaled for more.

He regarded me with a tender sort of delight as he swirled the liquid in his glass close to the lone tealight on the table, waiting patiently for my second pour. "This wine is of vines older than the whole of the British empire. Or that of France, Italy, or Spain. Older than your churches. Than your Gods. From the times of the Romans and the Israelites."

I nodded my fascination around another gulp, doing my best not to correct him. According to we Irish, no gods on Earth were as old and abiding as ours. We clung to them with such tenacity, the Holy Roman Church had to canonize a few of them before we relented to the invading Christian faith.

"The best wines are not from the west, as you Europeans like to claim," he continued, unaware of my unspoken argument.

He waited for me to engage with him, and so I did. "Wine is a different warmth than whisky, I'll give you that."

His short breath threatened to become a laugh before he sobered, regarding me over the rim of his glass. "What were you doing in town today, Fiona?"

I attempted my next swallow twice before I finally succeeded. I had no wits left in me for lies, and so I gave him the truth. "I was on my way to Scotland Yard."

"To give them the turquoise beads?" He took a sip, hiding his reaction.

I kept the beads in a jewelry box at home. I stared

at them all the time, making decisions then unmaking them. "To consult on a different murder, entirely. You remember I work for Scotland Yard as well as you? That connection has benefited us both."

"Yes, I am aware." After a wry, dismissive gesture, he reached for more bread, tearing it and dipping it into the dish of oil. "Is this a Ripper matter? Or does it have something to do with the latest murder in Whitechapel?"

He ate like he spoke, like he walked, like he gestured. Both decisively and gracefully, with lithe, exotic mannerisms. It transfixed me for a speechless moment before I remembered his queries demanded prompt answers. "Both, I think."

I had the distinct notion that he was more than mildly curious but didn't want to appear so. "They are connected, then?"

"That is yet to be determined. Did you know the woman who was killed in Whitechapel yesterday, Katherine Riley?"

He shook his head. "I've never met the woman."

"Like you'd never met Frank Sawyer?"

Abruptly, he thrust the breadbasket toward me, and I was ashamed to admit, I flinched.

"I insist you eat more." He annunciated every word with lethal precision. "The wine is stronger than you realize."

I obeyed, telling myself it was because I wanted to and not because I was afraid. The bread and oil were quite, *quite* good. However, I did feel a change of subject was in order.

"Do you know what all that hullabaloo was about in front of parliament? It seemed every organization in the empire turned out, ready to go to battle. I don't remember reading in the papers about a vote on anything particularly inflammatory today."

"That *hullaballoo*, as you call it, was about me."

I gaped at him. "You can't be serious."

A few muscles in his face twitched. "Several of the prominent gangs feel as though I require too much regulation and have acquired too much power. They decided to stage a unified uprising against me by hiding behind the colors and causes of organizations better than themselves."

"What do you mean?" Rapt, I lifted my glass to aid the waiter when he materialized to pour me more wine.

"Do you realize, Fiona, that over the last five years —with the extreme exception of the Ripper—there have been less violent murders of women and children in London than in a century?"

I had not realized that. I'd been so focused on Jack that such statistics evaded my notice. "What does that have to do with anything?"

"There has always been a king of the London Underworld, and I am the best this city has seen in decades." His hazel eyes glowed with a copper light, like two ingots heated in some inner forge. "I support the unions, who would keep children from factories. Who force industries to maintain a safe working environment for those in their employ. I retain more prostitutes than the East End Butchers, the High Rip Gang, the Red Blighters, and all the puny mobs of angry, unemployed youths who are a cancer on this city. Combined. Women line up to work for me because they are protected by my men, not used by them. In my brothels, they are not beaten, they are not starving, they do not die in the streets. I invest in many successful endeavors and charge less interest to enterprising entrepreneurs than the banks. Yes, I break the law, but I do so with a clean conscience."

That gave me more to think about than I was capable of processing at the moment. "What about...what about the bodies you give me?"

He shrugged a shoulder with very Gallic indifference. "Men. Only men."

"Yes. But dead men, all the same."

He leaned forward, capturing my gaze like a cobra. "Every single man deserved the execution I dealt them, Fiona. If you knew their crimes, you'd have wielded the knife, yourself. Believe that." He sat back, releasing my mesmerism, and drank deeply.

I never knew what to believe when it came to the Hammer, but I nodded all the same. "What do they have against you, these other gangs? Why don't they want you in charge?"

"Many do, and those men are currently squelching the rebellion as we speak."

"And those who don't?"

"People in this world hate anyone who is not familiar. Who is not them. Men are forever at war with their counterparts. The rich and the poor. The dark-skinned and the light. The law and the anarchist. The conqueror and the conquered." He made a flamboyant gesture around the café. "The gentile and the Jew. It is human to fear what you don't know. To hate what makes you feel afraid. To declare war against one who would bring peace. Because, in times of peace, a warlike man can too often only hate and destroy himself."

"You would bring peace?" I ventured.

"I would bring order. I am not like the government. Despite my reputation, I do not make money by killing innocent people and starting needless wars. To men like me, peace means profit."

"Are you not a warlike man? Do you...harbor such feelings about yourself?"

He tilted his glass at me. "I like you because you dare ask me such complicated questions."

I'd another one to ask. "If you are such a man of peace, why are you called the Hammer?"

The ghost of a smile haunted his lips. "It comes

from a hero of ours, a legend. Judah, the Hammer, was a rebel. A brilliant strategist, and a man who prevailed against unconquerable odds."

"I see."

"That isn't to say, I haven't used a hammer a time or two in my life."

After what I'd watched him do today, I no longer doubted it. I hadn't realized a man could kill with such grace. With such ease.

The thought chilled me to my core.

"Is your name Judah?" I asked, desperate for a distraction.

"No," he answered simply.

"Then he is...someone to whom you aspire?"

"Fiona," he said with a wry sort of impatience. "Men like me—men who have titles rather than names—we do not choose them, you understand? They are allocated to us by way of distinction or infamy. Which, depends on who you are speaking to in my case."

"Do your friends know your name?" I wondered aloud. "Your real name?"

He made a caustic sound. "Friends? A man like me does not have friends. I have enemies and allies."

He was like a king in an empty castle, I realized, surrounded by a moat that not only kept people out but also imprisoned him inside his own fortifications. How very sad.

"You pity me," he remarked with a droll sigh.

I was irritatingly expressive when sober, I couldn't imagine how easy I was to read after nearly three glasses of strong Israeli wine. "I just...such a life sounds awfully lonely."

"Perhaps, but someone like me is never betrayed."

"No?" With such a large army—such a dangerous and lucrative lifestyle—betrayal seemed not only likely but also inevitable.

"It is only possible to suffer betrayal at the hands of

someone you love or someone you trust," he explained, reading my thoughts. "I only trust that a man—or woman—will act in their own self-interest. I am never disappointed. And I am never betrayed."

"Is that what you did today when you rescued me? Was that done in the name of self-interest?" Because it felt like altruism to me.

He stared at me for a heartbeat longer than I expected. "If something happened to you, who else would hide the bodies, Fiona? Who else would clean up the blood?"

"Plenty of people, I imagine, if you appealed to their self-interest."

His laugh drew the notice of many, but none so much as I. It was easy to forget how flattering candlelight was. And hard to remember its tendency to play tricks. In such golden, warm light, a cruel man could appear kind. An older man, younger. A lethal man, friendly.

"Tell me your name," I breathed.

The air around us altered. Thickened. Until the gilded haze became both a color and a sensation.

"I have many." I could tell his coy smile had been perfected on many women. That should have incensed me, but it didn't.

"Don't be obtuse. What is the one your mother gave you?" I'd not have dared speak so tartly some time ago, but I was beginning to understand that the Hammer enjoyed it when I challenged him. Whether he knew it or not.

"I never knew my mother. Did you?" he challenged back, though there was no real heat in it.

"For a short time, yes. She died in childbirth when I was young. I was raised by my father and four older brothers. And I helped raise two more."

"Then, you are well acquainted in the ways of men?"

Not in any meaningful way. The boys in the house I

was raised in were odious creatures with dubious hygiene and abhorrent manners. I could not even begin to imagine the poised, starched gangster stepping a well-soled foot into the Mahoney household of yore without dissolving into a fit of mirth.

I wrinkled my nose to hide a smirk. "I...suppose I am."

"Don't let anyone ever tell you that is an unremarkable thing." He regarded me for a tentative moment. "Would you like to stay here and have dinner with me?"

The thought of taking another hansom back to Chelsea dropped my heart into my belly. Furthermore, I most certainly didn't have the courage to walk the streets just yet. "I might as well. Until the streets are safe."

"You might as well..." he repeated as though the phrase delighted him. "Women do not generally accept my invitations with such blatant insouciance."

"You'll have to forgive me. I'm not well practiced in what women generally do."

"Decidedly not." He didn't seem to think that was a mark against me.

"I'll need to send word to Polly, my maid. My Aunt Nola is expecting me for the evening meal, I don't want to worry her."

"Let me take care of it," he offered. "Aunt Nola will be fed and cared for. Do you like lamb?"

Warmed by his generosity as much as the alcohol, I grinned. "We Irish love lamb."

"As do we. Lamb it is, then." He made a gesture that produced a waiter as if by magic and ordered something I assumed was delicious and expensive.

I sipped wine and took dainty bites of salty bread, unsure of where to look or how to behave.

"Jorah."

I forced a dry lump of bread down with a healthy sip. "What?"

"The name my mother gave me, is Jorah. Jorah David Roth."

Impulsively, I reached my hand across the table for a cheeky handshake. "I'm Fiona Ina Múireann Mahoney. It's a pleasure to meet you, Mr. Jorah David Roth."

He laughed, and his eyes danced. In that instant, I forgot he'd gutted a man not half an hour before.

"The pleasure is mine." He kissed my hand. "And, please, when we are in private, I'd rather you call me Jorah. As I'll never profane your entire name by attempting to pronounce it."

Did this mean we were friends?

"Jorah, then."

Our meal was both pleasant and strange. I enjoyed myself so much, it did not occur to me until after the Hammer—Jorah—deposited me safely at Scotland Yard just what his initials were.

Jorah Roth.

JR.

CHAPTER 18

I couldn't tell you why I neglected to inform the Hammer about the letter in my pocket. Perhaps merely because his given name shared initials with a certain notorious sobriquet. Maybe because I could not, in good conscience, convince myself Jorah David Roth was definitively *not* Jack the Ripper.

And I'd had dinner with him anyhow.

Not because I was afraid to decline his invitation but because I enjoyed his company and the way he looked at me. I could confess, I spent most of my time feeling either ordinary or odd. In his presence, I was neither of those things. The Fiona I saw through his exotic eyes was not exceptional, but she was at least remarkable. She was someone worth listening to. Someone with whom he shared his own intimacies—however benign those might be.

Jorah Roth indiscriminately made love to a great many women. Still, I doubted he dined, engaging in two hours of uninterrupted conversation, with any of them.

To say I didn't take a heady gratification in that would be a rank lie.

It wasn't something I was proud of.

Or maybe it was.

I could ignore the tiny voice in my head whispering that the Hammer, himself, might be the author of the Ripper letter that had been delivered to me. I could reason with it. I could admonish it for being so puerile.

But I could not silence it.

The voice grew louder after the spell of Jorah's presence no longer held me in thrall.

Inspector Aberline reacted exactly as expected when I presented the letter to him at Scotland Yard that evening. His expression never changed as he devoured the words again and again, scanning through them and then starting over. His lips blanched and compressed, disappearing behind the mustache. The letter shook in his right hand as his left fingers hunted for the comforting familiarity of his watch.

I stood in his office, patiently waiting for him to process the subtle—and not so subtle—insinuations contained in the Ripper's words.

"What time did you say this arrived at your house?" He collapsed into his leather chair, and the springs made such a protestation, I worried about its structural fortitude.

I took his actions as an invitation to sit, as well. "Late morning. After Inspector Croft and I visited Mr. Thaddeus Comstock's office, in hopes of ascertaining his involvement or lack thereof with these latest Whitechapel murders. I don't know if Croft updated you on our progress, but we are convinced Comstock is the man with whom I had an altercation in Crossland Alley."

"I've been so busy this afternoon with that bloody riot, I've not had the time to give the case a second or third thought." He nodded his rather paternal approval. "I'm glad you had the good sense to take Croft with you."

I didn't correct him on those particulars. "We didn't

find him there. In fact, Comstock's editor said he hadn't been in the office since the day the article posted."

"There's a chance he could have been dropping this letter to you at the very same time you and Croft were investigating his office."

"I suppose. But we combed through Mr. Comstock's notes, and the writing isn't at all similar. Croft mentioned it wasn't difficult for a clever man to forge different handwriting. I brought this to you, hoping to ascertain if the writing matched any of the letters Scotland Yard has in its possession from the Ripper case."

His mustache curled into a tired smile. "I was just going to suggest that very thing." Heaving himself out of his chair, he opened the door to his office and told his clerk to fetch him the Ripper case file and letters.

I imagined that was not an uncommon request, judging by the clerk's prompt but unenthusiastic response.

Because of my near-sightedness, Aberline's features didn't become distinguishable until he'd settled himself across from me again. "You said the letter came to you in the late morning. It's nearly dusk, Miss Mahoney." His unspoken question screamed over the desk at me.

Where have you been?

"I took a hansom here right away," I explained. "I was caught up in the riot this afternoon."

"Crikey!" He finally paused long enough to take in my appearance. My pelisse, hat, gloves, and spectacles had become casualties of the day. Luckily, I'd chosen a simple chignon for my hair, which had been easily salvageable. However, I was still a bit disheveled-looking, if not unkempt. "How did you survive that nightmare without getting trampled? Or worse?"

"I very nearly was," I said. "But I ducked into a café just in time and hid there until I felt safe enough to venture out again." I didn't mention what café or with whom, obviously, as that would have caused both of us undue distress.

More my distress than his, but even so...

Emitting a gusty sigh, Aberline shook his head. "The entire police force rallied to put down the riot, but it seemed to be resolving itself by the time we were able to assemble. Say what you will about the Hammer and his Syndicate, but 'is methods, while ruthless, are effective. Without him, the gangs would dissolve into the chaos of the seventies. Turf wars, human slavery, utter butchery. I am no proponent of organized crime, mind you, but many of us 'ere at Scotland Yard fear the day the Hammer is overthrown."

Something to think about.

"Not Croft," I said.

Aberline snorted and returned to the Ripper letter. "Nah. Not Croft. There's a personal element to his vendetta against the Hammer, but no one knows just what that is."

I could confess that a part of me was glad we'd not found Comstock just yet. In his notes, he'd speculated that I'd been an associate of *JR*. At the time, I'd thought it a Ripper reference.

Did Comstock know the Hammer's real name?

Did he have damning evidence regarding my association with him?

On any other day, I'd have obsessively chewed on this. But it was hard to focus on anything past the red ink on the Ripper letter right in front of us. All other concerns seemed to blur like the distinguishing features of the rest of the world without the clarity provided by my spectacles.

In times like this, one must focus on what is right in front of them. What else could be done?

"I must say, upon first glance, this letter bears a remarkable resemblance to that of the *Dear Boss* letter, doesn't it?" Aberline remarked. "Neat, even script. References to his emotions as 'fits,' and to his murders as 'work.' Short, simple sentences. Could be the same author."

"Could be someone who was privy to it." Neither of us liked what that implicated. "What about the handwriting? Does that match?" I tried not to let my eagerness show.

"I don't think so, but it'll be hard to say definitively until Watkins returns with the boxes of letters from storage. Wot's this then?" Aberline smoothed his thumb over three roundish ripples in the paper caused by my earlier hysterical tears.

"I—must have gotten some rain on it."

He flipped the paper over. "On the inside?" Once he glanced up, he must have read the truth on my features because his softened and then drooped with equal parts exhaustion and compassion. He knew the storm had been from my eyes, not the sky. "You'll forgive me, Miss Mahoney. Sometimes, I forget that for all your strength and cleverness, you're still just a woman."

Just a woman.

When a man is weak and errs as humans tend to do, he shakes his fist to the sky. *I am not a God*, he rails. *I'm just a man.* What Aberline said to me was done in the same spirit.

I wasn't a man. He exempted me as such. I was just a woman. The expectations of me regarding almost everything were less than his. Tertiary.

First, God made man. And then because he had to, woman, whose strength and cleverness could never entirely be relied upon, not like a man's.

Aberline had meant it as an excuse, not a slight. As a reminder of my emotional gentility. But it rankled me still, enough for me to press my tongue between my teeth to render myself mute, lest I say something I'd later regret to a man I fondly admired.

He mistook my silence for something else. "You

must be terrified to have attracted *his* attention after all this time."

Must I? *Was* I?

In short, yes. But I could confess to a great deal of other reactions battling within me, as well. If the Ripper watched me, then he was close.

And if he was close, he could be caught.

Unless he caught me first.

Apprehensively, I licked my lips.

"Have you been drinking?" Aberline regarded me oddly.

Stunned, I squirmed in my seat like a naughty child reprimanded at primary school. "What makes you think that?" A few hours and a few heavy courses of food had all but wiped the effects of the strong wine from my hearty Irish blood. I wasn't feeling at all drunk, though perhaps still a bit warm and relaxed.

"Your tongue is as purple as your dress," the inspector remarked.

"I had a few glasses of wine at the café," I confessed sheepishly. "For the nerves, you understand. Not to worry, that was some time ago."

"Which café?" His eyes narrowed. "Did it have a license to serve alcohol in the middle of the day? Or at all?"

"You'll excuse me if I didn't have the wherewithal to inquire at the time," I retorted wryly. "I was more grateful for the libation than suspicious of it."

"Of course. Of course. It's just...you never struck me as the drinking sort," he mused.

"I'm not, but these were uncommon circumstances."

He conceded with a few vigorous nods. "I'll grant you that, Miss Mahoney. I'll grant you that."

"Inspector Aberline!" A stout, round-faced constable burst into the office without a cursory knock.

Astonishment drove us both to our feet.

"What is it, Johns?" Aberline asked in a voice that left the *this had better be good* unspoken but unmistakable.

"Another Whitechapel murder, sir. Inspector Croft sent for you." Police Constable Johns glanced at me before muttering. "He says to prepare yourself. This one's...right bizarre."

Aberline was already punching his arms into his coat. "Ready a coach," he ordered.

"Already done, sir."

Patting different pockets of his vest, Aberline took stock of his office, conducting some sort of mental checklist. "This week has become nothing more than a constant stream of disasters interrupted by a few catastrophes." He lifted the letter from his desk and handed it back to me. "I don't suppose there's any chance that you'll stay away from this murder."

"I'm afraid not, Inspector." I took the letter and tucked it into my pocket.

He scrubbed a hand over his face, swiping at eyes already burdened with bags of exhaustion before opening the door for me. "After you, then."

─※─

GHOULSTON STREET WAS NOT unknown to me, nor to anyone familiar with the events of the Autumn of Terror. That a gruesome murder should have occurred here seemed both macabre and apropos.

Just after the bustle of Aldgate High Street gave way to the deteriorating Whitechapel High Street, Aberline and I turned onto the ghoulishly named road. It was positioned exactly equidistant from Mitre Square, where Catherine Eddowes' mutilated body had been left on the night of the double event, and Miller's Court where I—*we*—found Mary Kelly some weeks after.

Ghoulston Street struggled to accept our coach. It

was an ancient place never destined for two-way traffic. On the east side of the road, lines of filthy tenements barely fit for human habitation waited. And to the west, a long, dilapidated building once used for industry stood, now abandoned by all but every imaginable sort of vermin.

Two years before, on a frigid Sunday in September, after the double event wherein Elizabeth Stride and Catherine Eddowes had been slaughtered, a police constable discovered a scrap of an apron soaked in blood in the stairwell of a tenement on this very street. Number 108, if I remembered correctly. The remnant of material was later confirmed to have belonged to Catherine Eddowes, taken from her apron at the murder scene. Above it, a graffito had reportedly been scribed in white chalk.

I say *reportedly* because police Superintendent Thomas Arnold had ordered it scrubbed away before a photograph could be taken. It seemed like a right idiotic thing to do, but I believed his motives were pure. London had been plagued by riots then, as well, and they were largely anti-Semitic in nature. Three different versions of the graffito were noted by three separate investigators, who were supposed witnesses. They were as follows.

The first: *The Juwes are the men that will not be blamed for nothing.*

The second: *The Juwes are not the men who will be blamed for nothing.*

The third: *The Juws are not the men to be blamed for nothing.*

This is relevant because the Jews—one in particular—were under intense Ripper suspicion at the time.

John Pizer, a bootmaker by trade, had amassed a reputation for violence against prostitutes. He'd been dubbed *Leather Apron*, by those who knew him, and his arrest resulted in several vicious anti-Semitic demonstrations even after he'd provided an alibi.

Israel Schwartz, a Jew of Hungarian nationality, had claimed to have interrupted the attack of Elizabeth Stride, but he ran instead of helping her. Louis Diemshutz stated that he interrupted her subsequent mutilation. It is believed that the Ripper killed Catherine Eddowes out of the frustration caused by the interruptions of two separate Hebrew men.

Three schools of thought circulate about the message:

One, that yet another Jew found the bloody scrap of apron, correctly guessed its origin, and hastily scribbled the message in a poor attempt to divert suspicion from his people.

Another, that upon fleeing Eddowes' murder scene, Jack the Ripper wrote the cryptic message to illustrate his frustration at the Jews, who'd repeatedly disrupted his work that night.

And the third, that the faded and almost illegible graffito could have adorned the stairwell of Number 108 Ghoulston Street for any number of days, and that the Ripper had discarded his blood-soaked trophy there was happenstance—thereby unrelated.

Neither Aberline, Croft, nor I had seen the message with our own eyes, but I'd visited Ghoulston Street on a few occasions. If only to stand where the Ripper might have stood, looking toward the direction of Miller's Court whilst contemplating what the message might have meant to him.

Had he been angry with the meddlesome Jews that night? Or...had he been one himself, and struck with a benevolent protectiveness of an innocent people suffering for his perverse deeds?

It all depended on numerous factors, I decided as I trundled up the filthy street with Aberline. I was still unable to make up my mind. To be honest, I'd always thought Jack a clever killer. At least literate, if not erudite. The rather crude execution of all three versions of the message never struck me as his.

I had to rethink things now.

He knew this place.

And if Croft had sent for Aberline again, then he suspected this murder might belong to the Ripper. That Jack returned here to commit a crime certainly squelched the idea that anything to do with Ghoulston Street was a coincidence.

Aberline had the door to the coach open and was stepping down before we'd even come to a complete stop. To his credit, he remembered to turn and reach in to help me disembark, as I was not far behind.

Scores of police held grimy gawkers at bay while others braved the dark unknown of the tenements in a tedious search for witnesses. Gas lamps were being lit across the city, but none could be found on Ghoulston Street.

Aberline ushered me across the gravelly yard beneath the archway of the industrial building, where we found a constable doubled over, retching up his supper.

"First dead body, is it?" Aberline kindly offered the young man a handkerchief with which to wipe his mouth.

The constable shook his head. "It in'nt my first, Inspector. But it's by far the worst."

We climbed the wide iron stairs abreast and in silence. Each heavy step echoed in the cavernous building where the skeletons of machines made eerie black shadows in what remained of the late-evening light.

At the top of the stairs, we found Croft alone, standing as sentinel to what appeared to be a foreman's office wrapped in purposely clouded glass windows.

The inspector didn't seem angry to see me. He didn't even seem surprised. In fact, he didn't acknowledge my presence at all.

"This building is slated for demolition tomorrow," he rumbled to Aberline. "He'd not have been found, otherwise."

"He?" I echoed, my fingers suddenly numb with cold.

"Comstock. I've not whispered the word *Ripper* to anyone, but he's done in Comstock as an act of retribution. He made that perfectly clear." The look he sent me held a hint of accusation I didn't at all understand.

Not until I saw the body.

The Ripper had gone to work. He'd warned me, hadn't he?

Unlike the poor constable downstairs, Comstock's murder was not the worst I'd ever witnessed.

That distinction still belonged to Mary.

I would say this, Comstock's scene was undoubtedly the most creative. Artistically speaking, anyway.

We could consider the Ripper unblocked, then. No longer paralyzed by his previous masterpiece.

I wasn't certain if the Ripper himself had whitewashed the lone brick wall, the stone floors, and the wainscoting beneath the windows of the old office, or if someone else had recently done so, and he'd taken full advantage of a perfect opportunity.

Painting an entire room would have taken a great deal of planning and forethought, and the Ripper was known as an opportunistic killer.

Perhaps he'd evolved beyond that now.

Maybe his fury had become more patient.

Mine certainly had, out of sheer necessity, if nothing else.

Had *I* placed a dunce cap on a corpse, I would have situated him in the corner to punctuate the significance. That this was my first thought before the horror set in should have disturbed me.

What actually bothered me was how long I waited before accepting that the horror wasn't going to show.

I felt nothing.

Entering the room by myself was exactly how I imagined stepping into a painting would be. Surreal. Impossible.

Vibrant.

Even the tactile altered. The dirt gritting beneath my boot as I lifted it didn't exist past the threshold. It was pristine and white in here. Silent. Empty.

Save for the blood. And the body.

My breaths were gunshots against a canvas. My footsteps cannon blasts. But an unholy, obsessive curiosity propelled me forward. I couldn't see the details until I moved closer.

In the center of the room, Comstock sat propped up at a masculine oak desk dressed in a smart tweed suit and a silk cravat that matched his pocket square.

His throat wasn't cut, at least as far as I could tell.

A lovely new typewriter sat perched before him, the metal parts gleaming. Two rivers of blood ran down the front of the desk like gruesome icing from a tall cake.

Comstock's palms rested on the wooden top, bracketing the typewriter. His fingers would have been splayed. If he had them. The rivers of red drained from ten symmetrical stumps.

The dunce cap came low over his forehead. Down over empty eye sockets crying crimson tears. A river poured from his mouth, as well, lending his chin a ventriloquist cut.

His eyes. His tongue. His fingers.

All gone.

I tested my inner sensory organs. Still nothing.

A white paper full of words fluttered limply from the typewriter in a breeze I didn't feel.

Another Ripper letter? A confession?

I had to bend down over the desk to squint at it.

Two sentences repeated for the entirety of the paper in perfectly typed rows.

I will not touch Fiona. I am not the Ripper.

I both recoiled and sagged with relief.

There it was, churning my guts and chilling my skin. It throbbed in the shallow cut on my neck and stung in the stitches there. It had arrived, finally.

The horror.

CHAPTER 19

He did this for you.

Why had the thought echoed through my mind in Croft's grizzled baritone?

Because it hadn't been a thought, I realized, as Croft stepped out from behind me and circled the desk, opening the drawer on the right.

Even his charcoal suit seemed lively against all the pristine white.

My heart violently rejected his words. "He did this chiefly because Comstock pretended to be him. Misrepresented the Ripper for his own gain," I argued. "The Ripper is no magnanimous altruist. He's a sadist. He took his own revenge, not mine."

Croft motioned to the drawer.

I shook my head. I wanted nothing to do with whatever dreadful truth awaited me there.

"He may have murdered Comstock regardless, but he did *this*..."—Croft gestured at the gruesome tableau —"for *you*."

"Easy there, Croft," Aberline admonished. "It's not as if she asked him to. And how do you know—?"

Croft cut Aberline off, his eyes boring into mine, electric with a barely concealed fury I didn't understand. "You may not claim the right to see this, to be

239

henceforth privy to what should be confidential to the police, to what your nemesis has done, if you refuse to look now."

He was right, of course. I had to look. There was never any question of that. But I'd never wanted Croft to be wrong with more fervency than in that moment.

Jack did not do this for *me*.

I ventured forward, regarding the drawer with the apprehension one would a thousand spiders.

It wasn't the tiny missing body parts all piled together in the rear of the drawer that stole my breath. It was the letter scrawled in red ink pegged to the bottom by the sharp end of a scalpel.

I did this for you, Fiona.

I slammed my lids shut. Grappling with my lungs, with my burning tear ducts, my careening heart. Those parts of my body betraying me.

Not now. I couldn't fall apart now.

I swallowed thrice. Once for my tears, a mad gulp for air, and the last to force my heart from my throat back to my chest where it belonged.

I opened my eyes to a blurry, silent Aberline, and steeled every part of myself to finish the letter.

Do you like my gifts? I say gifts because Comstock is the first, and the second is this instrument he used to cut your neck. He claimed it was an accident, hurting you. Screamed it. What a dunce. Barely a brain at all.

Do not mind the mess. The inspectors will gather the trifles. The coroner will take the body. The rest can be demolished with the building. There is nothing for you to clean. Consider that a professional courtesy. Not my first.

During our time together, Mr. Comstock convinced me he was not responsible for the recent Whitechapel deaths, and neither am I. Look elsewhere, Fiona. You have so many questions. If only your father was not already a dead man. He'd provide some of the answers you seek.

You must not fear me. You are safe now.

YOURS ALWAYS,
  Jack the Ripper

FUMBLING IN MY POCKET, I snatched out the letter I'd received this morning and hastily compared the writing.

An exact match. The script, the paper, the prose.

"What's this, then?" Croft leaned over my shoulder.

Aberline joined our little conclave around the open drawer, casting his shadow across the words, darkening the red. "Miss Mahoney and I were at Scotland Yard examining this letter she received from the Ripper this morning when you summoned me here," he told Croft.

"We still can't be certain it *is* the Ripper, can we?" My voice sounded high-pitched and desperate, even to me. "I mean, this could still be the work of some other delusional reprobate. Someone mad enough to believe he is the Ripper."

"Anything's possible," Aberline conceded. "But I think it's safe to operate under the assumption that it's him."

"May I?" Croft reached around me to pinch the first letter between two large fingers.

That he asked, surprised me. That he asked gently should have worried me.

As usual, the hairs on my body, the fibers of my skirt, all tuned to his nearness, following him with some strange, magnetic awareness.

My skin prickled with such intensity, it hurt.

I surrendered the note to him and retreated to the front of the desk while both Aberline and Croft scrutinized the letters written to me.

By Jack the Ripper.

He did all this for me.

Never in my life had I received a gift so utterly un-welcome.

Poor Mr. Comstock. I searched his unfamiliar face. I'd never actually met him but for our encounter in Crossland Alley. Of course, I'd fantasized about hurting him. Or worse. He'd terrorized me that night, after all.

He'd been unscrupulous and ambitious, but I did believe he never truly meant me any harm.

He knew—even before *I* did—that I was an inex-orable link to Jack the Ripper.

He'd been good at his job, and it had caused his demise.

What a death he'd borne for it.

Before Comstock, the Ripper had never developed a taste for live mutilations. I knew, beyond a shadow of a doubt, that Comstock had suffered these terrible things. Had lost his fingers, his eyes, his tongue, *before* he died.

He'd been threatened into typing out those sen-tences again and again before the blood was spilled. When he'd still been in possession of his fingers. Con-fessions that would not absolve him to anyone but me.

I will not touch Fiona. I am not the Ripper.

God, how he must have hated me before the end. Or, at least, my name. He'd been punished like a naughty schoolboy. Humiliated. Terrorized.

I couldn't fathom the torment he'd suffered. I didn't want to.

The Ripper knew me.

The comprehension struck me with the force of a rogue wave, threatening to shatter my entire life against sharp, treacherous rocks. He had to be an intimate of mine. A dreadful surge of guilt singed the last vestiges of my self-control. He wasn't just watching me as he claimed. He *knew* me. That familiarity was scrawled all over his letters.

The knowledge that I was innocent. That I didn't

tend to drink. He'd mentioned my dead father, who I rarely spoke of to anyone because his memory was sacred to me.

What could Francis "Frank" Mahoney possibly have to do with any of this madness? What did the Ripper know of him? What answers could he have provided me?

Sweet Jesus, had the Ripper been acquainted with my family? Was he an Irishman?

Not likely. He'd said I was unlike the drunkards of *my* island, not *our* island, which I took to mean Ireland.

Look elsewhere, he'd told me. *Look to the victims. They are chosen because they are the same. Like mine.*

Lord, maybe he'd been right in his initial letter. Perhaps I wasn't clever enough for all this.

I stared at Comstock. And stared. And stared. Forcing myself to meet his non-existent eyes until they were all I saw set against a stark, white canvas. A blank paper I could fill with notes.

How were the Ripper victims the same?

All penniless Whitechapel prostitutes. All famously uncontrollable drunks.

The Ripper had mentioned drinking twice. Praised me for being unlike the notoriously inebriated Irish, and again unlike the drunken whores of the East End.

Was that why he held me in some sort of esteem? Was it why he assured my safety? Said I must not fear him?

Because I was a relatively sober virgin? The opposite of his previous victims.

I could not imagine any other innocence I'd maintained but for the strictly physical.

I thought of his canonical victims. Each murdered in a unique way, and yet, there were utter similarities that branded them uniquely his. He'd stabbed them in intimate places. Taken from them, the parts that made them what he hated. Women. Whores. Drunks.

"Just how did Comstock die?" I breathed the question, almost to myself.

Aberline glanced up at me as though I'd lost my mind. "I should think that's rather obvious."

"None of the parts he lost were vital," I countered. "One can live without eyes, fingers, and a tongue, can they not?"

"Well...theoretically." Croft grimaced at the body. "But a man can die in any number of ways from something like this. Often the pure terror of such brutality can stop a stout man's heart, and you've already said that Comstock, here, was a nancy. He could have choked to death on his own blood, for all we know."

That was true, enough, but something still ate at me. Something we'd not yet discovered.

"We won't know the true cause of death until the surgeon arrives," Aberline supplied. "But I hazard this could be enough for a lean man like Comstock to have bled out. It would have taken hours, poor sod."

It didn't seem like even half as much blood as Frank Sawyer had left on the floor, but I imagined a great deal of it still pooled in Comstock's lower extremities.

Something I'd told Aidan at the Sawyer crime scene occurred to me.

The Ripper always takes something.

"I've a theory," I announced.

"What's that?" Aberline indulged me, while Croft didn't bother. He studied this morning's letter as though committing it to memory.

"When the Ripper kills, he directs his violence at what triggers his fury. With his female victims, he often damaged sex organs or took wombs. Livers. Kidneys. Intestines. Lips. The parts which could be used to ply their trade or to drink or process alcohol. He sliced their throats so they could not scream. So they could not speak. So they could not swallow. He took their voices *first*. And then the rest."

At this, I'd even recaptured Croft's attention, so I pointed to the drawer. "Are all Comstock's...bits...in there? Both eyes and all ten fingers?" I'd seen his tongue, one that would never lisp at me again.

Croft made the gruesome count. "It's all here."

"The Ripper was true to his form." I rounded to the left of the desk, examining Comstock closer so I could see properly. "He relieved Comstock of the parts that offended him. The tools of his trade Comstock used to tell sensational lies. If he left everything he cut off, what did he *take*?"

With grim syncopation, the inspectors blinked at me, and then looked down at the mutilated journalist.

Aberline patted Comstock's linen suit vest and lower. "I can't detect an open body cavity or aught in the way of sadosexual wounds."

Croft lifted the dunce cap, and we all gasped and retreated.

The Ripper had replaced the top of Comstock's entire skull with the dunce cap.

With surgical precision, he'd taken as his prize, the thing which had most offended him about the reporter.

His mind.

CHAPTER 20

I gazed out of the carriage window at the Strand, brightly lit against the velvet night, avoiding Inspector Croft's intense regard. He'd drawn the short straw, I supposed, and had been conscripted to conduct me home safely. I couldn't rightly say how the decision was made. Too many events had transpired that day. Too many deaths to remember the trivial things.

Compared to all of London's golden joviality, I felt like the word *stark*. Pallid. Bleak. Severe. As if all my sharp edges had been blunted, and my color drained until I was a iridescent copy of myself. A shade of Fiona. A ghost who hadn't yet died.

Who was I, that such ghastly violence painted my days? It seemed the years were now all demarcated by some massacre or another. My family. Mary. And now...this.

Was I being punished for something? Was all this blood God's own dunce cap for me?

What had I done?

I remembered being a very little girl, my pretty mother lecturing me about my possible place in Hell. *You can't pray with your eyes open, Fiona. Bow your head. Be humble. Close your eyes. Or the devil will take you where God can no longer find you.*

How can I see God if my head is pointed down? my six-year-old self had argued. *I can't close my eyes, Ma. God doesn't live in the dark, does he? How can I find him if I'm not looking up?*

She'd stared at me for so long, I'd thought she might reach for the switch. Finally, she'd knelt in front of me, Baltic blue eyes sparkling with unshed tears as she pressed my little hands between her palms. *Let me tell you a secret,* she'd whispered. *You'll never find God. No one does. Not really. He isn't here, with us, like we want Him to be. But we're supposed to kneel to Him. To bow. To supplicate. Not in hopes that we will look up and find Him, but with the faith that He's there when you are not looking. That He'll be there when you die. Faith is blind, Fiona. If your eyes are open, then you can't have found it. You don't find God in the dark.*

He finds you.

I'd never found my faith. I'd never really found God. I always prayed with my eyes open. *Lived* with my eyes open. Perhaps, even as a child, I'd known what kind of monsters lurked in the dark. And that God never stopped them from indulging their appetites.

The fear of standing alone and vulnerable in the darkness terrified me.

What if God didn't find me? Only the monsters. I didn't need to have faith in them, because they were tangible.

I never looked down. I never looked away. From anything. I never closed or averted my eyes.

I refused to be blind.

Eventually, because of everything I'd seen, I'd stopped praying altogether.

Everything my mother had said made sense now. Just as there was danger in darkness, there was safety, too. If your eyes were closed, you could believe that things could be different. That they might be better than they were. You could paint your own reality on the backs of your eyelids and look to it with all the hope your imagination could conjure.

It was too late for me now. Faith was something you had to learn early, something you could build with bricks of anecdotal evidence and pure, ecstatic hope mortared by unmitigated emotion.

I should have closed my eyes, I thought, watching the merriment bleed onto the streets. The laughing people, the gay revelers. They lived with their eyes closed. With their gazes down.

I should have closed my eyes. Maybe God would have found me in the dark...

Instead of the Ripper.

"You've something in your hair." Before I could stop him, Croft reached into my disheveled coif and plucked from it a small shard of glass. It winked and sparkled like a diamond in the soft light of the coach, distracting me from my grim contemplation of the night.

"I was caught up in the riot today in front of parliament," I answered his unspoken question. "My carriage was overturned by the mob. Both windows broken."

"You were in *that* carriage?" he thundered, pocketing the glass. "It was dismantled. The driver is in *hospital*. Jesus Christ, they found severed fingers inside."

I shrugged with a great deal more nonchalance than I felt. "I was able to escape the worst of it." With a wince, I remembered I hadn't the opportunity to properly thank Aramis Night Horse for his protection. He'd used his body as a shield for mine, and not an easily camouflaged one, at that. In any proper, pale British crowd, Night Horse was something of a conspicuous target.

I'd expressed my gratitude to the Hammer—to Jorah—over dinner. And while we were drinking ancient wine and enjoying succulent lamb, Night Horse had been the saber point of a militia charge.

I swallowed an absurd bubble of worry for the assassin.

"Christ." Croft repeated, his lip pursed into a caustic curl of disbelief. "You have nine bloody lives."

I began to wonder if Croft's outward displays of ire didn't stem from a more profound and primitive emotion. His skin stretched white over his knuckles as his hands curled into fists. A vein pulsed just below his hairline.

In my experience, anger followed quickly on the heels of something more vulnerable. Hurt, perhaps. Or fear.

I'd not want to meet whatever made a man like Grayson Croft afraid.

"Did they ever discover what caused all the madness this afternoon?" I prodded. I wanted to talk about—to *think* about—anything other than Thaddeus Comstock, Jack the Ripper, or the letters addressed to me that I'd left in police evidence.

Croft shook his head, staring out the windows with a blatant misanthropic cynicism that might have matched mine. "Madness is contagious. It spreads like a disease. Like wildfire. All it takes is tinder. And the entire world is just a pile of kindling waiting to catch on a spark."

"Is that what happened today?"

He dipped his grizzled chin in a sharp nod. "A mob turns reasonable men into animals, and no one knows why. They're just swept up in the firestorm. But I'd bet my life that the spark was provided by the Hammer. I'm going to retrace his every step today. I'm going to find where the match was struck and burn him with it."

It occurred to me that I should be alarmed by this, given the Hammer's steps intersected with mine for several hours today. Still, my inner alarm seemed to be broken at the moment. Like someone had cut the clapper from its middle so the bell swung wildly but made no sound.

"The Hammer," I echoed. "Aberline mentioned at the station that he had a hand in squelching the riots, not starting them. Do you disagree?"

"No, the Syndicate was there to scatter the rats. But I wouldn't put it past the Hammer to have organized the riot just so he could be seen resolving it. It's a masterful show of force within a city he intends to control."

I didn't like the part of me that felt defensive of Jorah.

I didn't like the part of the Hammer that made me as suspicious of him as Croft. Did I believe him capable of such deviousness as to incite a dangerous riot only to further his own ambition?

Absolutely.

"He's the key to all of this," Croft hissed. "I can feel it in my bones."

"Is that what you're basing your suspicion of him on? Sensations in your appendages?" I raised a dubious eyebrow at him. He'd have to do better than that to convince me.

Not that I didn't have my own reservations.

"As a detective, you learn to trust the reactions your guts and bones have." He pinned me with that hard, emerald glare of his.

I remembered what Dr. Phillips had said regarding this. That intuition was just the brain processing information more quickly than one's consciousness could comprehend. Or something along those lines.

What did Croft's bones know about the Hammer that his brain did not?

What did Croft's bones tell him about me?

I'd seen too many guts—too many bones—to trust them as reliable communicators.

"Those letters you received lead me to believe that my theory would convince even the Ripper."

I gaped at him. "What could you possibly mean?"

"Clearly, he believes the answer to who killed Frank Sawyer and Katherine Riley lies in what connects them."

My brows pinched together. "And you think that connection is the Hammer?"

He leaned forward, his arm draping over his knee. "I don't think it. I know it."

My heart stopped for a full second before sputtering to life again. "Frank Sawyer owed the Hammer money. But how is the Hammer connected to Katherine Riley?"

"How is that any of your concern?" Croft volleyed back.

"*Because*," I wanted to say but didn't. The Hammer claimed never to have met Katherine Riley.

Had he lied? Again?

I gazed back at Croft, dodging the waves of palpable tension and menace rolling off him like thunderclouds down a mountain.

I wasn't sure why I reached for him, I just did. My hand landed on his forearm and stayed there. "I think you're right, Inspector Croft. This is all somehow connected. Frank Sawyer, Katherine Riley, Thaddeus Comstock, Jack the Ripper, the Hammer...and me. If you can tell me anything—*anything*—that doesn't suggest that I'm the middle link to this gruesome chain of murders, I'd—" I broke off, unsure what promises to make. What gestures of *quid pro quo* I was willing to offer. Especially after our most recent conversation. "Well, I'd be grateful," I finished lamely.

He stared at my hand for a long time, the sinew and fibers of his forearm twitching and flexing beneath his jacket. After a moment, he relaxed, much of his tension releasing on a never-ending sigh. "Did you know I have a sister?"

I fought a growing sense of aggravation. What did

that have to do with anything? "I know hardly a thing about you," I hedged, hoping he'd make a relevant point.

"We were whelped in Northumberland. Street rats, mostly. Our mother died in a factory fire, and our father took off several years before that." He revealed this all whilst glaring down at my knuckles, a smooth, pale contrast to his.

"I'm sorry to hear it," I murmured. And I was. Truly.

He lifted one giant shoulder. "We were better for his loss, but not hers. We came to London in search of a cousin we'd heard word of, but what we found were the likes of the Hammer. I, being the youngest, fell in with a gang right away, and Amelia, she...she did about the only thing an uneducated girl can do in the East End for money."

His sister had been a prostitute. I understood immediately why she hadn't searched for factory work.

"Amelia had a baby several years ago," Croft continued. "A little boy. She placed him with Katherine Riley, as many girls in the business do. Including the Hammer's." He looked up at me then.

I had to be careful to temper my reaction. "How do you know the Hammer sent his girls to Katherine Riley in particular? There must be many such women who provide services like hers."

"Easy." He smirked. "I asked a few of them, and they told me. For a price. Always for a bloody price."

"It surprises me that any employee of the Hammer's would dare incriminate him, even for quid," I said.

"He's made no real secret of it. The Hammer tells his girls if they end up with a git they don't want, to take it to Katherine Riley. Said he'd pay extra money to place the child with the best family possible."

"It sounds like they had a profitable working relationship. Why would he want her dead?"

"That's what I intend to find out." Croft sat back, dislodging my hand from his arm. It grazed his thigh before I snatched it back. It didn't seem that he noticed, so I tried not to either.

"Whoever killed Katherine Riley stole my only chance of finding my nephew. Ms. Riley was trying to help me get in touch with the family who has him. But because of the illegal nature of her business, she's shite at keeping records. I think we were close, though, and now my sister is devastated."

"Where is your sister?"

"She lives with me. I take care of her...because of what she did to take care of me for so long."

I absurdly wondered if Amelia Croft's eyes were as green as her brother's. Then I realized this must have been Croft's reason for joining the Metropolitan Police. Not only because he could carve out a better living than down in the tube tunnels swinging a pickaxe or a hammer. Not only because he was the right height and build, but also because theirs was now a respectable life.

Come to think of it, an enterprising man could climb quite high on the social and political ladders within Scotland Yard. It was one of the only ways a man without noble blood could gain a voice in the system.

One of the only *honest* ways, rather.

"I hope you find your nephew," I told him earnestly. "I know what it's like to be without family."

That seemed to spark an idea behind his eyes. "What did the Ripper mean about your father?" True to his blunt disposition, Croft took aim at the most painful and mystifying words contained in either of the Ripper's epistles.

"I couldn't begin to imagine," I answered honestly.

"Were there any brutal murders of prostitutes back in Dublin or Limerick?"

"Not that I can remember."

"Perhaps your father investigated something. Or perhaps he..."

I stared at him with hard, bleary eyes, daring him to finish that thought. "I don't know. My father was a *good* man," I said from between clenched teeth. "He was both an altruist and an activist. One of those made him beloved and respected by all who knew him, the other got my entire family killed. He was *not*, however, a murderer."

It was impossible to read Croft's reaction to what I'd said, but his voice was low and soft when he asked, "How did they die?"

"Never you mind how," I spat. "It has nothing to do with this." I was *not* ripping open that wound. Not tonight. And not for him.

"Fiona, eventually, you're going to have to—"

"Oh, look, we've made it home." I sprang for the carriage door and half-stepped, half-stumbled down to the walk. "Goodnight, Inspector."

What I wanted to say was, "*Go to Hell, Inspector.*"

I might have fallen and humiliated myself had dear Oscar not unintentionally caught me.

"Here's trouble." He laughed as he caught my hand, wrapped his other arm around me, and swung me around in a perfect waltz. "We must stop meeting like this."

"Oscar." I squirmed in his grasp, acutely aware that Croft had emerged from the carriage and was glaring at us with tight-jawed disapproval. "What do you think you're doing?"

"You're a fleet-footed Irish woman, Fiona, dance like one!" He kept perfect rhythm despite my protestations, I'd give him that.

"You're drunk," I accused, finally managing to twirl out of his grasp, astonished that his breath, alone, hadn't inebriated me.

"You're sober," he slurred with equal dismay. He

reached out to stabilize himself on the closest, sturdiest object he could find.

Which happened to be Grayson Croft.

"Well, hello." Oscar's warm smile intensified from coquettish to brilliant. "Who is this brute in a suit?"

"Inspector, this is my neighbor, Oscar Wilde. Oscar, meet *Inspector* Grayson Croft. Now, please let him go."

Croft offered neither pleasantry nor presage. He stared at me, silently ordering me to make this inter-loper disappear so we could finish our discussion.

"Who died?" Oscar pressed a hand to the chest of his dinner jacket and glanced to me for verification. "Not Aunt Nola."

"Not Aunt Nola," I verified. But a great many others...

Relieved, he adjusted his white bowtie with equally pristine gloves. "Then why so grim, the both of you?" He glanced between us, still yet to release Croft's shoul-der. "I'd beg your pardon for interrupting a lover's spat but..." He leaned in close to stage-whisper into Croft's ear. "We both know our dear Fiona hath taken no lovers."

"Oscar!" I gasped, relieved to note our walkway was deserted at this hour.

"But *I* do," he purred, closer, I think, to Grayson's neck than any other man had ever been allowed to ven-ture. "Take lovers, that is."

As if that point needed any clarification.

Croft's expression warned that Oscar's life was in mortal danger.

Hastily, I clutched at my friend's elbow and dragged him away from the querulous inspector. "Let's have some tea in the garden," I suggested. "I can't send you up to your wife like this."

"She and the boys are visiting relations in Dublin," he informed me with a plaintive sigh. "I'm all alone in the world."

"We'll talk about it inside." I shoved all six feet and three inches of him up my front steps.

"Will the inspector be joining us?" The third word came out *inshpecter*.

"No." My gaze clashed with Croft's. "He was just leaving. He has a murder scene to return to."

"How *ghastly*." Oscar shuddered. "Tell me everything."

"Good night, Inspector," I said firmly.

I detected a hint of reluctance in the lines of Croft's body beneath his long coat.

"This isn't over," he rumbled.

"I know." It never was.

"Good night, then." He hesitated before swinging back into the carriage. "Lock your doors. And your windows." He settled in and shut the coach door decisively before opening the window and commanding, "And your grates."

"I always do." Unlocking my door, I shoved Oscar inside and did, indeed, lock the portal behind us.

Oscar made a derisive sound. "*Gray*son. What an apropos moniker. He's like a giant, fierce storm cloud."

"Tell me about it," I grumbled.

"I don't know whether to be frightened or fascinated by him."

I didn't, either.

"*You* should be frightened," I admonished. "It's reckless to all but proposition an officer of the law. He could have arrested you."

"Nothing ventured, nothing gained!" Oscar sing-songed through the foyer and down the hall toward the back kitchen, where he'd find the garden door. "I need a smoke."

I followed him, retrieving bits of his expensive attire as he abandoned them along the way. His cufflinks, his tie, his hat, his jacket. "I don't think Benjamin

Franklin was referring to homosexuality when making such a declaration."

He paused to roll his eyes at me before letting himself out to the garden. "You think that degenerate didn't sodomize a few beautiful boys in his hedonistic romp through life?"

I wrinkled my nose. I'd never really considered the private antics of great men. And why should I? Though now that the opportunity had presented itself, I'd imagine their tastes were often vast and varied.

I deposited Oscar's things on a table and joined him on the back stoop. I smoothed my skirts beneath me before settling on the steps, shoulder to shoulder with him. His legs were almost comically long next to mine, even though his feet rested a whole two stairs lower.

"He'd have not arrested me in front of you," Oscar said with more sobriety than I'd accredited him. "He wants you too much."

"Don't be so sure," I snorted. "He's that intense with everyone."

"It's a wonder he doesn't explode," the playwright murmured.

"He probably does, sometimes." Though I'd not like to bear witness to it and pitied anyone who did. I breathed in the threatening scent of autumn frost and expelled all the horrors of the day on a world-weary sigh.

Nudging me with his arm, Oscar asked, "Are you all right, darling?"

"I'm so tired," I whispered so he could not hear the tears tightening my throat.

"Of what, my dear?"

"Of blood. Of fear. Of all the terrible things people do to each other, and all the reasons and excuses they use to do them."

"Sweet girl. You are right to be tired. And afraid."

He kissed my temple. "It takes a great deal of courage to see the world in all its tainted glory and to love it."

"Are you still running away to Paris?" I asked.

"I wouldn't call it running away..."

"I would." I put my head on his shoulder. "Take me with you?" I was only half-joking.

"What are *you* running from?" he asked fondly.

"Jack the Ripper."

He grasped my hand with the force of his shock. "Tell me he's not after you."

"No, but he did kill someone tonight. We're sure of it, this time."

"How devastating."

"Not really." I was more upset that he'd killed Comstock for me, than I was by the journalist's actual death.

What did that say about me?

"*Fiona!*" Well, Oscar certainly disapproved.

"He killed a man this time," I explained. "A bad man."

"It is absurd to divide people into good and bad. People are either charming or tedious. *You* are both, if you were wondering." He took a sage drag of his cigarette.

"What about the Ripper?" I gasped. Surely, *he* was considered evil to everyone.

"The Ripper is tedious, obviously, because he is predictable. Above that, what is charming about murdering whores? Nothing. You're ridding the world of a lovely laborer, who provides a much-needed service to society. S'like—s'like why would one kill servants or wait staff for simply being who they are? Who, then, would bring you sustenance?"

I usually forgave Oscar for saying such silly things, especially when he smelled of absinthe. "Sex is hardly sustenance," I pointed out.

"Is it not? Is it not the sustenance of humanity, itself? Is it not necessary for the hunger of the soul?

The very mortar which holds the bricks of love together?"

"I wouldn't know." I rested my glum chin in my hand.

"That, my dear, is why *you* are tedious. Once your flower is well and truly plucked, you'll have a better understanding of things. You should see to *that* as soon as possible. You're not getting any younger, you know."

I scowled at him. "I'm starting to believe my flower, as you call it, is what keeps me alive."

"What could you possibly mean by that?"

"The Ripper wrote to me," I confided. "He praised my innocence."

Oscar made a comic sound of disgust. "I always maintain the reference to virginity as innocence is imbecilic at best. You are one of the least innocent women of my acquaintance."

"I confess, I had a similar thought," I agreed. "Of the many words I'd use to describe myself, innocent would never be among them."

Oscar was silent for a moment. "If the Ripper knows you're a virgin, he knows you."

I nodded, having come to the same conclusion.

"Just never *sell* your virginity, and you should remain safe." He shrugged as though figuring out how to safely deflower me was the problem of the day. "Besides, it's meant to be given away."

Isn't it considered a sin to give *or* sell your virginity unless you're married in the eyes of society?"

"Oh, please, there is no sin except for stupidity. And it's idiotic to let anyone in society truly know what sort of sex you're having." He tapped some ash to the ground. "Or not having, in your case." The end of his cigarette mesmerized me as it glowed upon his inhale. "What else did the Ripper say to you? Did he threaten you? I'm worried about you, darling. Perhaps you *should* come to Paris."

"He didn't threaten me." He'd killed for me. "He told me I was safe. That I need not fear him."

"Do you believe him?" Oscar murmured down at me.

I shook my head, more out of confusion than denial. "He mentioned my father. Said he'd have the answers I seek were he not already a dead m—"

"Your fahhhther." An offensively salacious purr escaped with some smoke into the night mist. "*Talk about* a tragedy. How you remain a virgin when you surround yourself with such beautiful men is beyond the scope of my understanding."

"I beg your pardon?" I gasped. "You've never met my father!"

"I have, too," he argued. "He calls 'round all the time. You and Nola had tea in the garden with him not a fortnight ago. Tall, lean, and golden enough to tempt a saint. I'd defrock him faster than—"

I surged to my feet, all weariness emptying from my veins replaced by cold, absolute panic.

Father.

All this time, I'd thought the Ripper had meant the word in the paternal sense. It had never occurred to me he'd been referring to the ecumenical interpretation.

My Father. Despite my endless protestations, everyone seemed to hand ownership of one particular father to me.

Father Aidan Fitzpatrick.

"I have to go." I dashed up the steps.

"Fiona. It's the middle of the night."

I paused in my back doorway, seized with indecision. What if the Ripper was even now visiting his sharp and terrible wrath upon Aidan? I burned to get to him, but I'd be a fool to go alone.

Someone had once said, "we are all fools in love."

That didn't mean I couldn't call for help. But assistance from whom? Croft? Aberline?

What if I ended up confronting the Ripper? What if he spilled my dark secrets to the police should they ever come to my aid? What if Aidan made a confession for me? I'd be in as much mortal danger from Scotland Yard as from any murderer.

Leaping down a few steps, I took Oscar's face between my freezing hands all but leached of blood. "Oscar. This is very important. I need you to send word to the Hammer at the Velvet Glove to meet me at St. Michael's in Whitechapel right away. Tell him it's urgent. Life and death. Do you understand? Tell him to *bring his Blade*."

I'd mostly convinced myself that Jorah wasn't the Ripper because he'd been with me during the hours of Comstock's death.

"The Hammer?" Oscar's inebriated eyes sharpened at the name. "The Hammer's Blade? Fiona, those are unspeakably dangerous men. What do you—what do *they*—have to do with—?"

"Just do it!" I commanded as I sprinted back up the stairs. "Please. Aidan is in danger!"

I only stopped to snatch a coin purse, another knife, and an extra pair of spectacles from my desk in the study before I burst onto Tite Street. I ran like a daft loon toward the thoroughfare where I was sure to find a cab to hire.

Don't take him from me, I begged. Tears formed by cold wind, panic, and the threat of grief streamed down my face. With whom did I plead? God? The Ripper?

Did anyone hear me?

One phrase from the letters ripped through my bones again and again, fraying at the edges of my sanity as I fought time and darkness and distance with desperation and despair burning in my chest.

Already a dead man.

Oh, God. While we were distracted by Comstock's murder scene, had the Ripper been with Aidan?

Suddenly, I understood. I understood the Hammer's wrath. Night Horse's lust for blood. All decency and humanity leached away from me with an unholy knowledge that if anyone harmed a single beautiful, golden hair on Aidan's beloved head...

I'd cut them to bloody pieces.

CHAPTER 21

T he screams echoing against the painted ceiling of St. Michael's mirrored the tortured sounds I'd imagined Thaddeus Comstock had made toward the end. It was the sound of a man losing a part of himself.

Parts of himself.

They stirred something inside me. Fractured my soul into many sharp and crystalline pieces, like a mirror I could no longer stand the sight of.

I couldn't say why I took the time to brush the cobwebs I'd snagged in the crypt from my shoulders and skirts as I raced down the hall toward the chapel.

Perhaps because I was as afraid of spiders as I was of death.

Or maybe because I was about to meet destiny, and a strange part of me wanted to look my best.

Either way, it was absurd. As irrational as avoiding the front door of the abbey had been.

I didn't know what I was thinking. At the time, it seemed more reasonable to gain access to St. Michael's by way of stealth, and I knew where Aidan kept the spare key to the crypt in the groundskeeper's shed. I must have figured if I were to gain any sort of upper hand with the Ripper, I'd need the element of surprise.

The agony contained within the sounds emitted from the chapel sent every plan or rational thought scattering to the night like a murder of crows picking at a corpse as wolves descended.

I picked up my skirts and sprinted forward when every instinct I had yearned to flee. I could not let Aidan suffer. I couldn't let him die. Not if there was a chance the Ripper would listen to me.

I skidded through the oratory, ignoring the candles warning me away with frantic golden flickers. The arched door dumped me at the front of the nave, where the shadows of empty pews were arranged neatly in the pious expectancy of a devout congregation.

I was still partially concealed by what was left of a rood screen. The ruins of an earlier time, of a more brutal, secretive church.

What I saw between the slats, crumbled the very foundations of my being.

I surged from behind the screen and tripped up the three steps to the sanctuary altar, holding my hand out in supplication. *"Aidan!"*

I didn't stop to think how foolish I was. I didn't process what my mind readily yearned to reject. I only knew that stealth no longer mattered. Only Aidan mattered.

Saving him.

Because he was *not* the half-naked man tied on his back to the cross, prostrate on the altar, the flesh of his shoulder and chest flayed away to reveal the fiber beneath.

Aidan—*my Aidan*—was the one wielding the knife.

I wished in that moment that I could rip everything I ever felt for him out of my heart and stomp it into the sparse rivulets of blood pooling beneath the altar.

But, alas, that wasn't how love worked.

Altars, it occurred to me, had been invented for this very purpose. The spilling of blood.

It shamed me to my soul that relief combined with the revulsion, the terror, and the shock of seeing him thus. A tiny, glowing bead in the Pandora's Box I'd just opened.

Aidan was alive. *Thank God.*

Aidan was a killer. Possibly *the* killer.

Oh, God.

I couldn't rely upon the Hammer to rescue me this time.

"Fiona." Jorah David Roth rasped my name from a throat made hoarse by screaming. His lovely, elegant fingers reached toward me from their bindings, even as he wheezed, *"Run."*

If I were capable, I might have obeyed him.

But what I saw burning in Aidan's dark eyes—brighter than the heated blade in his hand—planted my feet to the ground across the sanctuary from him.

Devotion. Pure, true, brilliant faith. No anger, wrath, or hatred as one would expect from the perpetrator of such a vicious act.

"Aidan?" My first instinct was to reach for the knife, but logic reminded me of folly. "Aidan, what in God's name are you doing? You'll kill him."

"Yes," he confirmed clinically. Not with relish or with regret. "Yes, eventually, I will."

I gaped at him in dumb astonishment before I finally struggled through my outrage. "It's *murder!* You can't atone for murder." I tried to speak to him in a language he might understand. To bring some semblance of reason back to what my mind didn't want to process as reality.

Patiently, Aidan returned the knife to a brazier of red and white coals as he addressed me. "This is *my* atonement. My sacrifice to the Almighty. It's what He demands of me. I'm not murdering them, Fiona. I'm martyring them."

"Go," Jorah moaned. "Get help. Get the Blade." He

gave a few weak struggles against leather bonds already slick with blood from his wrists and ankles.

The Hammer was not one to give in to such a fate without a fight. That he was so exhausted, revealed just how long he'd been in Aidan's custody.

Hours. Maybe since he'd left me at Scotland Yard.

"It's okay, Fi," Aidan soothed. "You can go. You are safe. I will come to your house and explain everything later."

I could admit the promise of safety tempted me more than it should. *This is Aidan*, my heart told me. Steady, brilliant, gentle Aidan. If he planned to kill the Hammer, he must have a good reason.

If he kills the Hammer, a dark voice whispered to me, *you'll be free of the gangster's illegal demands...*

No. I violently rejected the awful temptation. I didn't listen to that voice. We were all of us alive, and I'd do what I could to keep it that way.

Had tears not already been streaming down my cheeks, the sight of poor Jorah would most certainly have produced a flood of them. His well-hewn body trembled. The multitude of sacred candles half-mooned around the altar glimmered across the sweat slicking his pale skin.

Except for the places he'd been relieved of that flesh. Aidan had stripped the epidermis from part of Jorah's shoulder to the clavicle and had begun working down toward his chest when I'd interrupted.

Every nerve of mine seized with a strange sympathetic pain. It would not have surprised me to look down to find my flesh burning away, leaving a red, sinewy chasm beneath.

I could not fathom the agony Jorah suffered.

"You cannot believe that this is the will of God. Aidan, what could he possibly have done to deserve this?"

A transformation overtook him, then. Something

wicked. Demonic, even. "You know his sins are legion," he declared in a dark voice I'd never heard from him before. "Not the least of which is daring to touch you with his heathen hands."

What was he talking about? "He never touched me, Aidan, not in the way you think."

"You always were a terrible liar, Fiona." He shook his head like a disappointed parent.

"I'm telling the *truth*!"

"You're saying he didn't relieve you of your clothing? Your blouse?"

"Only to doctor a wound!" I touched the still-healing cut near my clavicle. "I *told* you that."

"He didn't half-carry you to the café today?" he challenged. "He didn't stroke your cheek and kiss your bare knuckles when he dropped you at Scotland Yard?"

Well...he'd done that. "Have you been watching me, Aidan? Spying on me, your oldest friend?"

"I've been watching *him*." Aidan stabbed a condemning finger at the Hammer. "That I often see you nearby is disturbing happenstance."

I heard none of this. Or maybe I did, and it refused to register because all I could focus on were the wet, awful sounds of several East End prostitutes as he cut their throats.

"It's *you*," I breathed. It all made sense now. Aidan knew my past. My secrets. He knew me better than anyone. Anyone left alive anyway. He'd been trained as a soldier and then as a surgeon. He'd been in Whitechapel long enough to carefully select his victims and reap this sort of bloody judgment upon them. He'd written me letters before, and his script was as dear as it was familiar.

But he could have changed all that.

"You're the Ripper?" To scream both a question and an accusation made the most ludicrous sound, but I did it. My chest expelled the words with all the fervency of a poisoned purge. Heaving the tortured conclusion into the air.

I kicked a few candles aside in my enraged advance around the altar. I was lucky my skirt didn't catch on fire. I was so hot, so inflamed with fury, I might not have noticed imminent immolation until my flesh began melting away. "Did you murder those prostitutes? Did you butcher them? Did you kill Comstock? For me? Because so help me, Aidan, I'll—"

"No!" He actually backed away from my wrath. Something in my frenzy reached him, and he was again the hapless youth who'd been caught keeping watch as my brothers slipped worms into my stockings. He shielded himself with spread palms as though they would protect him from my onslaught. "God, Fiona. How could you think that of me? Those women, the victims of the Ripper, are like the Magdalene. They needed mercy. Not brutality."

I thumped his chest as I'd done all my life when displeased with him. "Don't lie to me, Aidan!"

He grasped my shoulders, then. His fingers bruising with a strength I'd forgotten he hid behind the long, black cassock. How could it have taken me so long to be afraid of him? All my life, I'd taken Aidan's goodness for granted. Until the moment I realized he could—he *might*—kill me if he wanted to.

But he didn't. He merely brought his forehead close to mine until his doe-brown eyes became my entire world. "Fiona." He shook me softly. "Do you really think I'd hurt Mary?"

My every breath was a shaking mess. "Up until today, I never thought you'd hurt *anyone*."

To my utter shock, he pressed a fond kiss to my forehead. "Bless you, Fi, but you've never been so wrong in both your estimations of me. I am a warrior of God. And, therefore, I am unquestionably *not* Jack the Ripper. He is a servant of the devil." His hands on my shoulders turned me to face Jorah.

"Who else could it be but the Hammer?" Aidan whispered in my ear.

"The Hammer..." Jorah David Roth. "Jack the Ripper?" I blinked down at the man beneath me. Like a bear in a trap. I felt pity and a strange sense of disappointment. How did someone so canny, so clever to the point of devious, fall prey to a priest? It was difficult to see someone so powerful bound and helpless.

More difficult for him than I, I was sure.

An animalistic fierceness blazed from the gangster. His lips curled back from his sharp eyeteeth in a wolfish growl. His hazel eyes raged at me with silent demand. With threats and promises of retribution.

If he survived this, I'd have yet one more reason to be afraid.

"Everyone knew the Ripper was a Jew, and the Hammer is the perfect suspect," Aidan continued from behind me. "What's another dead whore to him? Less competition. He's a snake, Fiona. A serpent. And the devil makes him do unspeakably evil things. He's coerced you to commit egregious sins. Sins for which you'd hang. You said so, yourself."

For a moment, the Ripper had a face. A beautiful, exotic visage. He cut women open for sport with those deft fingers I so admired. He dominated them. Penetrated them. Took disgusting little trophies he might keep in a hidden golden Shiloh room, gleefully gloating how he'd outsmarted us all. That he ruled us all.

People not only feared his name. They feared his shadow, too.

He'd shrugged his shoulders when we blithely discussed our dealings. The bodies he gave me were only men.

Did he leave his women in the streets with their

throats slit and their legs open? Did he hate women that much?

"You know that it is not *me*." Jorah's ferocity drained away from him, replaced by a foreign sort of uncertainty. "Don't you?"

Did I?

I knew it was a bizarrely heady thing, to have the Hammer fear *me* for once. To have power over his life where before I'd had none.

I'd suspected him every now and again. Even this evening, when we'd dined together, the worry had whispered to me. Would the "*Juwes*" be blamed?

Weren't they always?

It wasn't fair, I realized. To condemn a man for suspicion. For public outrage. For the general opinions of the populace against his people.

I'd felt his pain as we'd spoken together. I'd commiserated with him about the prejudice of the majority against both of us. The blood that ultimately spilled because of that hatred.

The family we'd each lost.

"He's...he's not the Ripper." I spoke my conclusion with dubious conviction, but the Hammer's eyes still fluttered with relief. "Jack killed a man today, and Jorah was saving my life when Thaddeus Comstock died."

"He could have had an accomplice. That heathen with the blade," Aidan insisted. "I watched this man lust after you, plying you with drink, with charm, like a godless swine. He's always surrounded by an army of brutes, by his pagan protector, or walled away in his fortress of sin. But not today. 'Vengeance is *mine*,' sayeth the Lord. He presented a path, and I took it."

I turned in Aidan's hands, facing a wrath I'd never before witnessed as it clouded his visage. "Aidan, listen to yourself. This is all a lot of malarkey. Your guilt has driven you mad, I think."

He ignored me. "I could not bring the others here

to face their Lord as they died." He gestured to the life-sized crucifix hanging like a sword above the sanctuary. "But the Hammer makes a perfect offering. An eye for an eye. One of the same people who nailed our Lord to his cross will die upon it."

I pinched my brow. "But wasn't it technically the Romans who—?"

"He's one of *them*, too." Aidan made a dismissive gesture. "Half Italian and half Russian Jew."

There was that word again. *Them.* It sparked a memory of what Aidan had referred to earlier.

I'm martyring them.

"Who *else* have you visited vengeance upon? Who else did you martyr?" Why did I ask when I didn't want to accept it?

When I already knew.

Crossing himself, he raised his arms to the crucifix as though making an ancient, Abrahamic offering.

"Answer me!" I demanded. "Did you kill Frank Sawyer? Katherine Riley? Did you make martyrs of them, as well?"

He didn't have to say yes when he turned to face me. I read it all over him. I saw pride in his stance, in his secretive smile.

So many emotions flooded through me, I choked on them. Gagged. Struggled to draw in the life-giving breath I needed. I retreated a step, well aware of Jorah at my back. "They were innocent."

"They were damned!"

"You do not know that. You are not the judge of their eternal souls."

He swept his hand up at the cross. "*He* told me to send them to their reward."

"You're speaking madness!" I gasped. "Blasphemy. You cannot know what is in a man's heart any more than you can know what a God thinks."

"By his *actions*, ye will know them." He stepped

closer, and I began to decipher what was behind the devotion in his eyes. Rage. Desperation. A lethal combination. "I knew their sins."

Another hot tear tracked down my cheek. "We are all sinners. Will you kill everyone? Would you compel us to be obedient? Doesn't that make you the devil?"

At that, his shoulders slumped. "Of all people, I'd hoped you'd understand me. You always have."

"I *never* have." I didn't understand why he'd kissed Mary when he loved me. I didn't understand why he left me to join the church. And he was certainly making no bloody sense right now. Maybe he'd always been mad... and I'd been too naïve, too blind with love—to see it.

Perhaps he just made a sport out of breaking my heart.

"Do you remember the last time you were here?" he murmured softly. "When you tempted me? When you kissed me?"

I said nothing. He'd been just as culpable in that kiss as I, but now was certainly not the time to press such a point.

"Do you remember the little girl I held in my arms that day?" he continued. "All of nine?"

I did. I remembered the sadness in her eyes.

"*She* was Frank Sawyer's temptation. And not his first. The man never fought his wicked urges as I do. He admitted that to me when I confronted him." I saw the disgust written all over Aidan's face. One mirrored in my own heart. "What if the child Agnes carries were a daughter? What if he'd turned his perversions for little girls to her?"

I had nothing to say to that.

"Frank confessed eventually." Aidan turned from me to stare into the flames. "He begged, sobbed, and pleaded with me to take his weakness from him. To grant him absolution. And so help me, Fiona, I *did*."

Holy God. Despite my heresy, my own disbelief, I

crossed myself. Aidan had unsexed Mr. Sawyer. He'd taken from him the weapon he used against a nine-year-old girl.

"You sent him to Hell," I whispered.

"Like you said, I'm not the judge. I only do what I'm told. I sent Frank to St. Peter." He gestured to the stained-glass window beneath which we had kissed. To the martyred man hanging upside down. "A man who knew his unworthiness. Who only received his reward in the afterlife."

Aunt Nola had predicted that the Hanged Man deserved to die.

Oscar had told me to find Frank Sawyer's Salome. His desire. His muse. It never would have occurred to me to look for an innocent child.

I searched myself for sorrow over Frank Sawyer's death and found none.

"What—what about Katherine Riley?" I asked. "You butchered a woman exactly like the Ripper had done." Exactly as I had explained to him the very morning Ms. Riley died.

Had I given him the instructions for Katherine Riley's death?

He made a sound of pure revulsion. "She was the worst of the lot. Worse, even, than the Hammer, here."

Worse than a gangster and a child molester?

"Those sweet, innocent babies." Aidan's voice broke, and tears filled the seams of his lids, darkening the whites of his eyes. "They never found homes, not on this Earth."

My stomach rolled, and I put a hand to my corseted waist. "You can't mean..."

"She murdered them," he confirmed. "She took money from desperate mothers, left them with false promises, and strangled the unwanted children in... Cold. Blood. I *found* her, Fiona, burning wee remains in her cavernous fireplace."

I'd almost forgotten about Jorah until he emitted a tortured groan from behind me.

Aidan ignored it, staring at me as though I were the only person in the world. As if I were his confessor. "I stabbed her once for each woman I sent to her when I thought her an angel here on Earth. Each innocent baby I *knew* she'd killed. Fifty-three times in all."

My heart broke then. Just shattered. Aidan and I wept together as he unburdened his soul, making mine heavier and heavier until I thought I might be ground into the dust by the weight of all the evil in this world.

"I stayed with her most recent victims until they were naught but ash." He looked down at his palms, fingers spread as though the remains ran through them. "I tended to their little souls, prayed until I lost my voice."

Sweet Christ. Aberline had rubbed that ash between his fingers, tested it, not knowing the unfathomable contents. I'd scooped out the ashes from the fireplace and dumped them in the rubbish bin, clapping the dust from my gloves and wiping it on my skirts.

The rubbish bins. What a dreadful urn for innocent little souls.

And Croft!

I shed a tear for his poor sister. All this time, he'd been searching for a nephew likely years dead. God, would I ever muster the strength to tell him?

How many children had become victims of Katherine Riley's greed?

Hundreds, perhaps.

Bile clawed up my throat, washing my gorge with an acidic realization.

"You took her womb," I realized aloud. "Because she didn't deserve one?"

"I offered her corpse as St. Inocencia. One of the many named saints who were stabbed to death for their purity as a youth."

I closed my eyes against the barrage of pain searing

the rivers of my tears. Katherine Riley murdered *infants*. She hadn't deserved to live. I hoped she was burning in Hell alongside Frank Sawyer and anyone who stole the innocence of little children with their lust, greed, or cruelty.

"The Hammer is complicit in these crimes." Aidan reminded me. "He sent many of his own women to Mrs. Riley."

We both whirled on him, and I saw my ferocity reflected in the Hammer's dread.

"I-I didn't know." His struggles renewed, with more vigor this time. He sensed my mercy being depleted with each blow Aidan delivered. "I was trying to keep the women in my employ from turning to dangerous back-alley abortions. To give their bastard children better lives. I thought she was a good woman, a reformed prostitute who would be kind to my girls."

"The devil speaks with a honeyed tongue," Aidan hissed. "Him, I turn into St. Bartholomew, flayed alive, then crucified. His pain will purify him, Fi. But, unlike the others, there is no chance of paradise waiting after death, not for a Jew."

"Your Messiah was a Jew, was he not?" Time had seemed to rally the Hammer's fighting spirit, and his lithe body flexed and strained against the ropes.

Aidan struck him, his hold on the calm of Christian devotion slipping into true fanatical fury. "*Your* people slaughtered him!" His robes flared around him as he turned toward the brazier.

"Wait! Just wait." Frantically, I placed myself in between Aidan and his prey, holding my hand up, fully aware of what his coal-heated knife could do.

As much empathy as I had for Aidan's helpless rage in the face of true evil, I couldn't stand by and watch him brutally slaughter another human being. This wasn't right. Not only did I suspect that his fury, in this case, had as much to do with me as it did with piety, but his motive was also ethnic in nature. Such motivation had nothing to do with a misguided love.

And everything to do with hatred.

That, in itself, was evil. And if there were such a thing as a soul, as an afterlife, as Hell...this act would surely send Aidan there.

"I...understand your motives for reaping vengeance against the others." I did. And I didn't. I'd have *wanted* to kill both Frank Sawyer and Katherine Riley once I learned of their crimes.

But I wouldn't have. That's the difference. I'd have called upon the law.

What about when you find the Ripper? the dark voice inside my head asked. *Will you leave him to the police?*

Now was not the time to answer that question.

"Jorah is no Pharisee." I maintained as even an intonation as I could. "He's just a man. A sinner, like me. Like all of us. The repercussions of his demise could evoke more evil than you could possibly imagine. There is a gang war brewing in this city, Aidan, and he's the only one keeping it in check. If you kill him now, you doom more innocent people to death, and worse."

"I'll repent, if that's what it takes," the Hammer conceded evenly. "I'll offer your church atonement for any sins you deem necessary."

"Jorah?" Aidan repeated my use of the Hammer's given name with a treacherous deliberateness. "He is *Jorah* to you now? What do you mean, your sins are like his?"

"Nothing." I'd never been more thankful to have kept a confession to myself. Aidan knew I'd sinned for the Hammer, but at the moment, he placed blame for those sins on the Hammer's own head.

Lord, help me, but I wanted to keep it that way. Even if that wish made me a selfish woman, I couldn't bear to see condemnation in Aidan's eyes. Not so much out of love anymore.

But out of terror.

"I just meant that we all have sins that we must repent. We are promised mercy, are we not? It's not only criminal to do what you've done—what you mean to do —it's a mortal sin. Unforgivable. It's murder, Aidan!"

His calm had returned, and it did exactly nothing to restore my serenity.

"You think I hate these people. I don't," Aidan said. "That's what you don't understand, Fiona. I love them. As unworthy as they are, I do. And so does God. I offer them a path to forgiveness. Their only way."

He softened further when he read the utter confusion on my face.

"I am a sinner, too," he murmured. "Those beads you found in Frank Sawyer's blood were mine. Did you know that? They came from a rosary an Apache man made for me in America. I paid him in tainted blankets and faulty weapons. His entire clan died of cholera not three weeks later."

My lungs deflated. "What?" I thought this day could contain no more declarations of horror. How wrong I'd been.

"You lived through the war on our soil, wrought by these blood-thirsty English hypocrites. You know what it is like. The Republicans were dying. Starving. Desperate. A faction of us with powerful kin in America went in search of aid. We found men of industry, government, and military, Irish Americans who supported our cause. We did whatever they asked to save our country. We made land deals at first. Then arms deals. And, finally, we were told we could keep whatever we looted from native tribes. We were paid for their scalps."

I'd never seen a man more riddled with remorse. It buckled my knees. My joints ached with it, froze with it. I became paralyzed by *his* pain.

And still, he continued, his confession clawing at

that little was left of my own sanity. "I've been the cause of the deaths of more innocent—more innocence —than Frank Sawyer, Katherine Riley, the Hammer, and the Ripper *combined*. I had a hand in the slaughter of thousands, Fiona. And the whole time, I thought my cause was just. Those heathens had rejected Christ. Declared war on Him. They lost the war, and I knew it was because He was on our side. I prayed every night, and I heard the voice of God. I felt his righteous wrath. But then...there was this village..."

He pressed his lips together and turned his head, clearly fighting the rise of his own gorge at the memory.

"Oh, Aidan," I whimpered through my never-ending tears. "What did you do?"

He didn't seem able to bring himself to look at me. "There are no words for it. Butchery comes close...but not close enough. After that, God was silent to my soul. And in the silence...I heard your voice calling me home. But by the time I made it back, there was nothing. I was alone. Forsaken by the Lord."

He took my hands, and for the first time in my life, I wanted to wrench them away.

"I could not inflict my sins upon you, Fi. Upon our house or our children. So, I made my atonement the only way I knew how. I devoted my life to God. I asked to minister in the capital city of my enemy. To love them as Christ told us to love them." He bent his neck to gaze up at the celestial mural on the ceiling. "And still, when I prayed, I heard nothing but the pagan supplications of those slaughtered people. I wondered if He heard their prayers, I wondered if He heard their screams. I asked Him again and again. Do you know what my answer was?"

I was crying too hard to speak, so I shook my head.

"Silence. It's *always* been silence." His hands tightened on mine until the small ring I wore on my right hand bit into the fingers next to it.

My engagement ring. From Aiden.

I wanted to cut it off. It caused me more pain than just the physical, but I dared not move.

Aidan's eyes turned distant as he gazed into the past. "I heard his voice when Frank Sawyer begged me for help. When Katherine Riley tried to explain the little boxes of bones in her fire. When the Hammer caressed your cheek." To my relief, he released my hands to trail his fingers through my tears. "I love you. I've always loved you. But you must allow me to finish what I started. What God has commanded of me...or I cannot promise that God won't tell me that you're next."

"Me?" I recoiled, snatching my other hand away from his. Panic laced my blood with shards of ice. "But I don't hurt people. I'm not a murderer."

"You've enabled one." He gestured to the Hammer. "You've hidden him from justice. Your sins are many, Fiona. Purifying you would be the greatest sacrifice I could possibly make. God has asked for such a sacrifice before, from many of his saints. Think of Abraham."

I'd begun my retreat in earnest until my hip bumped against the altar. This couldn't be. To fear the man I loved, the boy I'd trusted with all of myself for so many years, was the worst loss I'd suffered thus far.

He reached out, and I shrank away.

"Don't be afraid," he soothed, pointing back up at the stiff, ever-merciful visage of the crucified Lord. "He will forgive you, too. If you take up the sword for Him." Aidan reached toward the knife, and my stomach plummeted to the floor.

We weren't all surviving this, I realized. He wasn't going to stop until someone was dead. Jorah. Me.

Or him.

"Do not tell me I have to kill this man in order to prove my love for God," I sobbed. "Such a death is not justice, it's *murder*."

'Tell that to Mary. Tell that to little Fayne as they ∴ung his body—"

I slapped him, hoping to knock the insanity away. How dare he bring my youngest brother into this. "*No*. Stop it! Stop this lunacy."

He shook his head at me, unfazed even though a red mark spread over the pale beauty of his cheek. Slowly, he slid the knife from the brazier. "The Lord is my shepherd; I shall not want."

No. Little needles of black punctured my vision. *Anything but this prayer*. The only one I knew by heart anymore. Psalms 23. The prayer of death. It had been said over every person I'd ever loved.

And now the only person left recited it over me.

My shattered heart turned from glass to stone.

"There has been enough killing," I shouted at him. "Enough! Do you hear me?" I spread my arms across Jorah, though I knew the action was both puerile and ineffectual. Why would Aidan listen to me when he heard the voice of God?

I took my own knife from my pocket. One I'd replaced from a collection in my home after the riot. The blade was longer than his, but I knew that meant nothing. I'd never used it to kill before. Aidan was stronger than I. Taller. A trained soldier. And still, I'd do what I could to stop him.

All my pride had vanished. "Aidan. *Please*," I begged. "You are the last person in the world I have left. My only link to home. Don't be this man. The voice telling you to do these deplorable things doesn't belong to God. It's the same demon who whispers to the Ripper. Can't you see that?"

He advanced on me. "...though I walk through the valley of the shadow of death..."

"Fiona. *Move*," Jorah barked. "There's no reason for both of us to die."

Aidan's hand snaked out to grab me, his knife raised,

aimed at my heart. The heart he'd broken time and time again. It leapt and jerked like a captured rabbit, but he was simply too strong. I meant to slash at him first, a desperate and futile grasp for salvation. Still, a lightning-quick movement from my periphery stunned me to stillness.

Aidan dropped his knife. It sizzled and sparked against the cold marble floor of the sanctuary. He coughed. Released me. Wheezed in a deep breath and coughed again.

A dark arm slid around his front and held him fast as Night Horse drove his blade deeper into Aidan's back, into his lung, and then wrenched it out, allowing the air to hiss out and the blood spill over his hands.

I couldn't fathom where Night Horse had come from, but I was both unutterably relieved and devastated to see him.

As Aidan rattled out another cough, blood erupted from his mouth.

Night Horse met my stare of astonishment with hard, black eyes as fathomless as any hellish void. He bared his teeth in what could have been a silent snarl, or a smile.

Today, vengeance didn't belong to the Lord.

It belonged to Aramis Night Horse, and to many of his slaughtered people.

With a cry, I caught Aidan as his knees buckled, and supported his fall to the cold floor. His blood pooled instantly beneath us as I held his head on my lap. My sobs had turned to whimpers. They became softer than the almost indistinct *whooshing* of the candle flames.

"Pray for me, Fiona." Aidan's voice was even darker than before. Wetter. "And remember me."

I made a terrible sound. How could I forget such horror? This would paint my nightmares red for eternity, if not beyond.

"Not like this." He read my tormented expression

correctly. "Like we were. By the river. With Finn and Flynn and... And Mary. When we were still...innocent."

I nodded. My last gift to him was an utter lie. I'd remember his confession. I'd recall that he tried to both save me and kill me. That he'd not felt worthy of my forgiveness, and in the end, he'd not deemed me worthy of his.

"Pray for me," he begged again. "Finish it."

I don't know how I managed, but I warbled and sobbed along with him as he gurgled and drowned in his own blood. "Yea, though I walk through the valley of the shadow of death, I will fear no evil..."

I was dimly aware of noises. Maybe I should have been afraid, but anguish smothered any fear, and I whispered the words I knew by heart.

Aidan's mouth filled before we were done, the blood overflowing until it streamed from the seam of his lips. He didn't fight it anymore. He no longer struggled for breath.

I finished the last stanza of the prayer with a stronger voice.

My tears died when he did.

I stared down into his vacant eyes, swathed in a cloak of grief and pain. Agony he'd inflicted on me, yet again. For the final time. His golden, cherubic aspect a mask for such deep wells of madness and violence.

I gazed at him for what felt like ages but was only enough time for Aramis to free Jorah from the cross on the altar.

"I tried to be quiet." The dazed gangster said almost apologetically as he sat up. "I was when he started on my shoulder. But...once he reached my ribs, I could no longer swallow the screams."

I knew that would happen to me, eventually. I could remain quiet now, but the day would come when I could no longer swallow the screams.

"Only you white men find shame in screaming.

When we kill, when we die, we make enough noise to alert the dead that more are coming to join them." Aramis looked over at me. "Unless silence means survival."

I wondered if it meant survival for me now. *All to the good*, I thought. I had nothing to say.

Did they blame me for this? For Aidan? Had I become someone on the other side of a chasm they couldn't cross? A liability. An enemy?

I waited for either of them to strike, my fingers clutching my knife.

They didn't.

"You are not bleeding much," Aramis noted as he examined Jorah's heinous wounds.

"No," Jorah groaned. "I'll live. He cauterized as he cut with that infernal blade. I think he hoped to flay as much of me as he could before I gave up the ghost. Tell me the carriage is here. I'm embarrassed to admit that I cannot make it home on my own power."

"It's here. Though I did not wait to bring anyone else to aid us. We'll have to send for the doctor."

Jorah patted Aramis's amber shoulder, then clutched it, his gratitude unspoken.

I used my sleeve to wipe my tears and blot at my nose as I sniffed. I had no handkerchief, and one was not offered.

The shadow of numbness crept through me. Much as I imagined the biblical Angel of Death had crept through Egypt so many thousands of years ago. It snuffed out everything it found. First, the terror, utter and unutterable. Then, the anger, cooling it like the marble had cooled Aidan's tempered blade. And, finally, loss and despair. They folded into a void infinitely emptier than the well of grief threatening to drown me.

I'd found power here. I couldn't explain how. But for a pure, empty moment, I was untouchable. I stared up at the Hammer and the Blade and, while I couldn't feel what my features were doing, I silently dared them to move on me.

It wouldn't matter. I had nothing left to lose.

A fraught silence became a death knell as they stared back.

The Hammer leaned heavily on the altar, his chest struggling against his uneven breaths. His teeth bared slightly in a now ever-present grimace of pain.

I couldn't lock gazes with Night Horse. I was afraid I'd find regret or pity in his regard.

I was afraid I wouldn't.

Did I hate him for killing the man I loved? Even though he'd saved my life?

I closed my eyes, returning my knife to my pocket. I placed my hands beneath Aidan's scalp, threading fingers through his golden locks as I lifted his upper body from my lap and extracted myself from beneath him.

Gently, so gently, I settled his heavy head on the white marble. No one helped me to my feet.

I stood on my own.

I skirted the growing pool of Aiden's blood as I took an altar cloth from the sacristy beside the lectern. I might have floated rather than walked. I couldn't feel a single limb.

As I covered Aidan's face, I felt as if I should say something, but words failed me. Other elegies I'd read or heard flitted across the silence of my thoughts like errant, unwanted moths looking for light or warmth and finding none.

Goodnight, sweet prince.

Better to have loved and lost...

Today shalt thou be with me in paradise...

It all meant nothing.

Woodenly, I surveyed the scene, almost too weary to draw more breath.

I turned and addressed the Blade, though my gaze found nothing higher than his chin. I harbored no hatred for him, no real condemnation, but neither could I summon gratitude.

Not yet.

In a way, Aidan was the embodiment of *his* Jack the Ripper. But infinitely worse. The scale of his loss was unimaginable, even now. All of this pain, all of this emptiness he carried in his heart, along with the ghosts of thousands.

"I'm not cleaning this up." My declaration echoed through the cavernous cathedral like a celestial commandment. I wouldn't survive it. If I were ever to remember Aidan fondly, I couldn't look at his empty eyes again.

Night Horse's chin dipped in acknowledgement.

I turned to go home, but Jorah stopped me with a grip on my elbow I'd not thought him capable of in his weakened state.

"I owe you a debt for what you did today. No one, not even Night Horse, has so fiercely protected my life with their own." Overcome for a moment, he glanced at the floor, grappling with his emotions. "It is currency I'm not certain how to spend."

I nodded politely and extracted myself from his grip, making my way down the long aisle toward the doors of the cathedral. I wasn't sure how to spend it, either.

But I'd think of something.

CHAPTER 22

Forgive me, for I have sinned. It's been...

Lord, how heavy my soul must be if I couldn't even remember the last time I'd been driven to confession. Long enough to be laden with damnation, some would say.

I'd locked myself in my grand house for several weeks, waiting for the screams to come. Waiting for the tears to find me.

But my voice never rose above a hoarse murmur. My eyes remained eternally dry.

My body betrayed me in other ways. Guilt and shame became a cancer proliferating through every vestige of my awareness.

There was no corner of my mind safe from my pain.

I trembled at night. For no reason at all, my muscles erupted into cold shivers of bone-wracking weakness. I'd lose my breath upon climbing the stairs. I'd sleep the days away, waking occasionally to the sensation of a wrathful specter smothering me. I'd gasp in a few desperate breaths, willing my heart back into its place, hissing at shafts of unwelcome afternoon sunlight only to reject consciousness and force myself back into oblivion.

I ached everywhere. My bones, my guts, my head.

My heart.

Nights were a paradoxically welcome nemesis. Too dark to reveal how pale and gaunt I'd become, but also a lonely void in which I had to keep company with my worst enemy.

Myself.

I'd haunt my own hallways like a ghost. A shade of grief and regret. My entire world, this grand, endless city, had been pared down to my narrow walls.

Autumn slipped into winter. Somehow, I failed to notice. I was already so cold. Most days, my fingers hurt to bend. My skin hurt to touch, often riddled with waves of prickly goose pimples.

Every moment felt as though a demon danced on my grave.

Nola stood vigil over me as best she could. She consulted every spirit within her domain. She read cards and plied me with broth. After a while, she wrung her hands and asked when I was going to get up. *If* I was going to get up.

"You can't be a spirit yet, Fiona," she reproached as she cleared away yet another untouched breakfast. "They say you've work to do. You've secrets to uncover. You can't lose your wits, or *he* will win."

He? Jack?

What did it say about me that a confirmed lunatic worried after my sanity? How could I tell her that I'd uncovered enough secrets to last a lifetime?

"You were right," I told her with no inflection, then held up my hand before she corrected me. "*They* were right about the Hanged Man."

Her soft eyes welled with tears. "I know," she whispered. "I'm sorry."

I didn't see her again for a while. Polly brought me my toast the next morning.

Several days after Aidan's death—I couldn't tell you how many—a note arrived scrawled in rather rudimentary script, accompanied by an article neatly cut from a paper.

St. Michael's Cathedral had burned in a mysterious fire.

I'd stared at the photograph. A greyscale skeleton of ancient stone. The beloved priest and local philanthropist, Father Aidan Brendan Connor Fitzpatrick likely perished in the blaze, though no remains had been uncovered.

So, that's how they'd done it.

An efficient disaster, was fire. It saved nothing but cleansed everything.

The note had simply read:

I have his ashes if you want them.

~Aramis

I heard nothing from Jorah.

I imagined his wounds healed faster than mine. But not his pride. He was likely once again the Hammer, at least to me.

Condolences came to me in the form of other notes, some accompanied by flowers. Dr. Phillips' arrived first. Then Aberline, Oscar, Hao Long, others I'd employed, and a few people who remembered me from home.

Aidan's mother wrote to me.

I was certain her heartfelt letter full of pride and regret would have left me in a soggy, sobbing heap on the floor. But I discarded it on the growing pile with similar apathy. She'd expressed her secret wish that he'd married me instead of joining the clergy. She wished she had a grandchild to remember him by. But he was never the same after he returned from the war. He'd needed the love of Christ more than the love of a woman.

I wasn't convinced. I didn't think a woman would have told him to torture anyone to death.

Depended on the woman, I supposed. There were the Katherine Riley's of the world...

I'd read the concise script on Dr. Phillips' perfunctory note and thought about the livers I'd promised him. The lecture would have been over by now. I'd completely forgotten. And, even if I'd been capable of working, I couldn't have faced the Hammer or the Blade just yet.

I'd let Dr. Phillips down, and he'd not mentioned a word about it.

What a dear man.

When the weather turned, no corpses landed for me to clean.

Mary Jean showed up on my doorstep with little Teagan. I'd almost forgotten about her.

Polly was certainly grateful for the help, as she had been nervous to tell us that she was engaged to be married and might not work for much longer.

Nola took to Mary right away as the girl was both gullible and fanciful enough to see spirits in shifting shadows. She even blamed one of Nola's wayward guides when she knocked over a crystal dish, and we let her.

Teagan was a happy baby, if louder than I often wished. Some children screamed their discomfort, and she certainly did that. But she yelled her delight, as well. She warbled, cooed, burped, and yawped just about every moment she wasn't asleep.

Sometimes, the sounds of the child reminded me of all the infant ashes shoveled from Katherine Riley's fireplace. Sweet, chubby Teagan could have been one of them.

If Aidan hadn't done what he did.

Mary was both kind and careful around me. She suspected my grief. I saw it mirrored in her eyes when she wasn't trying to appear chipper.

She'd lost her husband not so long ago. She spoke to him when she cleaned sometimes, when she thought she was alone. She nagged him. Berated him for leaving her. For being careless when she'd warned him not to.

She told him stories about Teagan. Told him she missed him.

Funny. I'd never speak to Aidan whether he haunted me or not. It was believed that ghosts were tethered to a moment in time. Or a place. Or, if they were very unlucky, a person.

I never felt Aidan's presence. And, I imagined, if anything of his spirit remained in this world, it wouldn't be condemned to revisit me.

He'd be in America, somewhere. On the bloody ground of that village. Tormented by the souls of the innocent.

I read the paper every day. Only because I had one thing left to fear...

A murder in the East End. A mutilated corpse.

A victim of Jack the Ripper now that he'd been coaxed out of hiding.

He was still out there, I knew. Watching me? I almost felt sorry for him. How bored he must be.

He never sent me *his* condolences.

Or did he? Hidden in the notes of another?

One morning, Mary brought me breakfast on a tray. "Thought I'd brighten such a dreary morning wif a flower, miss." She drew the drapes, and I moaned at her. "It's going to snow, I fink."

Let it. What did I care?

She bustled out, not waiting for a thank you, and for whatever reason, I rolled toward the tray. Butter actually smelled good this morning, and my stomach made a rude noise.

I stared at the flower in the vase as I gobbled the toast and tea like a doomed man would his last meal. A lily of the valley. Trimmed from a hot house, obviously, and drooping like shy little church bells. A waterfall of white.

I washed and dressed early, for once, and arranged my hair, surprised that I'd not forgotten how.

A sudden and intense need to unburden myself drove me into the cold of the approaching winter. God help me, a church was the last thing I wanted to see.

Forgive me, for I have sinned.

I'd lived my life for so long with one purpose in mind: to find Jack the Ripper.

A body needed a purpose in order to keep on ticking. So many people worked themselves to exhaustion, only to die the moment they retired.

Because what did they have left to do?

I still had Jack. I was no closer to finding him, but he'd crept closer to me.

And that meant something.

But first, I had to confess. I had so many secrets. So many sins. I had to cast off the heavy burdens and make some sort of recompense, or the weight of it would crush me like some inconsequential vermin beneath guilt's unrelenting boot heel.

I'd found that God was like the law—His reason for being to judge and punish you for your dastardly deeds. To warn others away from breaking long-standing tenets. In my life, He'd been more vengeful than benevolent.

But perhaps because I'd gone about it all wrong.

God, like the law, had a tendency to be merciful if a supplicant were willing to do two things.

Confess. And atone.

I could do both. It was time I unburdened my soul. I knew where bodies were buried. I knew the sins of so many others.

But I'd only confess my own.

I knocked on the imposing wooden door, not surprised to find it locked. The arch was taller and wider than most.

It'd have to be, I decided, to house who lived behind it. I knew the hour was early, that now was not the proper time for revelations, but if I didn't unburden myself now, I'd explode.

The door opened, and a surprised breath released a fragrant cloud of smoke from the person on the other side. I shivered on the doorstep while he inspected me with eyes that glinted, his expression shifting from hard, to uncertain, to concerned.

And then, Inspector Grayson Croft took my elbow and pulled me inside his home.

I opened my mouth before I could change my mind and inhaled deeper than was necessary to speak seven words.

I need you to take my confession.

"I told her not to write to you," he growled, less helping me out of my cloak than yanking it off me.

My lips slammed shut of their own accord. To whom was he referring? Had Inspector Croft not sent his own condolences?

I didn't want to examine my feelings on that score, so I took in my surroundings while gathering the thoughts that had scattered like moths. I'd been mistaken. Inspector Croft's dwelling resembled nothing close to a lair. If I were to pick a word for it, I'd choose *cozy*.

I wasn't sure what to do with that information.

"You don't have to do it," he continued. Resuming his grasp on my elbow, he conducted me through the oddly feminine front parlor and down a hallway cluttered with paintings, portraits, and photos I suddenly ached to examine.

His home smelled like bread and vanilla.

"How do you know why I've come?" And was he, of all people, doing his utmost to talk me out of confessing?

In a strangely solicitous and almost careful gesture, he nudged me into a room done in dark blues and masculine leathers. Bookshelves lined every wall and were not so much orderly as well-used. A fire crackled almost diffidently in the hearth, and on a side table next to a high-backed leather chair, his half-smoked pipe rested next to an open book.

I'd been mistaken...about being mistaken...

This was Grayson Croft's lair.

"Amelia is just about as likely as you are to heed an edict. I told her not to bother you, not so soon after the death of your priest." He didn't so much as look at me as he said this. Instead, he bustled around the room in a decidedly un-Croft-like manner, tidying up.

"He wasn't my priest," I whispered around a knot of emotion as he pushed another chair close to the warmth of the fire.

"He was something to you." He gestured for me to take a seat, and I did everything but collapse into the comfortable furniture.

Yes. Aiden had been everything to me once. I didn't know what he was to me now. A mistake? Both my sweetest memory and my most terrible one. The keeper of my heart and the breaker of it.

My reason for being here.

"Inspector," I started.

He held up a hand, and I noted the ink stains on his fingers. "I've come to accept that if a prostitute is murdered in Whitechapel, there's nothing I can do to keep you from the investigation, short of locking you up and losing the key."

Had he allowed me to speak first, that's exactly what he'd be able to do. Except now, I had a reason to be silent. A prostitute. Dead. In Whitechapel.

"I've not read of anything new in the paper," I said breathlessly.

"I'm unsure how long we'll be able to keep it from the press." His lip lifted in a semblance of a snarl.

"What does your sister have to do with this?" I

asked, a flare of panic chilling my skin at the same time my palms bloomed with sweat.

"Did she not mention?"

I made a negative gesture. I'd never received a letter, but I'd be damned if I allowed Croft that information before I gleaned what I could from him.

"She knew the victim." His gaze shifted to the floorboards, then he studied the hemmed cuffs of his trousers as his hard jaw worked over something that looked very much like shame. "From earlier days, when the only law we knew was the law of the streets."

I leaned forward so I could hear him properly over the thundering of my heart. Had another woman lost a dear friend to Jack? And why would Croft's sister call for my help?

Grief had blanketed my fate with doubt and self-recrimination, but there was no time for that anymore. All thoughts of confession dissipated into the London fog as I leaned forward and captured that flinty green glare with mine.

"Tell me everything."

Coming 2020: A Treacherous Trade – The Business of Blood Book 2
Coming 2021: A Vocation of Violence –The Business of Blood Book 3

ALSO BY KERRIGAN BYRNE

THE BUSINESS OF BLOOD SERIES
The Business of Blood
A Treacherous Trade
A Vocation of Violence (Coming 2020)

VICTORIAN REBELS
The Highwayman
The Hunter
The Highlander
The Duke
The Scot Beds His Wife
The Duke With the Dragon Tattoo
A Dark and Stormy Knight

THE MACLAUCHLAN BERSERKERS
Highland Secret
Highland Shadow
Highland Stranger
To Seduce a Highlander

THE MACKAY BANSHEES
Highland Darkness
Highland Devil
Highland Destiny
To Desire a Highlander

THE DE MORAY DRUIDS

Highland Warlord
Highland Witch
Highland Warrior
To Wed a Highlander

CONTEMPORARY SUSPENSE
A Righteous Kill

ALSO BY KERRIGAN
The Highwayman
The Hunter
The Highlander
The Duke
The Scot Beds His Wife
The Duke With the Dragon Tattoo
How to Love a Duke in Ten Days
All Scot And Bothered

ABOUT THE AUTHOR

 Kerrigan Byrne is the USA Today Bestselling and award winning author of THE DUKE WITH THE DRAGON TATTOO. She has authored a dozen novels in both the romance and mystery genre. Her newest mystery release THE BUSINESS OF BLOOD is available October 24th, 2019

She lives on the Olympic Peninsula in Washington with her dream boat husband. When she's not writing and researching, you'll find her on the water sailing and kayaking, or on land eating, drinking, shopping, and taking the dogs to play on the beach.

Kerrigan loves to hear from her readers! To contact her or learn more about her books, please visit her site: www.kerriganbyrne.com